About the Author

I was born in South Africa and moved to a small city in the East of England when I was twelve years old. As a child, my favourite thing to do with my father was write short stories about frogs and giraffes (drawing questionable illustrations to accompany these), and in my teenage years I found a passion for writing and singing songs. I qualified as an Occupational Therapist in 2018 and have since been privileged to engage individuals recovering from mental health conditions in creative writing workshops, where my inspiration to write my own novel was founded.

Unearthlies: The Keeper of the Chrysalis

Cara Knox

Unearthlies: The Keeper of the Chrysalis

Olympia Publishers
London

www.olympiapublishers.com
OLYMPIA PAPERBACK EDITION

A CIP catalogue record for this title is
available from the British Library.

ISBN: 978-1-80074-355-7

This is a work of fiction.
Names, characters, places and incidents originate from the writer's
imagination. Any resemblance to actual persons, living or dead, is
purely coincidental.

First Published in 2022

Olympia Publishers
Tallis House
2 Tallis Street
London
EC4Y 0AB

Printed in Great Britain

Dedication

I dedicate this book to my dad and my Omi, who showed me
the wonder of getting lost in stories.

Acknowledgements

Thank you to those who made this novel possible — you know who you are.

Chapter 1
The laws of witchcraft and sorcery

Monday 2nd September 2020, 7.05 a.m. (way too early)

The creaks in the wood whisper to me. This old oak house tells many stories to eager listeners, but it will keep the golden secrets that protect its occupiers. I grew up here, spending most of my weekends learning from my ancestors, whose voices echo the halls. My grandmama, Asteria, is a powerful being, but certainly not more so than her mother before her, and before her, too. While my mama was shamed for her overt indifference to the 'Wand' (here, the name of our Lore, not the imaginary stick which supposedly possesses magical powers, like the earthly children are taught), I was branded as the redeeming daughter of the Orenda line. "A miracle", the townspeople gossiped, "this child has been blessed with the powers that only three generations before her have known" (I'm not so sure about that though, I spent four weeks learning a simple spell of turning water into ice, which any sorceress could learn in a matter of days, and worse yet, a fridge freezer could accomplish in a matter of hours).

'Lorelei', I was named. My papa, being an earthly man, was banished not long after I was conceived. "What a disgrace, a sorceress and a mortal!" I was realised as a confusing invention of hope and humiliation, which had even the truest of 'Wand' devotees perplexed. Hemlock House is where my destiny has been cast. Mama made a deal with the devil, so to speak, the newly elected Mother of the Wand, that she shall not face punishment for her crimes so long as my Grandmama (a once highly regarded sorceress) takes us both in and raises me by the ways of our Lore. Long were the nights with disturbed sleep, interrupted by the murmurs of the walls, and by those of my ancestors who were desperate to witness my promise accomplished: their path to redemption. "Sleep child, tomorrow we learn the five ways of the sun" were the very words to keep me from my dreams. My mama could not bear to listen to the voices telling her of her shame, and so one day she begged the Mother of the Wand to let her hear silence while she sleeps. This was granted but it secured her debt, which is never a good position for any sorceress, or mortal, to be in.

While every weekend saw me creating potions, casting spells and learning the Oath of the Wand, my weeks were filled with 'earthly' studies. It was a pact made to ensure peace between the mortals — the landlords — and us — the tenants, who are powerful enough to rule them, but are ultimately intruders on their land. How we came to be? It is still something of a mystery. Old men claim to know. Stories have been told and history books written, even. But the truth is, if we do not know, how can they? All that *is* known is that there once breathed a very powerful sorceress, named Parisa, born in the stars, the first known of our kind. She was said to possess a power beyond all, and some say she was even the creator of all life, mortals included (although evidence gathered so far suggests that she arrived on earth *after* the mortals). Old spell books and ritualistic items were traced back to where she was thought to have lived after she landed upon earth. Her word quickly spread throughout the villages, and although no one ever caught sight of her, she was felt as a presence in every sorcerer and sorceress to come after her, as if she was living within them. I haven't felt her though, at least I don't think I have. If a power born in the galaxies was within me, Parisa would have made sure that I could turn water to ice, in an instant.

I spent the summer reciting an original edition of *'The laws of witchcraft and sorcery; the words of our Mother'*. (Newly edited to exclude the word "witchcraft" — it scared the mortals, gave them the impression that we fly around on broomsticks and turn men into frogs. How gullible and foolish they are.) The script is a little shy of three hundred and fifty-seven pages, and although I am proud of my heritage, I nearly lost the will to live after reading through it for the eighteenth time. It's a dull read if I'm honest. It basically lays out the rules of when and when not to use our powers, how and how not to, and why and why not to. It's Parisa's survival guide to being noticed in the realm of powerful beings, while remaining unnoticed in the realm of earthly beings. Personally, I can't quite fathom how these can occur simultaneously, especially when dark powers brew, as they have before. While I consider myself to abide by our shared code, and by that of the mortals, I inherently place a higher value on my own; I have a purpose and a prophecy, which may be unknown to me, but will one day be known to all. These are the words spoken to me by my ancestors, repeated like a broken record.

Where I go to school, along with the mortals and daughters and sons of our kind, is a particularly unpleasant place, for the most part. Each school in our county has a certain number of "places" allocated for the "unearthly students" (yes, that is actually what we are officially called, but I take it as a compliment). I started school at the age of eleven, which is when unearthly children can start receiving a formal education. I suppose it is because earthly children are "innocent" and "impressionable", and the mortals were worried that we would corrupt them at a young age, perhaps. I am now fourteen years old, and today marks my third year of attending Weyborough High. I learn all of the typical, boring and utterly irrelevant subjects. Science, English, maths, art, history… Chemistry is one of the only subjects I can honestly say that I enjoy — It helps me with my spells. The earthlies (what *they* are called) must also attend two lessons of "unearthly history" a week. I guess it was part of the pact to make it seem as though our kind weren't the only ones who had to compromise (although, we really were, all things considered). My first year at Weyborough was long and tiresome. The mortals had an unusually confident way about them; they were intimidating and didn't hold back on the insults. "Big nose witch", "potion making pig." It was unusual because, although I joke about turning men into frogs, we literally could do that, with the flick of a finger if we wanted to. But by my second year, the novelty of a few new unearthly students wore off, and we were mostly left alone.

I'd be lying if I said I had high hopes for my third year. My plan is to get through it, really. Lay low, don't look the wrong way at the earthlies, or do but only when they're not looking. As much as I would like to blend in, the different coloured collars make it pretty hard. The earthlies wear a green ring around their necks, while ours is blue. It was set to be red, initially, but the school governors settled for blue as they figured it would go down better with the *'Unearthly Parent Teacher Council'*, of which they have three unearthly teachers, and a fourth one starting this term. The purpose for this, they said, is to help the teachers identify which students have to stay on at the end of the day to attend the earthly after school activities (we all get to go home and practise our spells). We all know though that it is a clear attempt to maintain the division and ensure the earthlies aren't unknowingly mixing with us without supervision — we could lead them astray! Well, we wouldn't want to mix with them anyway, their simple brains could never comprehend the things we've seen, the powers we have. They act all unbothered by us, but deep down they're just jealous. How could they not be? I try to avoid them at all costs when I can. In our first year, the thirty new unearthly students were each paired with an earthly who had the unfortunate job of showing us around the school grounds, telling us about the rules and reminding us how we totally do not belong. At least, that's what my earthly did.

Dean O'Malley: he is still assigned as my earthly. We meet twice a week to discuss the lessons we've learned about our respective cultures, watched by eager eyes belonging to Mrs Mapleton, who supervises every one of our interactions (although she doesn't have much to supervise, we barely exchange one word and instead pass the time by directing looks of pure disgust at each other). Dean's blonde, shaggy hair often covers his crystal blue eyes, but I can still feel the weight of them. They're nice eyes. Cold, but sometimes, and only sometimes, I catch a spec of warmth in them, too. We've been taught to despise one another — it's nothing personal. But I don't hate our meetings, I just don't look forward to them, either. The only thing we can agree on so far is our mutual animosity towards organised sports. He hates them, I think they're a joke. So, when our silent judgement of each other wears thin, we continue filling our meetings with the topic.

"Did you see that ridiculous ad campaign about that footballer, you know the main one that plays for Carvery United, and something to do with how he only wears the Flipso trainer brand?" Dean awkwardly brought up in our last meeting.

"Yeah, well no actually, but I bet it's stupid", was my unmotivated reply.

End of conversation.

Last time we met, the day we broke up for summer, I could tell that Dean wanted to ask me something about my spell book. He glanced over at Mrs Mapleton, who would disapprove of such a conversation, and looked back over at my book, which I slid out of my backpack and placed on the edge of the table. I was hoping he would, it would have been a far more interesting subject. But he didn't. How could he? It would not have looked good that an earlthy was *actually interested* in finding out something personal about an unearlthy, especially on the topic of magic. So, we spent the last fifteen minutes of last term watching the clock and contemplating what we were going to do with our summers, instead. Mine was, of course, already planned out for me, but I did wonder how he would be spending his. Not in a 'curious about Dean' way, just in a 'curious about earthlies' way. I thought I might ask but no doubt he would have probably given an answer like: "not much" or "haven't thought about it", and either way the conversation would have drawn to a close fairly quickly, as it always does. I did hear something about how he works in his papa's garage over the holidays, and I almost felt guilty that mine would be filled with learning to grow a tree from a root in under a minute, and about how that would make Dean's plans seem completely underwhelming — they were. No wonder we have nothing to talk about, you could call it his one and only magical power: the ability to put me to sleep instantly, just by talking about himself.

So here I am, packing my bag and getting ready for the new school term. I did learn to grow a tree from a root, but I only managed to do it in one and a half minutes, so I still need to practise. I was given this journal by my mama. She said, "One day, you'll want to remember your youth. I used to keep a diary, I still have it somewhere, and I like to think about the fun, normal times I had with your grandmama, and with your papa." That's when she tends to start tearing up, "your papa." So I said I would give it a go. Mama doesn't have much she can bond with me over; she hates any mention of spells and sorcery stuff, so I think it was her way of trying to give me a part of her, and I took it, with a smile, and with a limited intention of actually writing in it. But oh well, I promised I would try, at least for a month, and write down my thoughts and anything that isn't strictly magic related, like potion ingredients — I have a separate book for that. Every day I'll write one entry, after I get home from school, and after my evening lesson with Grandmama. I hear Mama calling from downstairs, "You're going to be late, Lorelei, come down, I've made you some toast." Deep breath, I suppose summer couldn't have lasted forever.

Until tonight, Diary.

Chapter 2
Little witch

Oh, Weyborough High, how little I missed you. Your tall, cement buildings are nothing if not downright depressing, plastered in variations of the shade of grey. Did a little colour ever hurt anyone? You can tell the school had been designed and constructed by mortals — so little creativity, so little inspiration. When Mama drove me up to the brown steel gates, I was almost tempted to use the vanishing trick that Grandmama and the ancestors have been teaching me. I've nearly done it, a couple times, but I can't quite seem to master it. Last time I tried it, I managed to make almost all of myself invisible, aside from my scarf. Imagine that, a floating scarf! I caught sight of a mirror and nearly wet myself; how peculiar it was. Even Stumbles, the grouchy guinea pig that belongs to grandmama, gave a faint half smile. Blink and you would have missed it, but it was there! Though I don't think Grandmama was much amused, and I know the ancestors wouldn't have been; they don't seem to have a very good sense of humour, judging by the time I've spent with them so far.

Anyway, looking at the sorry sight that is Weyborough High would surely have been enough motivation for me to perfect the trick. The only thing stopping me was knowing I get to see Melusine today. Mel is my absolute partner in crime (if the crime was sneaking out of earthly lessons and casting spells on Morton, the school groundskeeper). But don't feel sorry for him, Diary, he's a grumpy old character, much like Stumbles, and the worst we've done is turn his gardening hoe into a giant candy cane, all in the spirit of Parismas (the unearthly version of Christmas)! You should have seen his face, his expression even changed from his usual look of sticking his tongue in a squeezed lemon to one of puzzlement, and back to squeezed lemon again. Mel swore she saw him take a lick of the cane, after he scanned his surroundings to make sure no one was watching, but I didn't see it.

Mel has a bit of a habit of, how do I put it… fabricating stories. Call it… 'the curse of the imagination'. But I don't mind it though, she's fun to be around, and we've been best friends since we were infants. She lives across the road from us with her parents and twin brother. Her papa is quite the controversy (not more so than mine, of course). He works for *'The Council of Sorcery and Enchantment'* — an independent regulatory body who reviews the rules and guidelines put in place by the Mother of the Wand (MOTW) and her cabinet, and oversees the handling of misuse of power, including incidents of dark magic. The reason for his controversy is that *he* is a suspected practitioner of dark magic.

Earlier this year an elderly neighbour (a sorceress) reported that someone in Fickle House was practising dark spells. You can tell when someone does because there's a sort of energy that anyone in Parisa's bloodline (any true sorceress or sorcerer, because unfortunately we do have 'mortal pretenders' and fortune telling scammers) can feel, when in the immediate area of the cast spell. It almost feels like a heavy weight, as if your body is filled with lead and your insides go all tingly. Although there is no explanation for this, it is thought to be our one-thousandth sense (we have nine hundred and ninety-nine others). Grandmama tells me it was gifted to us by Parisa to ensure the easy identification and banishment of those who misuse their magic. But dark magicians argue that Parisa's true purpose was to use her powers *against* the mortal beings; bring torment to their lives in a ploy to take over the land and rule as superiors, with them as our servants, not our leaders. There have been a few known dark magic enthusiasts, and someone from my school was even expelled for practising a dark spell in the school toilets a couple of years ago.

The punishment for such a felony is unclear; those deemed guilty of serious dark magic crimes by the Mother of the Wand Crown Court of Justice are exiled to a discrete island off the coast of Vormera; our mainland. The Island, given the name of '*Soulas Lossesta*' (meaning 'souls that have been lost' in Parisa's early writings of her language), is said to be bound by a powerful spell, known only to a handful of individuals in the MOTW cabinet. This spell is rumoured to be the most formidable of all, with no others strong enough to break it. It was cast by four influential figures in magic evolution said to be hand-picked by Parisa who appeared to them in a vision while they were asleep. Parisa supposedly relayed to each of them a separate part of the spell and gave them clear instructions of how to find each other, thus completing the jigsaw with their individual pieces. The spell was first cast on the island when a wicked sorceress by the name of Sereia and her lover were caught devising a curse to turn all earlthy blood into *poison*. This would, in a moment, destroy all mortal life in an excruciating transformation, and leave them as nothing but carcasses; objects to satisfy Sereia's gaze. She and her lover were sent immediately, without trial, to the barren island. It is there they will remain forever, joined by others who are bound by the spell that lets only dark souls in, but lets none out!

Mel's papa was investigated for a dark magic crime about three weeks ago, but there was no proof other than witness testimony and, coincidentally, the elderly neighbour who reported the misdemeanour disappeared the following morning. She was reported missing but hasn't yet been found. Mel said that her parents told her the lady had probably moved to the Isle of Gormer to live a quiet life with her grandchildren, but the suspicions held by the community are far more sinister. I can't speak much for Mr Magus, he seems like a nice enough man whenever I come across him during my visits to Mel, but he is certainly quiet and there is an uneasy feeling about him, perhaps because of the stories I've heard. Mel doesn't talk about it much, but she maintains his innocence whenever she is taunted by the earthlies, or unearthlies, for that matter. Grandmama isn't too pleased that I spend so much time with Mel, but she knows how close we are and how much we need each other to survive this school.

As I stepped out the car, I saw Mel and her brother, Cleo, saying goodbye to their mama. I waved over at them. Mel grinned and waved back and Cleo did his usual thing of staring at me with a smirk, but typically didn't respond. They both started heading towards me.

"Have a good day, Love, it'll go better than you think," Mama said as I turned to her before closing the car door.

"I'm sure it will," I replied with a smile, not believing my own words but trying to sound confident enough to fool her.

Mel and Cleo were stood behind me after I shut the door. Mel embraced me with a hug. "It's so good to see you, Lorrie. I have a feeling about this year you know, I think it'll be our year." I wasn't sure I shared her sense of optimism, but I told her I missed her too (we'd seen each other the week before but that felt like ages ago now). I said hi to Cleo to be polite and he returned my greeting with a nod, saying:

"Hi little witch, how you doing?" Again, with that smirk!

He was quite handsome, really, but very annoying. He carries himself as if he is better than everyone. His dark brown hair with a tinge of auburn and his caramel eyes are held by a tall, slender body. He looks much like his sister, although not identical. Cleo is well known for his tyrannous ways, perhaps taking after his papa. He's popular with the girls at school, or at least he *was,* and I've even seen a couple of earthlies give him a second look. But he has the courtesy of a pig, and he isn't afraid to show it.

"I'm good, thanks!" I replied, hoping he wouldn't extend the conversation, and knowing he would.

The three of us walked up to the open double doors of Weyborough High. Our Headmaster, Mr Goddard, was standing by the threshold "welcoming" everyone in. He's a mortal, of course, and it shows. He has these thick round glasses (the kind that belong in the sixties) and wears the same pair of dusty brown trousers with a paint mark by the left pocket. He is less than intimidating, and he doesn't even *try.* I orientated my head towards him but avoided direct eye contact and said hello. Mel did the same and Cleo commented: "I like your tie, Mr G, very hipster." 'Mr G' never knows how to take

Cleo, perhaps he's a bit scared of him: the child of the suspected dark magician. I made my way to my locker which is a few away from Mel's. I opened it an unpacked my bag, taking out my books and a pencil case. I saw an old Biology worksheet titled *'Mitosis and Meiosis'*. The topic had the earthlies mesmerised but bored the unearthlies to death. Why would we concern ourselves with something that didn't even apply to us? It did get me thinking of how we came to be, and whether any of the 'evolution' stuff rings true to our kind. I don't like to think about it much though, it's hard to make sense of.

My thoughts were interrupted by the bell. Students were scrambling to collect their things for their first lesson as I caught sight of Dean, who was walking out of the bathroom. He must have noticed me as he directed a slight nod of the head, his face remaining neutral. I suppose he sees my dark — almost black — hair, pale skin and emerald, green eyes as something of a horror, the way he looks at me. I smiled back. I was due to meet with him at the end of the day, but I wasn't sure it would go ahead. The first day of term is never *that* predictable. There's always additional assemblies and prolonged breaks. I made my way to my first lesson, which was English. We were studying Shakespeare at the end of last term. Don't get me wrong, it's interesting learning about the history of playwriting, I just prefer learning about mystical creatures — most of which are mythical, but some of which really *do* exist. Like Blubbers — I've had a few unsavoury run-ins with the snail-like creatures (and by 'run-ins' I mean run-*ons*).

After re-learning about the infamous tragic death of the young couple in a forbidden love affair we had art class, which is not one of my strong subjects. We were drawing a picture of a bowl of fruit, which was stationed on the table at the front of the classroom. I don't even have the vision-reduced excuse of being near the back — my desk is in the second row from the front! I personally prefer unearthly art. My favourite technique is completed using '*Potion la flay*'. If the correct proportions of the core ingredients are mixed and used as ink — and the spell is spoken word for word — then when you draw an image on paper, the lines wiggle on the spot and can sometimes even jump *off* the paper (although this is usually when too much of the main ingredient, tumbleweed, has been used, and is not the intended effect!). Last year, Alfreda drew a stick figure version of a monkey. At first it began to dance on the page, and then one by one each of its stick arms and legs started to *come out* of the page! Next thing we knew, there was a badly drawn monkey running about and jumping between the desks. He nearly landed on Mrs Kelpie's head, before she caught him and popped him back in the sketch book! Normal ink is boring; it never moves on the page and certainly doesn't go running around. I started drawing the fruit bowl, only really touching on the apple.

Next thing we had was lunch. It was a decent tasting spin off of chicken pie. The meals are hit and miss here, but overall, they do the job. After we ate, Mel and I went off to the forest where we knew Morton would be lurking. He has an odd fascination with picking up the leaves, which inevitably get replaced by new ones almost immediately (it is a forest, after all). We watched him for a while, but I started to feel a bit sorry for him, so we refrained from casting any spells and gossiped instead. Mel told me about this boy she fancies, Easton, who isn't much to look at but he's nice enough. He helped her carry her books to biology the other day (what is it with Biology and masses of textbooks?). Mel swore they exchanged looks of deep passion and is confident that they will end up getting married one day and grow old casting spells and creating potions together. She went on to talk about her assigned shadow, a despicable earthly named Jessica. I don't know her too well, but Mel doesn't describe her in the best light. "She's awful… she's SOOOO ungrateful!" Unlike Dean, Jessica apparently asks way too many questions, which is almost worse. Although, according to Mel, she does that thing where she doesn't let you answer but instead changes the topic or talks about herself, generally choosing the subject of her nails or hairdo. "Do you like them? I got them done at Layla's beauty boutique. They charge a FORTUNE, but she did a tacky job, don't you think? Daddy said that next time I can ask for the *premium* mani pedi deal. Do you get yours done? I suppose not, but you should really, they could do with a touch up." Mel blocked her nose as she impersonated Jessica's whiny voice.

Mel couldn't care less about her nails. Why would she when she's learning to master the very complicated, Grade 5 trick of locking secrets — ACTUAL spoken secrets — in a box. I'm on Grade 6 spells now — they go all the way up to Grade 13. They start with simple tricks at Grade 1, things like learning to manipulate small objects in space by purely willing it to be (like bending, twisting, lifting twigs and other light objects) and reading palms — although we are not to perform this unsupervised; it has been known to bring up dark fates, and that's simply too much responsibility for a young sorceress to handle. Grade 13 is the highest level of magic mastery; only a handful of our kind have reached it, and they tend to be working in the cabinet of the Mother of the Wand as lawmakers and professors. The four unearthlies I mentioned before (the ones that Parisa hand-picked to perform the imprisonment spell on Soulas Lossesta) were Grade 13 wizards and witches. As a Grade 13, you "possess a power to collide the earths", whatever that means. I personally think it's just a snappy catchphrase conjured up to encourage the young prodigies to strive for greatness and undertake the gruelling tests which secure them their advanced qualifications. The test for Grade 5 was tough enough — three hours later and I only just passed.

Mel was due to see Jessica later today, but it never happened because Jessica was "off sick" with a "sore throat." Mortals, how feeble. Try snakeweed poisoning from a spell gone wrong — it is not pleasant! I also didn't see Dean because we had assembly instead after lunch. What a shame (not) I missed out on guaranteed awkward silences and slander of the silly rules of basketball. But assembly was as uninteresting as usual, and the last lessons to conclude the day were maths and more maths.

At four p.m., Mama picked me up and boy was I relieved that my first day was over! After I got home and had some fried duck legs, Grandmama took me to her study — my classroom — where I recited more of *'The Laws of Sorcery'* (*'The Laws'* for short) for my upcoming Grade 6 test next year, and then went outside to practise turning a wonky root into an even more wonky tree... you should see grandmamas back garden, it's a random collection of half-grown trees, trees missing leaves and leaves missing branches. I cut my time down to one minute and three seconds though, and with a few more tries my ancestors are sure that I'll get it in under a minute. Grandmama gave me that look as if to say she wasn't as confident as them.

I was absolutely exhausted after that. Channelling your powers together with reading fifty pages of archaic language (much like the Shakespearean tale of Romeo and Juliet) had me longing for my pillow. I'm writing this before signing off for an early night, but one sure to be disturbed. It's loud out there tonight… the wind is howling, and my ancestors whisper to me words of reassurance that promise me my dreams, but simultaneously keep me from them: "Tomorrow, trees will grow and your strength will, too."

That's it for tonight, otherwise I'll fall asleep on top of you!

Until tomorrow, Dairy.

Chapter 3
Two percent Mortal

Tuesday 3rd September 2020, 6.15 p.m.

My wind chime alarm greeted me again at dawn, the sun only just starting to rise. Who on this unearthly earth decided that we should wake up when it's still dark outside? A mortal, I would guess. A myth about unearthlies: we 'like' the dark. Who *'likes'* the dark? Sure, it's fun when we're casting light spells or watching scary movies with a big bowl of sweet 'n' salted popcorn, but seriously, not to WAKE UP in! I snoozed my alarm once… twice… for a fleeting moment of silence. On the third alarm, I opened my eyes just wide enough to catch sight of Stumbles, laying at the bottom of my bed. How he gets up here is a mystery, but then life is full of those. "Get down, Stumbles." We entered into a staring competition, which he was always destined to win. It was a battle of stubbornness, and it was far too early to be stubborn.

Stumbles and I have a complicated relationship. I don't mind him much, but he usually avoids me unless I'm the only one home and he's seeking food scraps, then I'm his favourite. You would have thought he would do more than use me for food — I gave him his name after all. He kept finding his way under my feet which led to plenty of stumbles and banged knees. Mama thought it was ever so funny. "A name so peculiar that it could only be given to a naughty guinea pig on a mission to knock little children over," she said as she chuckled. But after my third bruise in over a week, the humour was lost on me.

When I finally convinced Stumbles to kindly make his way off my bed (encouraged with a slight shove) I heard a knock on my door so gentle it could only have been Miss Michaela, our earthly housekeeper. Miss Michaela is one of the few mortals I am fond of; I've practically grown up with her around. During the summer holidays she was my only real company (aside from the many ghostly inhabitants of Hemlock House) and I still look forward to her arrival every morning. When I've asked, Miss Michaela says she is fifty years young, "give or take a couple." Although the other day I was trying my luck for a few more minutes of my favourite programme on the television, so I attempted flattery and told her she didn't look a day over twenty-eight. She laughed at me but declined to hand over the controller, proceeding to ruthlessly hit the 'off' button.

"It's getting late," she said, "and you don't want to be tired for all of your sorceress business tomorrow."

"Oh please, Miss Michaela, I won't be tired, just ten, maybe fifteen more minutes, max."

She shook her head which was carrying her very kind smile and even kinder blue eyes, as her thick salt and pepper hair followed, and instructed me to get ready for bed.

Miss Michaela has worked for our family for thirty-nine years. Her papa worked as the Hemlock House groundskeeper when she was ten or eleven years old, and when her mama tragically passed in a car accident, he had no one to look after his daughter and so brought her into work with him. Grandmama tells me she used to help him with the garden, but on the rainy days she felt sorry for Miss Michaela and offered her to come inside until it passed. Grandmama spent some time getting to know her, and she started playing with mama too, in the early years. They formed a close friendship, sharing secrets and telling stories, but mama was sent to a boarding school attended only by unearthly students (before the pact was introduced some nineteen years ago) for most of the year. During this time, Miss Michaela started to pick up some chores around the house, tidying the study and dusting the windows. After a while, Grandmama offered her a few pennies for her time, and soon Miss Michaela would formally become our housekeeper. When mama returned for the summers, they would still play (much to the dissatisfaction of both communities), but only after they each finished their unique duties in the evenings, and for forty minutes between the hours of twelve a.m. to one p.m.

Miss Michaela often tells me stories of when her and mama were little (and whispers stories of when they were older, too, pretending that the ancestors won't hear, but knowing they probably will). She actually introduced Mama to my papa. He was a distant cousin of hers who had recently moved to Vormera when they met. His papa — my estranged grandpapa — was reassigned to another job within his organisation. He worked for a bank that operated exclusively for unearthlies and earnt a fine wage to compensate for the shame that was cast upon him for it. Miss Michaela introduced them at an earthly party one summer evening, which mama snuck out to once grandmamma had turned her light out for bed. They gravitated towards each other, as the story goes. My papa spotted her from across the room and their eyes locked as their bodies drew closer, synchronously, as if they found themselves as the protagonists of an award-winning romance film. I try to believe in that, in true love, but I've always been taught that the power love is unfortunately not as great as that of magic. And so our loyalties should, above all, lie with our craft.

"Are you up, buttercup?" Miss Michaela's soft voice permeated through my wooden bedroom door. "School time, sunshine," she sang.

I take great pleasure in waking up to her voice, it's far more friendly and gentle than my wind chime alarm, which consistently shrieks at me as if it has just witnessed an atrocity. I murmured back:

"Miss Michaela, please make the sun go back to sleep so I can too."

"No can do, Lorrie, I asked it the same question this morning but it told me no."

How rude. I decided to give in to my fate after a while of resisting and fumbled of bed, careful not to catch a glimpse of myself in the mirror — now that really *is* the sight of an atrocity! I contemplated using a very well-practised spell of compelling my bed to make itself, cushions and all, but mama disapproves.

"You need to learn to do things the *normal* way too, Lorelei, like every mortal has to do."

"But why, I'm NOT a mortal!"

"Because you're being lazy, and you need to appreciate the wonder of mortality!"

I'm not sure what 'wonder' Mama keeps referring to, I would be downright *bored* if I was an earthly, that's for sure!

32

Mama always had a longing to be earthly, she doesn't keep that quiet, and I sort of understand it, but I don't *feel* it. I mean I know it's probably to do with my papa and how she had to lose him to keep me (and to keep her freedom), and I know that it's not a decision anyone would choose to make. Of course, I wish she didn't have to, either. I didn't *choose* to grow up without a papa, I would have loved one. But then I never knew him so I can't *miss* him, just the *idea* of him, really. I once saw a faded black and white photograph of mama and papa sitting on a picnic blanket; his arms wrapped around her in a bed of autumn leaves. They looked happy. *Mama* looked happy. I hadn't seen that expression on her face before and it felt strange, they both felt like strangers. I felt for her, not the lady in the picture but the one in her bedroom, now, two doors down the hall from mine. I also felt for the man. He had lost his wife and daughter all in one fell swoop. But I didn't feel sorry for myself, really. As I said, I didn't *know* him. But for a second, when I studied his face, I could see mine in it too. Just for a second. And that's when I felt a brief feeling of longing. How would it have felt if he held me like that? Would his mortal arms be weak or strong, cold or warm?

I quickly placed the photograph back in the old chest, hidden by dust in a room not used any more, when I heard footsteps in the hall. I wondered when last someone gazed their eyes upon the chest, and the memories it kept hidden. I do hear mama wander into the room sometimes, late at night when the ancestors have kept me awake. Maybe she meets him in the dead of night, re-living the moment in the picture and staying with him for a short while. I've even wondered, when I've heard whispers belonging to a strange voice to which Mama answers, that she surely can't be talking to the ancestors she resents so. Could she be summoning her powers, the ones she so often rejects, to connect with him in another space and time, or a place, perhaps? I've thought about how I would feel if that were the case if I'd want to meet him too. I'd be curious I guess, how much of him lives as a part of me. How much of him Mama sees in me. She tells me I have his nose (not literally of course, although some sorceresses do keep organs and limbs suspended in liquid-filled glass jars as part of their spells).

If you're wondering, Diary, how a child born from a sorceress and a mortal could be the redeeming prophecy of the late Malasea Orenda, I'm wondering that, too. In biology we learn about "unnatural intimate relationships" between unearthlies and mortals. Of course, such a courtship — although very rare — is considered a great tragedy and both communities tell tales of babies born with crooked fingers that have trouble casting unerring spells as a threat to deter the idea. I don't have misshapen fingers, though, I'm pretty certain of that (I've studied them for long enough). In fact, I had some of the experts baffled. It would appear, from the many experiments conducted on me by scientists from both kinds, that my veins pump blood which is infused with the powers passed on to me through my unearthly parent. They reckon I share some of my papa's blood, too, but that it's sort of "inactive" because the blood of my ancestors was strong enough to render it so. This had them conclude that I am roughly ninety-eight percent witch, two percent mortal. It's odd because I've only known of one other 'demi-sorcerer', and while he didn't have crooked fingers, he did have trouble with his spells; they never turned out the way they were intended (he managed to shrink a lizard to the size of a pea by trying a simple grade 1 spell of changing its colour).

He is a boy who lives on the unearthly side of the Vormera Cathedral, where not only enchanted creatures are forbidden to enter, but all earthly creatures, too. It lies on the border of the earthly county, ironically. History books have described it as a centre of dark magic, though no one knows why. But all who pass its grey steel gates and enter its grounds are overwhelmed with a sense of dread. Even birds have been spotted altering their path to avoid flying over it. Speculation has grown over the years, and some believe that a true horror occurred inside its walls. One so evil, so dreadful, to establish it as the birthplace of dark magic itself.

In old books found during a seize of Sereia's underground temple (as it was called) there were drawings of the cathedral, capturing its architecture with illustrations of its floor plan. There is no doubt that she chose that ghastly place as a site to carry out her final malevolent spell. While there is no clue as to when it was built — and by whom — a small silver plaque on its heavy door is engraved with its name. Over the years, a series of troubling accounts given by visitors who dared take a step inside led to its closure. One woman told her friend how she saw a face in the window above the alter, right before the air was taken from her lungs and she struggled for breath. Were it not for her husband, who was by her side at the time, dragging her out of the gates, her breath may never have returned to her!

When more tales of bad experiences and sightings of the mysterious face in the glass spread amongst the communities, the Council of the Mother of the Wand, and the opposing Council of the Mortal Beings, finally had one thing they could agree on: the Vormera cathedral is a threat to all and shall be open to none. It was thereby shut to the public in 1981. Shortly after its closure, a group of teenage wizards seeking a thrill entered the cathedral one night, carrying bottles of cheap honey whiskey and blasting music from a stereo. Screams were faintly heard by passers-by who couldn't be sure of where they came from or who they belonged to, as the church bell sounded simultaneously at midnight, and the boys were never seen again. Informal search parties were arranged by their parents and neighbours, but then even the official search teams did not enter the building. Location spells and seances were performed but no trace of their spirits, were found. Not in this world, or in another. It was assumed that whatever sinister forces lie within Vormera Cathedral had taken them as prisoners, swallowing them up and stealing their souls.

Anyway, sorry to go all dark there, I think it's all nonsense; stories to scare children so that they do not wander alone into earthly territory at night. I lost my trail of thought, where was I? Oh yeah, so a boy who lives on the other side of the cathedral has an earthly mama and a sorcerer for a papa. He used to go to my school, but he was pulled out after only a term in. His teachers argued over which lessons he needed to attend, and he never had much luck at making friends. No one really knew where he fit in. There was pressure from the board to withdraw him, with the suggestion that his parents rather provide him with home-school education. Everyone agreed that it was probably for the best, school was a rather confusing place at the best of times, I can't even *imagine* what it must have been like for him!

Because I was pretty much all unearthly and tiny bit earthly, I didn't get any trouble from anyone. It was kind of accepted that my place was with the unearthlies. But I did feel sorry for the boy — I saw him sitting alone in the lunch hall every day, and one time I nearly felt bad enough to go over and say hello. But I'll admit, and I feel awful about it, that I did think about how people would talk... what they would say. "Look at the two demi-unearthlies getting along," was what came to my mind. "Maybe they should teach each other how not to mess up spells and how not to shrink reptiles." I was building up the courage and even spoke to mama about it all, and she of course was horrified that the school would let a child be treated that way, just by who his parents were. I had every intention of introducing myself to him (or I'm pretty sure I did) but then one day he just didn't come into school, so I never gave it much thought after that. I'm not proud of it and I do *still* feel bad about it, even just writing it down.

School today wasn't much more eventful than yesterday. After I eventually got dressed in my uniform and went down for breakfast, Miss Michaela wandered into my bedroom to tidy it up a bit and inspected my bed. She could tell that I made it without channelling magic, and mama says that just to be stubborn like Stumbles, I put in extra effort to make sure my pillows are *not* aligned, and my duvet falls to the floor on one side. That *might* be true... Mama drove me in again, and this time Cleo greeted me at our car, unaccompanied by Mel. I remember her saying that she didn't feel too good at the end of the day yesterday, so I guessed she wasn't feeling any better and stayed home. I was hoping Cleo wasn't planning on hanging around with me *all* day; he had an annoying habit of doing that. Luckily, we had different lessons in the afternoon, so I managed to get rid of him by lunchtime and boy was I ready to. He spent the whole morning trying to show me a trick he'd learnt and finally managed it but was spotted by Mr Goddard and got into trouble for practising magic in the hall. It wouldn't have been so bad if he wasn't so smug all the time. My lessons in the afternoon were long and boring, and when I got home grandmama was resting, which meant I got to rest, *too*! No spells tonight, time for TV!

Until tomorrow, Diary.

Chapter 4
I won't bite

Wednesday 4th September 2020, 7.45 p.m.

Mel was back today. I was EXTREMELY relieved that I didn't have to entertain her brother for a whole morning. They seem to stick together, Mel and Cleo. I guess it's partly because, following the scandal of Mr Magus and his supposed dark magic practices, our other friends seemed to keep their distance from Mel, and Cleo's friends' sort of stayed away from him, too. Mel was, of course, very hurt by it all, and I was disappointed in the ones who I thought would be there for her no matter the rumours. Cleo did his typical thing of pretending he didn't care that his closest mate, Regin, also decided not to associate himself with the son of the dark wizard. "Whatever... it doesn't bother me. He wasn't much company, anyway." But Mel could tell that he was hurt, and so could I. He tries to hide it but one day last term I came into school late (we had an unfortunate episode involving Stumbles peeing on my skirt) and I found him loitering in the hall. This was just *days* after his papa was investigated for his crimes. As I approached Cleo, he turned his head away from me, but I caught his eyes, and I could tell they were red. His cheeks were also flushed while the rest of his face was pale.

"You okay, Cleo?"

"I'm fine, little witch. You better run along, you're late!"

he commanded in a husky, stern tone.

"Thanks for that, I can tell the time you know."

I felt for them both, but Cleo really didn't help himself. His bitter, arrogant persona certainly didn't nurture sympathy.

"I'm seeing Dean today," I said to Mel as we walked into the English classroom.

"That bad smell? I feel for you, little witch." Cleo butted in, uninvited, while Mel rolled her eyes and replied:

"Could be worse, you could have got paired with Queen Jessica the mighty and rude."

"True" was the only word appropriate to respond with. "He's not too bad I guess, but it's a whole hour of true earthly bore."

"You sure you don't fancy him, witchy? I hear he's quite a catch with the ladies!"

"Cleo, would you stop putting your nose where it doesn't belong!" Mel snapped back. "You don't though, do you, Lorrie?" Mel turned to me and asked with caution.

"What? Don't be ridiculous, he's an *earthly*! I couldn't think of anything *worse*!"

I was almost offended that they could ever think I would fancy Dean. I could see why the earthly girls fancied him though; he wasn't bad to look at, for a mortal. I was scheduled to meet him after lunch, which was after music, which was after English. English was all right, we studied Gothic Poetry. Do you ever feel like you read way too much into a meaningless string of words? Our teacher is CONVINCED that every single reference to the colour red is a metaphor for periods. PERIODS, of all things! But I kind of like the gothic as a genre, I mean it's far more inviting than Chaucer and his Pardoner, which you basically need to learn another language

40

to be able to interpret.

I normally look forward to my Music lesson. Although I usually get stuck with the triangle (I have about as much musical talent as a goldfish!). My favourite thing to do every evening before bed is to lose myself in orchestra soundtracks and violin ensembles. Music is like chocolate to the ears; sweet and addictive. The other week, I compelled my instruments to play a symphony so glorious that I can almost never listen to the radio again. There's something about music that speaks to me. I struggle to relate to any other art form, especially when created by earthlies, but music is one thing I can generally always appreciate, earthly or not.

I walked into the music room, greeted by Mr Maguire. He was a music fanatic and was totally open about it. Good morning, Miss Orenda, ready to rock that triangle? 'Rock' is one word for it — tap gently, more like. "Yes, sir, ready!" I replied awkwardly and unconvincingly. As I took my seat, I spotted Dean two rows in front of me. He was poised with his tuba. An intriguing instrument, the tuba. It could sound so dreadful and so beautiful, depending on its master. It's surprising that we hadn't spoken about music before and relied on mocking sporting celebrities to fill our time. We clearly both *enjoyed* the sound of classical instruments.

For some reason I paid particular attention to Dean today. Maybe it was in apprehension of our meeting scheduled for the afternoon, or maybe it was just curiosity; my two percent earthly curiosity. But from the back of the room, I observed him as each instrument began to sing out. He joined in after the fourth bar, and I couldn't help but admire how he lost himself in his instrument. He seemed so absorbed, but so free at the same time. An image of peace if I were to try and describe how he looked. After the second verse I was dreading having to come in with my 'big solo'. As if the triangle ever deserved a solo! I braced myself for every pair of eyes to turn to me at once, which is exactly what happened. I struck the metal precisely nine times with the intention of maintaining a rhythmic pattern. On the ninth strike, I gazed up prematurely in relief of having almost finished my part and hit the bottom right corner of the metal.

CLAAANNNNGGGG! An awful ringing noise sounded which had everyone reaching to cover their ears. As I said before, musical talent is NOT something that I possess! I gazed around the room while I felt my cheeks burn. Dean lifted his head and caught my eye. I think he could tell how much I wished in that moment to retreat into a dark hole forever. He directed me a grin which I sensed was one of empathy, even of reassurance, perhaps. It was one of the few I had seen from him. After my total fail, which ruined the entire piece, the bell rang for lunch. Thank goodness for that!

On the menu today was beef bourguignon (which I only know how to spell because I saw it written on the board outside the lunch hall). It sounded fancy and I wasn't sure I had it before, but when I went to taste it, I caught a whiff of the steaming sauce and it reminded me of something. I couldn't quite put my finger on it, but it had a taste of happiness. Maybe I had it over Parismas one year, that is my favourite holiday! Parismas day presents as one of the few exceptions where Mama and Grandmama lay down their metaphorical swords, so to speak, and forget about their life- long disagreement over magic. Even the ancestors remain quiet (well, not totally, but more so than usual). I cannot WAIT for it this year! Grandmama has already hinted as to some of the gifts she's arranging for me. She spoils me, I must admit. Mama does too, but in her own 'advocating for mortal presents' kind of way.

Take last year, for example. Grandmama hid a small jar under my pillow… It was filled with a potion that, if ingested by any creature, would cause them to giggle hysterically. '*Giggle-grub*' was the unofficial name we gave to it. Of course, the first creature I used it on was Stumbles; I mixed it in with his lettuce. He ate the whole lot, too! Stumbles giggled for what felt like twenty minutes straight, pausing momentarily to catch his breath every few seconds. Me and grandmama nearly wet ourselves! Mama walked past the dining room to investigate the sound, and even SHE found it difficult to hold back her laugh. The same day, mama wrapped up some earthly makeup for me, as well as a pair of Chewy Trainers, made from 100% earthly materials. I was grateful, but not quite as amused as giggling Stumbles. Can you blame me, Diary? I had never witnessed a laughing guinea pig, after all.

Anyway, I enjoyed the beef thingy today, which I ate with Mel. Cleo rarely joins us for lunch, though I'm not too sure where he spends his hour. Mel says he needs some "alone time", and when I asked her where he goes to receive this, she shrugged her shoulders and said: "not sure really, probably to the forest to get away from everyone!" ("Everyone" being earthlies and unearthlies alike). I've noticed that she never questions him when he returns, which is usually after the second bell call. She just greets him, and he says "hey" back, so I pretty much do the same. I do wonder though, but I've learned not to question Cleo. His short, defensive responses don't give much clarity, and end up leading the conversation into silence pretty quickly. He's a lot like his papa in that way, according to Mel. It's no wonder they get along so well. They spend most weekends together and every summer they go on an extended papa-son holiday (without disclosing the location, in true Magus mystery style).

Speaking of family trips, Mel was rambling on about "the adventure" that her family had planned for the long weekend. They're going to the Isle of Dominia where they have a "fantastic three-day schedule" planned. Within their 'schedule', they're spending a day at *'Musea de Potin ela Charmus'* (The Museum of Potions and Charms stores *hundreds* of mystical objects which have been found and collected over the years) where they will explore the temporary exhibition of the collectibles hand-picked by the Mother of the Wand. I think they're also planning to go on a guided tour through the old caves once thought to belong to Parisa, and earlier witches. I've seen photos of the caves in unearthly history, with confusing writings and abstract images smeared into the walls.

I zoned out as Mel went into more detail of her family's plans for the holiday, until she asked me if I would like to come with.

"You should totally come, Lorrie, we'd have the best time! Tell your grandmama it's for research purposes, to learn more about your heritage. Just think, we could spend a *whole week* together. Oh, it would be wonderful!"

It sounded like fun, but I wasn't sure Grandmama would bite.

"I'll have to ask, she's already planning every single spell I'll be practising with my grade 6 test coming up."

I think I told you that Mel is on her Grade 5. Did I also mention that Cleo is only on Grade 4, which you might have guessed, Diary.

"Oh do, Lorrie, do ask! And tell her that I promise I'll make sure myself that every day you spend at least three hours reading some more of the Laws of Wit — I mean Sorcery, The Laws of Sorcery."

I smiled at Mel; we both knew she would do nothing of the sort. If anything, she would steal it from me the moment I hop into the car to make sure I would focus on nothing but gossiping and plotting more harmless spells to cast on Morton. The truth is, not that I could say it to Mel, that I could probably convince Mama and Grandmama of the cultural value of the trip, were it not for those rumours about Mr Magus that had everyone in a tizz. But I told her I'd try, mostly to shut her up. I love Mel, she's my best friend, but sometimes... just SOMETIMES... she can chat your ear off, if you let her. And I'd rather keep my ears where they are.

Tick. Tock. Tick. Tock. Dean was late for the first time since, well, ever. He was *always* on time, for *everything*. It's one of the things I like about him if I have to dig really deep. I turned to Mrs Mapleton who, of course, had her eyes glued on me already. She shrugged as if to share my confusion. Ten minutes and counting... I thought to myself that at least if he doesn't show up I could probably get off a bit early. No point sitting here like a potato if I'm not joined by another one. I was just about ready to walk over to Mrs Mapleton and plead with her to let me leave when Dean walked into the room. Our meetings always take place in the sports hall, which is separated into four quartiles, each with a table and two chairs. Also positioned against the walls were two isolated chairs, one on each side of the hall opposite each other, which seat the eager eyed supervisors (usually Mrs Mapleton and an unearthly teacher). At the tables, the pairings would take their seats across from each other. Approximately four pairings would meet at any one time, but there were only two others there today.

Dean walked towards the table, pulled out his chair and took his seat while Mrs Mapleton forced out a loud sigh. He was quieter than usual and avoided my eyes.

"Sorry," he spoke silently and coughed as if to clear his throat. "Sorry I'm late," he continued while looking at the floor.

"That's all right, another minute though and you'd have done me a favour — I'd have been out of here like a bolt!" I tried to lighten the mood.

He smiled slightly, but still at the floor.

"Sorry I wasn't late enough then, I guess."

Something was odd about Dean today. He never usually says much, neither of us do, but this *felt* different. Usually, it's our shared awkwardness and acknowledgment of how little we have in common that keeps us from talking. But this time, it was more like he was sad… sombre. He didn't seem that way before lunch, when he fired me that grin in Music (remember, when I totally embarrassed myself *and* my not-so-trusty triangle). We probably spent five or so minutes basking in our usual silence. Dean was twiddling his fingers below the table, and I was glancing between my notepad and Dean. I wanted to say something. I don't *choose* to spend my time with earthlies, but that doesn't mean I enjoy seeing them all upset like that. I'm not a dark witch, after all!

"So I saw this crazy…"

Dean shifted in his seat but didn't raise his head to meet

mine.

"I saw this stupid…"

I was intending to make up a story about how I'd come across an interview with a snobby tennis player or something like that, but I couldn't quite bring myself to. He was just SO quiet.

"Dean?" I wanted him to look at me, for once.

He raised his head and met my eyes, not making a sound.

"Let's talk about music, for a change, eh? I could've died in that lesson, everyone staring at me. It was mortifying! I think even my triangle was judging me for my careless handling of it!"

He smiled again. This time it was wider, and he held my eyes.

"Yeah, I mean it was rather unfortunate. Wasn't the most pleasant of sounds I've ever heard."

"All right, no need to rub it in." I actually got a laugh, this time.

"Sorry, Lorelei, it wasn't all THAT bad, it just could've woken the dead, is all!"

I returned a laugh. I noticed that he used my full name and, come to think of it, he always has. The only other person who does that is my grandmama when I've messed up a spell, or sometimes Mama when she spots me using spells outside my practise hours.

"Remind me not to come to you for comfort, Dean!"

It was the most natural, easy flow conversation we'd ever had, and he had a sense of humour, too. Who would've thought? I thought that maybe we should stick to music, for a while, instead of the obnoxious sporting industry. Dean had the same idea.

"Do you listen to music much, Lorelei?" Dean's voice softened again and he brushed his hand through his hair as he asked me the first personal question probably EVER.

"Some, I guess. Mostly in the evenings before bed, or after I've studied with my grandmama."

"Studied?"

"Oh yeah, I mean, uh, once I've studied my… spells." I was hesitant to say the word.

"Oh, yeah, makes sense." We were tumbling rapidly into awkwardness again!

"I like classical stuff. I clearly can't play it, but I like to listen to it." I tried to recover the conversation before it completely died a lonely death.

"Me too. I usually put my headphones on when I'm working on cars at my father's garage! It helps me to focus, I guess."

I found myself sort of *enjoying* our interaction. I was kind of glad he was perking up, too. I didn't think about him much, obviously, but I certainly didn't think that I'd almost feel *sorry* for Dean. He just did look *so* sad when he came in. I wondered if anything had happened, I wondered if I'd ever find out? Unlikely. After about twenty more minutes of actual conversation, with to and fro chatting and laughing, Mrs Mapleton had to remind us — actually *remind* us — that we had come to the end of our time.

"All done for today." She spoke sternly and without hesitation, as if waiting for the clock to strike three so she could end this disgraceful interaction. All other tables were silent — I suddenly noticed that as Dean came to the end of his sentence. They always were though, that was no different, but what *was* different is that ours *wasn't*. We both stood up after Mrs Mapleton clicked her heel on the floor to signal the end of our time. Dean retreated back into his solemn mood, curling his shoulders and looking at his feet again. It bothered me that he was bothered, and it bothered me even more that *I* was bothered that *he* was bothered. Why? I had never cared before...

Dean walked towards the door as I followed him out the hall, with Mrs Mapleton trailing us both.

"Dean?"

"Yeah?"

I turned my head to catch enough of Mrs Mapleton's disapproving eyes.

"Can I show you something? It won't take long, it's just something I think you might like..."

"You have FIVE minutes before your last period." Mrs Mapleton adamantly reminded us. She was starting to really annoy me now (I wonder if I could use a silencing spell on her, I thought to myself).

"It won't take long, Dean!" I spoke with persistence, for Dean's benefit and Mrs Mapleton's.

"Yeah, I suppose..."

He didn't sound as confident, but he followed me as I turned my direction and we drifted off from Mrs Mapleton. I knew the Music room would be free; all the teachers meet up and gossip in the staff room (separated by their kind, of course) when the pairings have their meetings. As we were navigating the halls, I could feel Dean staring at me through the corner of his eyes. He was probably speculating as to where on earth this unearthly was taking him. I shared his confusion. I wasn't sure *why* I wanted Dean to perk up, it's not as if I'd be spending any more time with him this afternoon.

As we approached the music room, I peeked in the slightly ajar door to make sure no one was in there. Our instruments lay as we left them; my triangle resting limply on the edge of one of the wooden benches where I abandoned it after it betrayed me. I looked at Dean as he hesitated at the door threshold.

"I won't bite, ya know!"

He entered the room, still very unsure. I paused for a minute until I worked out what I was going to say to him… how I was going to explain it. This wasn't really allowed, what I was about to do. "Magic should *not*, under any circumstances, be performed outside of unearthly lessons", as stated in the school rules.

"Dean, I… I wanted to show you something and it's… I suppose it's because you like music and all…"

"Lorelei, are you about to get us both into a lot of trouble?"

Dean realised that I probably was, but his voice picked up as he said it and I sensed a hint of excitement hidden beneath his reluctance.

"So it's basically… it won't scare you, or it shouldn't anyways…" I was seeking his permission, but he remained quiet.

"I'll just show you then, I suppose…"

"Remember, Lorelei, you told me you wouldn't bite!"

"Lorrie!" Mama's calling me from downstairs, Diary. "Come and get your dinner, it's getting cold!"

My thoughts ran away with me. I'll have to finish my entry tomorrow evening.

Until tomorrow, Diary.

Chapter 5
Pandymonks

Thursday 5th September, 6.50 p.m.

So, where was I? Oh yeah, Dean reminded me that I promised not to bite him. I wasn't planning on it, anyway, I'm not a vampire (those don't exist, obviously)! Besides, earthly blood would be disgusting I bet. I imagine it would be tasteless, utterly unsatisfying. So, there we were, alone together in the music room. In hindsight, Dean was probably *terrified*. He didn't seem it though, he seemed maybe a little nervous, but then I certainly wouldn't feel too comfortable in the presence of a sorceress who had just led me into a room, on my own, and told me they "wanted to show me something". And I'm still not sure whether it did bother him, what I showed him yesterday, because he avoided me all day today like a smelly sock. But he seemed to enjoy it at the time, but then maybe I'm not good at reading earthlies, in all their lack of expression and general enthusiasm about everything.

I knew Dean wasn't feeling cheerful, I could tell it by the way he carried himself, and by the fact he was late for our meeting. I guess I'm no good at watching people be miserable — I've seen Mama do it all her life. It didn't suit *her*, and it definitely doesn't suit *him* either. I think I was also excited that we finally had something to talk about besides a mutual dislike for our athletics programme at school (which I couldn't figure out if we had both invented to occupy the hour-long sessions). But either way, I felt an urge to open up a gigantic part of myself to Dean: my powers. I gave him one last glance before casting my spell. While I closed my eyes, I could feel his were fixed on me. In apprehension, perhaps, or curiosity — maybe both.

I whispered the words to Parisa's *'Instramalus Vocus'* spell I had practised in my bedroom (which has been modified since her earlier recordings of it where a whole load of instruments hadn't existed at the time). With the flick of a finger (literally) the instruments in the room started to sing, in harmony. The strings on the guitars came to life, the piano keys sounded, and the flutes echoed. Dean's tuba made a sound so beautiful, as if it had finally achieved its perfect tune. Even my triangle rang out in a sweet but quiet melody; complimenting the other instruments, instead of disturbing them.

I turned to Dean. His eyes were closed, and his face was neutral. Oh dear, was this all a mistake? I thought to myself. I desperately wanted to use one of the Grade 7 spells of mind reading to figure out what Dean was thinking, but that can only be done to willing participants through a tedious process; one that even involves a formal application! Otherwise, location spells set by the Council of the Mother of the Wand can identify and sanction any unearthlies who cast such spells on those who are 'not approved'. It was another pact made to keep peace with the earthlies, I suppose. How I wished I could break it in that moment.

I let the melody carry on for a few more moments, but gradually each one of the instruments faded out in my trepidation. When the last violin breathed its final note, I hesitated before glancing at Dean again. His eyes opened gently, as if he was waking up from a deep sleep, and we both stood in silence. His gaze shifted from the chairs beside the instruments and halted on mine. They were so blue, the kind of blue you see in the sky on a clear, sunny day. Before he could say anything — and I thought he was about to with the slight break in his lips — we heard a few pairs of footsteps in the hall. It startled us both — the sudden sound that invaded the delicate silence.

"We should probably go, Lorelei", were Dean's long-awaited words. After what I just showed him, that was the best he could come up with?

I followed Dean out the door this time and we parted ways in the corridor. He uttered not a single word to me before he fled the scene of the crime.

After that, my afternoon was uneventful. I arrived home after school and was greeted by Stumbles, who I suppose was still in a grump with me after our falling out (and his falling out of my bed) the day before. I focused on reciting more of the Laws instead of my usual spell practising, as grandmama wasn't feeling too good. She's been having spells of awful headaches (not the magical kind, the brain kind) which have left her somewhat fatigued and mostly bed or couch bound. Mama's been taking care of her, despite their usual avoidance of each other. When I fell asleep last night, after eating dinner and watching half an episode of *'Sam and Marnie'* (a trashy but gripping reality TV programme involving two earthlies who adopted a bunch of unearthly children), my last thought was of Dean. Would he pull me aside tomorrow and tell me how irresponsible and outrageous I behaved by showing him my spell? Or would he run to me and tell me it was the most magnificent thing he had ever laid his eyes and ears upon?

Well, it turns out he did neither. He simply avoided me for the entire day today, and when I passed him in the hall or spotted him in the lunch queue, he made an obvious effort to look anywhere but in my direction. Mel asked me how it went with him yesterday, after she ranted about Jessica for about ten minutes straight.

"All right!" I replied, purposefully withholding the details of the events that occurred.

Mel probably would have taken great pleasure in my rule breaking and magic showing, but she's a loud-mouth and soon enough everyone in the school would have heard about it.

"Did you speak to your grandmama yet, Lorrie?"

"I…"

"I hope you told her I'd make sure you do some intense studying?" Mel had a bad habit of interrupting.

"I haven't yet, but I'll speak to her tonight after…" Cleo bounced up to the table and took a seat opposite me.

"What's this I hear, witchy, you joining us for the epic Magus family gallivant on the weekend?" Like his sister, Cleo also shared the tendency of not letting people finish their sentences.

"I'm not sure my grandmama will let me, she's…"

"She's what? Go on, finish that sentence!" Cleo's tone changed suddenly, and his face transformed into a shade of red while he leaned forward.

"She's just worried I won't keep up to date with my reading is all…"

"You sure it's not cause she's afraid of the big bad Mr Magus, like all these other gullible idiots?" His piercing eyes were anchored on me, as if they were intent on burning a hole in my brain.

"Cleo, don't be ridiculous, Lorrie's grandmama doesn't

believe all that stuff, does she, Lorrie?"

"No, of course she doesn't. She barely keeps up with the weekly edition of 'Magic Madness', never mind the silly town gossip!" I wasn't sure how convincing I sounded, but I must have done an all right job as Cleo's face softened and he slumped back in his chair.

"Aah well, I'll make room for you in the car then!"

"Thanks, Cleo, generous as always!" I rolled my eyes in return for his wink.

When I walked through the timber door of Hemlock House, Grandmama was sitting on the sofa, nursing a cup of lemontwine tea and reading a novel. I asked Mama in the car how she had been feeling.

"Oh, you know your grandmama, she's far too stubborn to complain. I've been feeding her bowls of Reece's Remedy soup with a sprinkle of opal stone salt. Always does the trick for me when I catch a nasty bug!

I picked up on a slight sense of worry in Mama's voice, disguised with an attitude of nonchalant. Although it probably wasn't the right time, I cautiously broached the subject of the "Magus family galivant".

"Mama, Mel and her family are going away this weekend to the Isle of Dominia. How would you and Grandmama feel if I tagged along with them?"

Before she had time to reply, I sensed hesitation coming and quickly continued:

"It'll be a factual, educational tour of our history and heritage with lots of opportunities to learn."

"Did you rehearse that speech, Lorrie?" Mama smiled, amused by my formal, teacher-like dialect before continuing.

"Oh, I'm not sure if it's a good idea Lorrie, you know how

we both feel about the Magus's, how *everyone* feels about them…"

"But it's not about THEM is it Mama, it's about Mr Magus and he's barely gonna be around… (lie)… I think he has some business planned so we'll basically be alone: Me, Mel, Cleo and Mrs Magus (total lie)." I had, to my advantage, Mama's fondness for Mrs Magus. In fact, that's how Mel and I met in the first place and became the best friends we are today. Mama and Mrs Magus were in unearthly baby class together, which Mama was forced to attend as one of the "conditions" of her deal with the Mother of the Wand. Mrs Magus is also not the most avid supporter of the MOTW council, so I guess they bonded over that.

Mama told me that if I could convince Grandmama, she would let me go with the Magus's. Although she made it clear that I shouldn't get my hopes up, as she doubted Grandmama would agree. But what she didn't know was that I had a few tricks up my sleeve that Mel taught me (not the magic kind, the conniving teenager kind). Turns out I didn't have to use them, Grandmama surprised us both with how easily she agreed to it.

"I suppose so, Lorelei, but I will be setting in every evening, eight o'clock, to check up on your readings."

'Setting in' is where unearthlies can 'jump in' to someone else's mind, so to speak, and directly observe their experiences. So, if I was eating a chocolate bar hidden under my bed which Mama told me I couldn't have before bedtime, she could 'set in' to my head and see through my very own eyes the very big chunks of chocolate I was guiding to my mouth (it has happened, once or twice…). Mama maintains that she despises magic, but she sure does use it to her advantage, when the occasion calls for it. Again, with all the rules set by the MOTW, this should only be done to consenting unearthlies, who are almost always direct relatives. And of course, should NEVER be done on an earthly. A crime such as that could be punishable with a temporary suspension on one's powers, or worse...

A couple of years ago, an unearthly set into an earthly student who was sitting at a desk next to his, during an exam. Unsurprisingly, he got caught because his answers were exactly the same, word-for-word, as those of the earthly. He didn't even bother to amend the silly spelling mistakes that the earthly made. It really wasn't very clever. Anyway, he was given a formal warning (by the school board AND by the MOTW council) and a week's suspension of his powers the first time it happened, but then the third time he did it and got caught, I suppose sympathy had run out. He was expelled and sentenced to a year of unearthly community service. I've obviously never *personally* experienced unearthly community service, but I hear it isn't a whole lot of fun. We walked past a group of unearthly delinquents once, when we went on a school trip to the '*Zoo of Unearthly Creatures*'. The three of them were in the Pandymonks enclosure, cleaning up their mess while being chased by the little racoon-like creatures. Pandymonks are ugly, adorable things. They're known for their mischievous behaviour, and they're not very intelligent, apparently.

No one is quite sure how they do it, but the most well researched powers of Pandymonks is that they can make you extremely forgetful, provided you get close enough to them. They have the biggest effect on earthlies, of course, but unearthlies have also been known to misplace their sunglasses (which remain on their forehead) or forget to pick up their handbag after viewing the little creatures.

It was hilarious watching the unearthlies that day. They kept re-cleaning the same spot of the enclosure, forgetting that the other had done it just five minutes earlier! Took them an hour to get through a ten, fifteen-minute job, MAX! Even the earthly students couldn't stop laughing, which may have been partly due to the Chucklebubs in the adjacent enclosure. Chucklebubs look a lot like shrew moles and release laughing gas (as in, their farts literally make you break out into fits of laughter). Giggle-grub is made from extracting the laughter-inducing particles from Chucklebub gas, and I have a bottle of it sitting on my windowsill. It's a little gross when you think about it.

If you're wondering about Stumbles, Diary, we aren't too sure if he has any powers or not, other than being astonishingly annoying. If he does, he's done a good job at keeping them a secret. Grandmama is convinced he's a mystical creature of sorts. She says she can "feel his unnatural energy." Mama and I surmise that what grandmama probably feels is the heat he emits when he releases a great blast of wind. That creature is disgusting!

Mama and I exchanged looks of surprise when Grandmama agreed to the trip without even the slightest battle. I was prepared for it, after having practised my "speech" once already on Mama. I perfected it, even. I kissed Grandmama on the cheek, gave her a huge hug and ran up to my bedroom to start picking out what clothes to pack. As I was removing my entire wardrobe and laying it out on the floor, I heard Mama and Grandmama having one of their rare, prolonged conversations.

"Mama, are you sure you think it's a good idea? I mean

Lorelei hasn't been away from home for more than a night, let alone three, and the Magus's… I'm just not sure…"

"Well, Fiona, she has to be trusted at some point, and it may be nice for the child to have a break. She has been working very hard, after all."

Yes, Grandmama, I sure have!

"Well, I know, I just worry is all," Mama responded.

"Worry about her, or about me?" There was a moment of silence.

"It's unusual for you to be so… accommodating, Mama. Are you *sure* you're feeling better?"

"Yes, Fiona, stop fussing, you fuss too much! If you were half as worried about me when you used to get up to your teenage antics, I wouldn't have *this* many grey hairs!"

I can't want to tell Mel tomorrow; she's going to be beyond herself with excitement. I suppose Cleo will have to make space for me in the car after all. I'm going to get a head start on some of my readings from the Laws. Hopefully then I won't have too much to read while we're away, and when Grandmama sets in, I'll have my book at hand. I am *slightly* worried though. Come to think of it, it was fairly unusual of Grandmama to be so "accommodating", in Mama's words. Maybe she isn't feeling as well as she says she is… Stumbles interrupted my train of thought as I caught sight of him scowling at me from my bedroom door. He provided me with just enough motivation to get up and close it on him. Time to read, Diary!

Until tomorrow, Diary.

Chapter 6
Mr Good Boy

Friday 6th September 2020, 6.00 p.m.

Mel couldn't believe it when I told her this morning as we collected our books from our lockers. Her eyes widened and her hands were held on her cheeks.

"You're kidding. No way, no way, NO WAY!"

I nodded with a gigantic grin.

"Oh, Lorrie, this is the best news EVER! We are going to have such fun I cannot *wait*!"

Mel only ever used my full name when she was either seriously upset about something or seriously happy about something. We started walking towards the unearthly science classroom.

"Of course, Grandmama will be setting in every evening and expects to find me by my book, which she will, won't she, Mel?"

"Oh well of course she will, where else would you be, Lorrie?" Mel remarked with a smirk on her face and sarcasm in her voice.

We both laughed.

"I'll just need to run it past Mama and Papa, but I have no doubt they'll be delighted for you to join us!"

I paused in my tracks and stopped Mel in hers.

"Wait, you haven't asked them?"

"Well, to be honest, Lorrie, I wasn't sure your grandmama would say yes. So, I didn't want to make a fuss about things that weren't likely to happen. But honestly, they'll be totally fine with it, I promise!"

Mel does this sometimes; she gets carried away with her own ideas and doesn't seem to involve anyone who would be affected by them. I find it slightly frustrating...

As I internalised my annoyance, I caught sight of Dean walking in my direction. He normally changes course when he sees me coming his way, and he *definitely* saw me. This time, though, he continued walking straight towards me. Closer... closer... He wasn't stopping...

"Lorelei..."

He halted in front of us, his focus shifting between Mel and I. I responded with silence, taken aback by the novelty of his approach. I could tell Mel was also a bit stunned.

"I wondered if I could have a quick word with you, maybe alone, though?" He spoke softly, but with purpose. I could sense Mel's glare.

"Um, sure, I have US in like five minutes though, so it'll have to be quick."

"That's fine, it'll only take two." Dean reassured me with his comforting smile, so trustworthy he seemed.

I ended up being ten minutes late for Unearthly Science (US, as we call it) but I didn't mind so much. Mel required some prompting to leave us alone.

"Mel, would you give us a sec?" I asked.

"Yeah, sure, Lorrie, I'll see you in US."

Once Mel walked on, I turned back to Dean.

"Is everything all right, Dean?"

There seemed to be a delay in my question and Dean's

response, as if he pondered this a while before answering me.

"Yeah, um, I'm okay."

The little confidence he had was dwindling, which was made obvious by the awkward silence that followed. I waited a while and then broke it by professing:

"You seemed to avoid me after, you know, what I showed you the other day…"

"That's what I wanted to talk to you about, actually," he quickly jumped in. "So I wanted to say that I'm sorry about all that, but I guess I just didn't know what to say at the time."

He's mortified, I thought to myself. He's completely disgusted.

"It was incredible, Lorelei. I haven't seen or felt anything like it."

Surprise.

"Really? I wasn't sure if you were afraid or… annoyed by it or something."

"Annoyed?" he remarked with amazement. "Lorelei, I hadn't told you this but the reason I was late to our meeting that day was that I'd just been through some difficult stuff and… well it doesn't matter but I wasn't feeling too good and you…you helped. I can't explain what it felt like, I really can't, but I'm glad you shared it with me and I'm sorry if I gave you the impression that I wasn't happy about it."

I couldn't quite believe what he was saying, and how *much* he was saying. This was the first time in my whole life that an earthly ever told me that they found my magic "incredible", and the longest string of continuous words I had heard from Dean's mouth. I didn't quite know what to say, and I think he could tell.

We spoke for a few minutes more. I was tempted to ask

about the "difficult stuff" he referred to, but I contemplated whether this would show I was *too* curious. I also got the sense he didn't really want to talk about it. So instead, I spoke about how I learned the trick from grandmama when I had a sore tummy and needed cheering up. Dean laughed and remarked that it was the most unusual thing he'd heard of to cheer someone up when they had a sore tummy, but that he was sure it made me feel a lot better (which it always did). He also said that when he wasn't feeling too good, his mama normally made him gooey chocolate brownies. At times he would pretend he was unwell and, although he was sure his mama knew this, she still made him the brownies.

"So, Mr Good Boy does tell lies after all?" I teased.

'Mr Good Boy' was a name commonly associated with Dean, probably because he never once got into an ounce of trouble. The perfect student; already set in line to be Head boy.

"I lie, Lorelei! I tell *hundreds*, even *thousands*, of lies! I am a terrible liar, it's a problem."

"Oh really? Is that a lie?" I said with an exaggerated sense of scepticism.

"Maybe," he smirked while his head dubiously fell to the floor.

Then followed a natural lull in the conversation, so we mutually decided that we probably better head to our lessons. I told Dean to have a nice long weekend, and he said he hoped I would have a nice one too. I was eager to know what he had planned but, again, *too curious*!

I walked into US and Mel's head shot up from her book.

"Miss Orenda, you're late."

Miss Celesti's glasses were poised on the arch of her nose as her stern eyes peaked above. What is the point in that, seriously? She doesn't need the glasses for two reasons. 1. She's an unearthly and she could easily book in to any of the Magical Medics who can temporarily enhance her vision (they haven't found a spell to permanently alter sight, so she would need to visit one every four months or so for a 'top up'). 2. She's not even looking *through* them; they're resting on her nose threatening to flop off at any slight nod of her head and providing her with no support whatsoever. But I suppose it gives her the 'teacher look'. You know the one, Diary.

Anyway, so apparently, I missed the register and all of five minutes of an introduction to the unearthly digestive system. Turns out it works the same as earthlies, really, when it comes to food. You chew, swallow, your tummy does some wacky things like churn it up, and then you poop it out. It's more complicated than that, but those are the basics. The only difference is that our stomachs work *faster* and *more efficiently,* and we can digest pretty much *anything!* Even things that have no nutritional value, like Sandstone flakes, which are actually delicious when you crumble them on top of custard or, if you're striving for health, yoghurt. It's a shame you can't try it, Diary, considering your lack of digestive abilities. You'd love it!

Although we can stomach most things, there's only one ingredient known to cause extreme sickness and agony to unearthlies when ingested, while proving absolutely harmless to earthlies. It's been the subject of all kinds of research, and it's something as feeble as *Thyme*! Thyme has been the cause of multiple conflicts between earthlies and unearthlies in the past. In a dispute between an unearthly man who owned and managed a pizza restaurant, and his earthly employee who waited tables there, the earlthy man sprinkled a few fragments of Thyme into the managers soup while he was on his lunch break. The manager practically inhaled his lunch and there was a short delay before he became suddenly and violently sick, decorating the restaurant's newly purchased ivory carpets in a shade of deep red, to match the tomato soup he had swallowed.

As Thyme is just about the only thing that could have incurred such a reaction, when the manager recovered a few days later, he stormed into his restaurant along with two unearthly policewomen and had his employee arrested. He even went as far as to hire the most expensive lawyer money can buy, and pressed charges on the man for *attempted murder*. It fell through and instead he was sentenced to four years in prison followed by three years of earthly community service (no pandymonks were involved) for assault.

Turns out, the reason he poisoned the manager was because he brought his dog, Pollock, into work just that once, as there was no one at home to look after him, and he knew that the manager wasn't due to come in that day. He kept the dog in the manager's office (bold move) and at the very moment the manager unexpectedly walked in to collect his briefcase that he mistakenly left the night before, the dog decided to unashamedly do his business in the corner of the room by the elegant looking pot plant.

The manager was FURIOUS. Some say he came close to mystically engulfing the dog in an ignition of unnatural flames. Instead, though, in a moment of anger he cast a covert spell on the dog to never be able to do his business again. The dog unfortunately became very sick as he ate and ate with nowhere for the food to go. He now has an artificial suction pump to relieve his bowels (gross stuff, sorry) and the employee spends every penny of his wage on the dog's extra digestible dog food, which doesn't even do the trick!

It reminds me of Stumbles a bit. He eats everything in sight but, unlike the unfortunate dog in the restaurant, he certainly does not hold back in letting it out into the world. He left a nice present for me ('nice' meaning repulsive) at the bottom of the garden once. It collided with my shoe in an unfortunate series of events, and I swear that Stumbles intended it to — I could see him on the porch staring in amusement, obviously pleased with himself.

"What was that all about?" Mel was seated at the desk in front of me and had turned in her chair as I took my seat behind her in US.

"What was what all about?" I whispered back while unpacking my books, my eyes on Miss Celesti who I was more cautious of now.

"You know, with Dean!" Her voice suddenly spiked in volume, alerting the entire class.

"Miss Magus, is there something you would like to share with the class?" Please don't, Mel, I silently begged.

"I was just catching Lorrie up with what she missed, Miss Celesti."

Obviously, no one bought that, Miss Celesti included, but she continued with the lesson after a prolonged period of directing her thick, intense, raised eyebrows at Mel.

"I'm watching you, girls, another word and you'll be explaining yourselves to Mr Goddard."

Nothing like the threat of being confronted by Mr Goddard to put a sense of fear in you, NOT! But we both shut up anyway, knowing that Mel couldn't for the life of her maintain a lower volume of speech if she tried. And she rarely tries.

"Wait for me, I need details." Mel ordered as we started packing away our things at the end of the lesson.

I took extra time, partly because I knew I would be subject to a hundred questions after we left the classroom, and partly because I was still a bit distracted by my earlier conversation with Dean. It was the first time we spoke outside of our monthly meetings, and I hoped we would speak again before the next. Though I would never admit that to anyone, especially not to Mel. An unearthly *choosing* to speak to an earthly. And *taking pleasure* in it? Almost unheard of!

"So, tell me Lorrie, what did you speak about? Why did he want to speak to you and in *private*? That's rather strange, isn't it strange?"

"Um, we didn't speak about much!" I intentionally kept my answers very brief, hoping Mel wouldn't continue prying, but I should know her better by now.

"Well, that doesn't tell me much. What did he *say*? He must have said something you took a good ten min—"

"All right, Mel" I turned to her as I sighed out the words. "I'll tell you, but you can't tell anyone, okay?"

"Not a word!" She gestured, zipping her mouth shut with her fingers.

I leaned in after looking around to make sure no one was listening in.

"So, basically, Dean told me he's completely and utterly besotted with…"

"With?" Mel's eyes were wide as she eagerly awaited the big reveal.

"With YOU!"

Mel was speechless, and I couldn't remember her *ever*

having nothing to say.

"With me?"

She seemed concerned at first, which changed to surprise, and then apparent flattery.

"I suppose I have noticed him staring at me a *lot* lately. We were in the lunch queue yesterday and I totally caught him looking at me... did he say *why* he has a crush on me?"

"He didn't say, but he made me promise not to say anything and I swore I would never speak of it, so do NOT go saying anything to anyone!"

I knew this was the one thing Mel wouldn't repeat. She would be mortified if everyone thought an earthly fancied her. Especially if Easton found out; their imagined love affair would surely come to an abrupt end. It was a white lie — one I hoped would get her off my back about Dean. It seemed to work too because she remained silent as she inevitably processed the news.

Cleo eventually caught up to us. He was in the US lesson, too, but he was asked to stay behind by Miss Celesti after she handed us our test papers back. I assumed that meant he didn't do too well. Cleo doesn't have the best academic record, but I had my suspicions that he was smart. He just didn't seem to care much when it came to schoolwork. He was much more interested in messing about and back chatting the teachers, which does not make him a favourable student. He got worse with it all and started caring *less* after the rumours of his papa spread around school, which they did like wildfire.

"So, what's this about Dean that my sister, in true Mel fashion, blurted out in front of the class, then?"

I began to reply.

"Well, Cleo, since you're asking..."

. "It's nothing!" Mel interjected. "He was just apologising to Lorrie for being late to their meeting. That's all, isn't it, Lorrie?" Mel was pleading with me, and I was enjoying making her squirm far too much. But then again, she does it to me all the time.

"Yeah, pretty much."

I showed Mel mercy by changing the topic of the conversation.

"I've started packing for tomorrow. Anything you'd like me to bring with? My camera maybe?"

Mel welcomed the diversion.

"Yeah, bring your camera, definitely! Oh and any chance your mama can make those delicious Sandstone flakes for the car ride?"

"Oh yeah good point, we normally pass a crummy earthly ice cream place on the way that could do with some added flavour," Cleo remarked.

"I'll see what I can do. What time should I be ready for?"

"Probably nine-ish. We always aim to leave for six, but I've never seen it happen!" Mel responded.

"That's because it's never happened, in the history of Magus family trips," Cleo confirmed.

They both laughed.

At just about the same moment, and I'm not sure how it all happened, but we were interrupted by a sudden '*booof*' noise and next thing I saw was paper flying everywhere. Cleo's exam sheets, each decorated with the letter 'D' in red, bold ink, were spread out over the floor. Cleo hastily and purposely dropped to the floor as he scrambled for his papers. While he collected them, I looked up to see Dean, frozen in his place like a deer in headlights. He slowly crouched down as if to help Cleo, but he never actually reached for any papers. Cleo rose and was followed shortly by Dean, who fixed his eyeballs on the unearthly boy who was known for his short temper.

"Watch where you're going, earthly!" Cleo's voice simmered with anger.

"Sorry, I was… I didn't see you there."

Before the collision we were making our way to the library for a private study period. I also needed to get a few books for a project I was working on in Geography. Geography was the only subject which *wasn't* differentiated for earthlies and unearthlies. The earth is the earth; some of its substances are raw, some of them are mystical. It always elicited interesting debates about who the earth serves best in regard to its inhabitants. The unearthlies view the discoveries of unnatural products as evidence of Parisa's rule, and the earthlies practise their lack of imagination and uninspired logic to prove that they are the original and intended inhabitants, and *we* are the unwelcome intruders.

The project we've been assigned relates to the formation of rivers. I won't bore you with the details, but basically direction of flow and erosion are involved somehow, and we've been set the task of building a model to illustrate this. It can be physical (and made only out of raw materials) or electronic, in the form of a poster or animation.

"Get creative, kids!" Mr Johnston enthusiastically chanted.

Of course, it is necessary to suck the fun out of the task, and so magic is strictly not allowed.

"It would be an unfair advantage to the unearthlies, and strength of character is not built by unfair advantages, kids!"

Blah blah blah.

"I smell like earthly now, ew!" Cleo shrivelled his face as he recalled the unexpected, unfortunate encounter with Dean.

I felt bad for Cleo; for both of them, but mostly for Cleo. He reminded me of a duck scrambling for bread by the way he rushed to conceal his test papers. I don't think he *enjoys* the bad results and detentions, they just seem to be drawn to him somehow, and him to them, like a dark magnetic spell. And Dean, he really looked like he was braced for a beating, not that Cleo has ever laid his hands on an earthly.

"It wouldn't be a fair fight, poor things!" Cleo pointed out as he exercised mercy.

He had a couple confrontations with unearthlies that resulted in black eyes or scratched faces (emphasis on 'a couple'), mostly with Cleo as the perpetrator. Again, after the rumours he seemed to go looking for trouble. He was seemingly desperate to both prove and deny his dark demeanour: a self-fulfilling prophecy.

It was the first time I had ever seen Cleo directly address Dean. Not once had I ever witnessed them utter a word to one another. They often directed cold looks of loathing, as did every unearthly and their earthly counterpart. I could see Mel switching her gaze between the boys as her brother fell and her "admirer" stood upright. She later theorised that Dean had obviously been so distracted by her that he smashed straight into Cleo. Or alternatively, he did it as an excuse to get close to Mel.

"If he was trying to make an impression, that probably wasn't the way to go about it!" Mel ruminated. "I mean, I suppose he did catch my attention. I suppose you *could* say it was a romantic gesture of sorts…"

I began to regret this rumour already.

"Mel, I really don't think that was his intention. I mean, no offence, but I doubt he would intentionally push your brother to the ground in a master plan to win your affection." Although I did wonder to myself, why *did* he collide with Cleo? It's a straight corridor, Cleo was generally careless in his motion, but surely Dean would have seen him. After Dean's nervous apology, Cleo reawakened his commonly used fire eyes (the ones he used on me when I spoke about Grandmama's hesitation with the trip) and held his position, prompting Dean to back away like a timid rabbit in a lion's den. I shot Dean a look of sympathy as he faded into the background of the busy hall.

The rest of the afternoon was dull, MUCH less eventful than the morning. I got home and started packing, only to be summoned by grandmama to practise some spells. She was feeling a bit stronger, although she mostly instructed me without any demonstration and she didn't join in, like she usually does. We had a lot to catch up on before my test, and I'm about to lose my long weekend to the Magus family adventure.

I'll write an entry tomorrow, Diary, before Mel's family pick me up at nine.

Until tomorrow, Dairy.

Chapter 7
Fortunaes

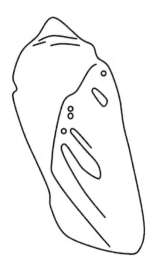

Saturday 7th September 2020, 8.20 a.m.
It's a miserable day, Diary. The kind of day where the clouds threaten to do their damage with an outpour of rain but hold it in just to toy with you. It's grey, and the wind is icy. I've packed a pair of gloves and my scarf is waiting for me by the front door. Even unearthlies get cold — it's one of our few misfortunes. The forecast tells me it'll get warmer by lunchtime, and the clouds should clear. Is the weather forecast ever right, though?

I walked past Grandmama's room; the door was half open. I could see her sitting on the edge of the bed, sliding her feet into her slippers, and taking her time to do so.

Knock, knock.

"Hello?" she sounded surprised.

"Morning Grandmama! Would you like a cup of spiced nettle tea?"

"Oh, yes darling, that would be wonderful." She said it as if I'd answered her prayers.

The ancestors kept me up last night, whispering to me of my duties to continue my studies while I embark on my adventure this weekend. It's as if they have eyes on YOU, Diary, and are reading my inner schemes to neglect my reading, for a day or two. I shushed them and threatened that I would be too tired to do my readings if they didn't give me some peace and quiet for a good night's sleep.

I've packed my copy of the Laws and I intend to bring it out into the world at eight p.m. sharp, every evening. Or, maybe a bit before to scan a few pages in case Grandmama questions me (which she most likely will). I had a suspicion that Grandmama would want to practise one more spell with me before I left, but when I asked her as I handed her the spiced nettle tea, she said that it's best I practise by myself today, as she wasn't "in the right mind". I actually wanted to practise my new spell. It'll be pretty great to show Mel and Cleo if I can master it. It's basically a spell called *Fortunaes.* It involves predicting fortunes but, more than that, if you really get the hang of it, you can predict them through your dreams. Which means you basically get to see someone's future when you're asleep. Like watching a boxset on the TV — free entertainment!

You may be wondering how you can *show* someone a trick which is displayed in your mind, Diary. Well, the proof is in

74

the pudding, so to speak. I could foresee Mel, for example, and the evidence of my trick could be written in a fortune cupcake. If it comes true (which it would if it's performed correctly and doesn't get distorted or misshapen, as it so often does) then that's the magic! Of course, there is a debate as to the cause and effect. If I've *predicted* it and it happens, is it because I've told her it's going to happen, and so she's *made* it happen, or is it because I've seen the inevitable future. Sorry to splurge some unearthly psychology at you. It's part of the theory behind the trick, though, so it's relevant.

The trickiest part is trying to channel a specific moment in time, and a specific event. Last night, I tried it for the seventeenth time. My task was to channel what Grandmama would be eating for dinner in three days' time, without telling her but writing it down in my spell book as later evidence of its success (or failure). So, I fell asleep having recited the spell and placing a drop of fresh dew on my tongue. In what felt like an instant, Grandmama emerged in my dreams, clear as day. I saw a chicken and pumpkin pie, which I wrote down as my prediction, but then Stumbles came into the picture (who else) and I was suddenly observing him doing his business in the spot of the garden where he normally catches people out. I suppose it's because I wrote about Stumbles and his excretory habits before-hand, partnered with having uttered the words *ever so slightly* incorrectly. It was nasty, though, I saw the up close and personal detail of it, which is something I neglect to observe when it happens in real life! No doubt my prediction on Stumbles will come true, but I'll have to wait to find out whether Grandmama had her pie.

"Lorelei, come down, the Magus's are here." I could hear

Mama and Mrs Magus chatting for a while, but they're half an hour early which was unexpected.

"Couple more things to pack and I'll be there, Mama!"

I can hear Mama whispering very loudly to Mrs Magus as I write…

"How have things been lately, Radella? Any more word from the council on Arion's caution?"

"No, Fi, he's confident they have no case now that the witness… well disappeared."

"Do you think he's right?"

"I'm not as confident…"

"And the kids?"

"Melusine is doing okay, she still has her head in the books. But Cleo… he seems a bit *off*. I've tried to talk about it with him, but he just shuts down and tells me there's nothing to discuss because nothing happened… 'Dad will be rid of the ridiculous rumours soon' is all he keeps saying, but he's getting into trouble at school, his grades are down, his teacher's… I'm not sure what to do about it, honestly."

"Oh Della, I'm sorry I haven't been there more for you all. It's just hard for me, with everything…"

"I know, Fi, I heard you defended me to that Witch Maraja the other day, and I really appreciate it, I do! And I don't expect anything more from you. Lorelei's friendship has already helped Mel, and Cleo. He talks about her quite a bit, I think she has really done them a world of good by sticking by them."

Cleo talks about me? I dread to hear what he says about the "little witch".

"But if there *is* anything I can do, anything to do with the kids, do let me know, Della!"

Beep. Beep.

I looked out the window to see Cleo leaning over his papa's shoulder and pressing the horn.

"That'll be Cleo," Mrs Magus remarked.

"Lorelei?"

"Coming, Mama!"

I'm afraid I don't have much room for you in my suitcase, Diary, neither do I have much room for you in my packed schedule (sorry). I'll be back on Monday. See you in a few days!

Until Monday... maybe Tuesday... Diary.

Chapter 8
Four-thirty tour

Tuesday 10th September 2020, 6.00 a.m.
So, Diary, there's a LOT I need to update you on.

We got back late last night, and I was EXHAUSTED! The trip back wasn't quite as… spirited as the trip there. When I walked out to the drive after Mama had a word with Mrs Magus on Saturday morning, Cleo sprang out the car and in true sarcastic gentleman fashion he held the door open for me, his arm extended out to gesture me in. In a formal accent with a deep voice, Cleo pronounced:

"Hello, Miss Orenda, please take your seat in your noble carriage, and strap yourself in for the ride."

I rolled my eyes as I passed by him and took my seat in my "carriage". Mel said hi to me as she grinned, her eyes filled with excitement and her smile wide, bearing every one of her teeth as if the grand curtains had opened to present a stage of performers. She was seated by the window, and I knew that meant I would be wedged in the middle of her and Cleo for the whole four-hour trip. Great! Mrs Magus followed me out and took her seat in the front passenger side.

"Hello, Mr Magus," I spoke softly.

He peered at me through his rear-view mirror as he mumbled "Hello." Man of many words is Mr Magus.

"You strapped in kids? All ready to go!" Mrs Magus

sounded as though she was trying hard to be brighter than she was ten minutes ago.

Cleo jumped in the car and announced:

"Ready as a gassy Chucklebub letting it loose!"

Classy. Goodbye sarcastic gentleman and hello Cleo.

"Eww" was everyone's unanimous reaction, followed by laughter and more eye rolls. The weekend was sure to be full of them — I just hoped I didn't lose my eyeballs in my head!

The journey there was long (clever us thinking we could miss the long weekend traffic). For most of the way, we listened to Mr Magus's fascinating but unnecessarily monotone audiobook about the origins of the rainbow tree. It's a bizarre yet delightful wonder of the earth, located just beyond the border of the Isle of Dominia, with origins unknown but suspected to be an unearthly phenomenon. They say it reflects every colour of the rainbow if you catch it in the right light.

We also stopped by the gross ice cream place, which was as gross as Cleo warned. I ordered mint choc chip with a dash of ground tulip sauce, which is mostly for decoration; it doesn't taste of much. But even though I was informed about the quality of the ice cream, I didn't *really* believe ice-cream could taste THAT bad. How do you mess up ice cream? Surely that's the work of dark magic, and the sorcerer should be charged as guilty! I drowned it in Mama's best batch of Sandstone flakes, which improved the taste massively.

Mel and Cleo started arguing when we were just one hour in, and Mr Magus threatened them with his audiobook if they continued. They did continue, and hence the audiobook. It was hardly worth it, the topic they chose to argue over. I wasn't listening much; I spotted a small but pretty butterfly out of the window, keeping up with the speed of the car, and then I started daydreaming (I do that a lot). I caught the odd word and from what I could gather, Cleo was teasing Mel about Easton, as a brother does, and Mel told him to "shut up" a few times, which of course he didn't. Does he ever?

We arrived at the hotel early afternoon. It was a lovely building, from the outside, but a bit less lovely on the inside. The carpets were tired, and the wallpaper was peeling at the corners of the walls. We had two rooms booked; one shared between Mr and Mrs Magus and the other reserved for Mel, Cleo and I. We checked in and Mrs Magus handed Mel our key, with '*Room 15*' inscribed on the copper tag. Mr and Mrs Magus were in the room opposite, number twelve.

"I heard there are earthlies staying here too, Radella," Mr Magus whispered with disgust as we walked down the narrow corridor.

"I can imagine there are. The Isle of Dominia attracts all types of visitors from around the earth. The mortals are also intrigued by our culture, I suppose. A bit scared too, I imagine."

Mrs Magus was right. I was told once by an earthly at school that learning about unearthly heritage was "creepy... like watching a horror movie. You're frightened — terrified even — and you cover your eyes but you can't stop watching and so you peek through." It was an awkward conversation cause the earthly had just joined the school and she must have thought I was one of her kind, too. She wasn't paying attention to the collar, obviously. But when she did spot it, she went bright red. Her complexion resembled a strawberry.

"Oh... I'm sorry, I didn't mean..." was all she managed to get out before she scurried away.

She definitely meant it though, but I wasn't offended.

"Better than watching a dull movie with no twists or turns. Just trivial earthly occurrences: brushing teeth, doing homework, working in your dad's car shop over the summer, like your earthly does..." Mel remarked when I told her later that day.

We laughed about it. It must have been *mortifying*, and if she was scared of unearthlies before, I bet she felt rather unsettled after blatantly insulting one.

"I bet she thought I was going to curse her!" I said as I reminisced over the incident.

"I think you should, Lorrie, you've had enough practise on Morton, time to move on to the next challenge." Mel winked and we still chuckle about it.

We agreed a plan to meet Mr and Mrs Magus downstairs by Reception in fifteen minutes. It was probably nearing three p.m.by that time, and Mr Magus was set on visiting the caves before nightfall.

"Shotgun the double bed!"

Cleo wasted no time in securing his spot after we entered the room, and before we could protest, he threw his backpack on the bed, placed his arms out by his side and flopped backwards onto the covers.

"Cleo, how on this unearthly earth does that seem fair to you?" Mel snapped back, but with minimal effort as she probably knew it wasn't worth the fight.

"I'm longer than you, I need more space!"

Mel and I relented and made our way to the bunk beds. I took the top one. I walked up the tiny ladder, which could barely hold my feet, and let my body flop face down.

"It's strange how you feel tired after a long drive. You do

nothing but sit in the same position for hours and you end up feeling exhausted, or is that just me?"

"Nope, not just you witchy, I feel the same!" Cleo agreed, and Mel did too:

"Yup, I could just fall asleep right now."

"Alas, the caves await!" Cleo said as he chucked a pillow at Mel. "What's in the caves, anyway?" he naively asked.

"Cleo, we learnt about this like three weeks ago. We had a four-page test on it!" Mel pointed out.

"Huh. I probably should have paid attention then. Makes sense why I didn't pass it."

I felt kind of bad for him in the moment, so I tried to sympathise:

"I also didn't click that it was the same caves, Cleo. Will be interesting to see them though, maybe you're just more of a visual learner!"

I peered down and saw Cleo sitting on the edge of his bed. He seemed relieved by my offer of reassurance, and even smiled at me — a genuine smile. Mel jumped aboard the empathy train:

"You're probably right, who can really learn from a textbook anyway?"

We arrived at the caves at four-ish after getting lost. Turns out Mrs Magus is not a renowned map reader, but that came as no surprise to her family, who have endured her navigation challenges every time they travel. I wondered whether there is a spell for that; it would save a *lot* of time and energy. There probably is, there's a spell for practically anything and everything, I just haven't discovered them all. I told myself to make a mental note to ask Grandmama later when she sets in.

As we drove into an area which was framed by a wooden

fence, we saw a sign reading: *'Parisa's caves: get your tickets here.'* We queued up for a while at the ticket booth at the bottom of the cave trail. When we reached the front, Mr Magus asked for five tickets for the four thirty guided tour. I offered to pay for mine, and I sensed Mr Magus was about to let me, but Mrs Magus interjected and said not to be silly, I was their guest. We were told by the ticket booth man to congregate at the *'trail begins here'* sign, when it came to our time.

While we waited for the start of the tour, Mr Magus's phone kept ringing, and he continued silencing it. The ringtone sounded like the one they set the phone to as a default, similar to the classic wind chimes that greeted me every morning — supposedly calming, but truly irritating. I almost wished he would answer after the fifteenth-or-so ring. He did after a couple more, prompted by Mrs Magus who elbowed him in the ribs and shot him a disapproving side glance. I think she noticed the stares we were getting from the other tourists; it was a really annoying ringtone!

I was sort of curious as to who would be so desperate to get hold of Mr Magus, seeing as everyone in the community has disowned him. But as Mr Magus answered, he distanced himself from us. Mel started reciting some facts about the caves, while Cleo obviously remained quiet, and Mrs Magus listened with pride at her daughter's knowledge.

"Did you know, they reckon that only seven witches have lived in these caves. They found the bones for three of them, but the rest are missing."

"How do they know that there were seven then? A bit of archaeologist imagination running wild, there?" Cleo sarcastically enquired.

I was half listening, but I knew the same facts Mel did, I

just didn't channel my inner know-it-all like her, on a daily basis.

I was distracted by Mr Magus. I wasn't sure why — I'm still not — but I had a peculiar feeling. I felt unsettled. I glanced at him. He was standing a fair few metres away, and I couldn't make out much of what he was saying, with Mel and Cleo jabbering. But I could almost sense his anger. He was gesturing with his left hand, almost like he was swatting a fly, and raising his voice while maintaining a whisper. I could hear a few words, but most likely out of context. I noticed there was a rubbish bin just to the right of him.

"I need to throw my gum away," I pronounced, without much of a thought.

"Yep!" Mel acknowledged as I walked towards the bin and continued spouting facts to anyone who would listen.

As I drew closer, Mr Magus was faced with his back towards me.

"I can't talk now, P. It's all set in motion and I'll update you tomorrow after I retrieve the package."

That was the clearest sentence I could get. Shortly afterwards, Mr Magus spotted me and lowered his voice, pushing his phone into his cheek and tilting his head so that his mouth was closer to the speaker. After that, all I heard were a series of mumbles, picking up on every fourth or fifth word:

"Pocket." "Alarm." "Boy." "Lemon."

Whatever he was talking about, it sounded very random.

"Four-thirty guided tour of the caves. Four-thirty guided tour of the caves. Calling all with tickets for the four-thirty tour."

We both heard the call. Mr Magus quickly said goodbye to whoever was on the other end of the line, and I threw an imaginary piece of gum into the bin. I walked towards the crowd as Mr Magus followed closely behind.

"I heard they do ghost tours, if you come after nightfall… spooky!"

Don't tell anyone, Diary, but I preferred Cleo's cave facts to Mel's (although it's debatable whether they are actually facts or not).

"I heard the carvings on the walls are drawn in blood!"

"Correct, young man!" The short, enthusiastic tour guide (who looked like he was dressed for a safari) turned to the group and confirmed Cleo's claims as we walked through the entrance.

"Mind your heads" he had warned us as we approached the dark hole, after a ten-minute hike up the steep, rocky terrain.

"Bathed in blood, these walls. It is thought that Parisa made the first mark. An offering to the caves who would house and protect her for some ninety-four years." He drew out the words "ninety-four" in the air with his finger, as if he was set in slow motion. I guess it was meant to add to the suspense of it all.

I was quite enthralled by the caves, I must say. It was dark and dusty inside, but the 'paintings' were crystal clear. Time hadn't seemed to disturb them; only slightly faded the ones in the direct path of the sun. One captured my eye. It looked like two figures, their shapes distorted by large cloaks that draped them, positioned one behind the other. Beside them was another mark, and I couldn't tell if it was part of the same image. I also couldn't be sure of its form, and so I asked the tour guide. His response:

"Ooh, good question young lady. Are you a sorceress?

You strike me as one. Although no one is sure, it appears to be a symbol… or a small, unusual creature… or just an unintended flick of the brush… Who knows!"

For some reason, I wanted to memorise every detail of the marking. Although I heard the rest of the group move forward into one of the tunnels, I found myself stuck; as if I had unknowingly walked over wet cement that dried in an instant. I can only vaguely remember it, but I could have sworn I *tried* to move but my feet wouldn't lift. In the moment, though, I didn't feel afraid (which is unusual cause if I really was stuck in a dark cave haunted by mighty powers roaming the space, I would have thought I *would* feel slightly unnerved). Instead, I lifted my head and faced the painting once more. I continued analysing it for a while, as I could feel my head pulling closer to the wall, and my eyes squinting. There was a moment, a brief but unmistakable moment, where I thought I saw the figures… well, where I thought I saw them *move*!

"Lorelei" I heard Mrs Magus calling my name, she was obviously more panicked than me.

Her torch rushed towards me and her shadow followed.

"Darling, did you get lost? We're all on to the next tunnel. Please pay attention, Lorelei, we can't have you getting lost on our watch!"

"Sorry, Mrs Magus, I… I hadn't noticed. I'll keep up, I'm sorry."

"Where were you?" Mel whispered as Mrs Magus and I re-joined the group.

"I… dropped something, I was just trying to find it…"

"You mean like your imaginary gum, Lorrie?" Cleo's voice called out from the darkness. How did he know?

The tour itself lasted half an hour. The guide started most of his sentences with "Although we can't be certain…" or "It is believed that…" I suppose if Parisa really *did* live there for some ninety odd years, she was most likely smart enough to leave many questions unanswered. We then got to wander around for a bit. Cleo was having trouble with his low-energy torch they gave us for the tour, and he was banging it against the palm of his hand while muttering insults to the poor thing. Mel and Mrs Magus were examining one of the markings, comparing it against its description in the tour handbook they purchased at the booth. I lost sight of Mr Magus for a while, but he emerged from the darkness as the tour was nearing its end. He is an odd man. We made our way to the souvenir shop which was mainly selling magnets. In a corner was a small rack of t-shirts and caps, all printed with images of the caves, or of specific paintings, etched with the logo *'Parisa's Caves'*. I spotted a magnet of the marking I was so entranced by. It was buried under hundreds of other cave magnets which were exact replicas. I felt a warm flow of air on my neck, which startled me. It belonged to Cleo.

"What you spotted?" he said in a husky voice, which sounded far too serious for Cleo, and made a change from his normal, jovial tone.

"Oh, just a magnet of one of the paintings. Not sure why, but I liked it."

Cleo was silent for a while, but then resumed his sarcasm: "Work of art!"

I placed the magnet down, and we headed back towards the car.

We had an early dinner at the hotel restaurant, and Mel and Mr Magus treated themselves to some edible ice-cream, which they seemed delighted with. We were all tired, so we walked up to our rooms together and parted ways in the corridor again. I was just in time for Grandmama's scheduled 'set in' at eight p.m. I grabbed my book from my suitcase and laid it wide open on the floor. I recited some of the "key takeaway messages" from pages one hundred and eighty-eight to two hundred and eleven (which I rehearsed last night) and Grandmama seemed satisfied, as she left me after just fourteen minutes. Mel fell asleep fairly quickly, but I suddenly didn't feel as tired once I staggered up my ladder. How annoying is it when that happens?

"Lorrie?" Cleo's voice once again surfacing from the dark. "You still awake?"

"Yep, I can't seem to keep my eyes closed."

"Neither can I! What did you like so much about the painting, anyway?"

"The painting?" I had a brief lapse in memory.

"The one from the magnet!"

"Oh yeah... I'm not sure, really. I think I just found the whole tour really good. And the painting, it was just curious, I suppose." I waited for Cleo's response, but it never came.

"Goodnight, Cleo."

"Night, little witch."

"Coming, Mama." I'm being called down for breakfast. I'll finish this off after school, there's still so much more...

Until... well you get the drift by now.

Chapter 9
Mortal or Magic

Tuesday 10th September, 7 p.m.

Where was I? Oh, so I fell asleep and dreamed of the cave marking. Why was I so fascinated by it? I couldn't remember exactly what happened in the dream, but it felt like I woke up prematurely, as if I had missed the most important part. I could hear Cleo snoring as I climbed down the ladder, while Mel was up and ready for the day; her hair drying from a wash, and a backpack crammed with tourist goods (water bottle, camera etc.). I glanced at Cleo. It was unusual to see him in such a quiet and serene state. It made quite the contrast from his awakened self. He looked quite peaceful, and I felt happy for him in his solace, but it seemed as though Mel was set on waking him up. She flicked the lights on and plugged her hair dryer in, right by his bedside, despite the many plug sockets located around the room. He pulled the pillow over his head as the dryer roared, and he uttered a groan.

"Wakey, wakey, sleepy head!" Mel shouted above the noise of the hair dryer, with zero ounces of compassion.

"Why so early?" he whined, his eyes closed, and his face still submerged by the pillow.

"Lorrie?" I heard him call as I walked towards the bathroom, slightly taken aback.

"Yes, Cleo?"

"Please can you ask your friend to turn off that hideous machine?"

"I'll try, but I can't promise anything!"

We had planned the night before to meet Mr and Mrs Magus for breakfast at the hotel restaurant that morning. We were told they were serving a breakfast buffet and honestly, it's what got me out of bed. The thought of limitless pancakes with birch sap syrup, my favourite! It was around eight thirty a.m. when we wandered downstairs. I could tell the Magus's were there already there as their bedroom door had an "open for service" sign attached to the knob. As we descended the stairs, with two flights to go, Cleo announced that he left something in the room, and turned back. Mel and I continued and were greeted by Mrs Magus at the bottom of the stairs. She said good morning and mentioned that Mr Magus had some business to attend to and would be joining us soon. We took our seats at the table and waited an acceptable amount of time before we hoarded our plates with delicious pastries. As I stuffed my face, I spotted Cleo at the entrance of the restaurant trying to place us, and so I waved at him to signal our position. We all enjoyed a feast. Mr Magus emerged at the end of the breakfast run and pocketed a small packet of three biscuits while taking a sizeable bite out of an apple. He was unusually quiet, which for him means saying less than his usual six words per hour (I counted and drew an average).

"Are you kids excited for the *Musea?*" Mrs Magus shrieked after we got in the car; me squished in the middle again (eye roll). *She* clearly was.

"Yes, Mrs Magus, I can't wait! Grandmama has told me so much about it!"

I wasn't lying, I had heard a LOT about it, and I was

curious to see the artefacts that it stores. In our Grade 7 test we're expected to be able to recite them all, and describe their powers, so it's all good preparation! But besides that, there was a specific relic that caught my attention. Now it doesn't sound like much, and when I tell you you'll probably be underwhelmed, Diary, but it really is believed to be one of the most powerful objects in the history of witchcraft, so try to be open-minded, okay?

Thought to precede even Parisa, and hold powers equal to, or greater than hers (depending on which archaeologist or unearthly artefact collector you speak to) is a small, shell-like, rust-coloured stone. I've only ever seen it in old drawings and photographs when we've studied it in Geography. So the story goes: Some sixty years ago, an earthly lady stumbled upon it on her journey home one evening. She was making her way home from the local earthly care home after a long shift, where she volunteered as a nurse. The walk was only three minutes, but it was a particularly cold and gusty night. A blanket of thick white mist descended, denying the old earthly lady her sight. With no way of knowing where she was, she had nowhere to go. But she continued, step after step, hoping she would collide with a building or landmark soon enough.

She was declared missing for fourteen days, and when she was found deep in the forest by a local hunter on his horse looking for wild boar, she had no recollection of the past two weeks. Expecting the lady to be frail and dehydrated, the hunter lay her on his horse and took her to the local clinic. Remarkably, the lady looked colourful and strong, but she did complain of a headache and a rash was found on her left palm, which needed monitoring. When the nurses admitted her and accounted for her belongings, the lady was found only to have the tin she took with her from the home that evening, planning to fill it with homemade carrot cake which were a favourite among the residents.

The tin was empty. That's important to remember.

When the lady recovered a few days later, she was handed back her empty tin and driven home by her friendly neighbour. Curiously, once she was left alone by worried friends and relatives that flocked to her aid, she picked up the tin to put it away and noticed a sound. At first, it was a near silent rattle, but then the sound grew louder as she waved it from side to side, and so followed her curiosity. She peeked inside the tin. Surprised; she shut it quickly. But when she opened it up again the next morning, there lay a single stone. It wasn't anything spectacular, just a stone. It was rough around the edges but heavy in weight. It was matte, but it sparkled in a certain light. And it *definitely* wasn't there when she inspected the tin in the long car journey home, wondering why she would have kept it with her, when she had lost even her shoes. She noticed later that afternoon that her rash had returned, in the same place as before; on her left wrist.

What's so special about that? I wondered this after five minutes into the story. But here's the best part: when she would dream at night, the lady unearthed memories of her time in the fog. She recalled seeing a glow of white light, even whiter than the fog, coming from ahead. Thinking it was a streetlamp or the window of a house, she walked towards it. She kept going for what she said felt like an eternity, but somehow never managed to close the distance. Confused, she stopped to catch her breath and re-evaluate her position. Only when she stopped, did the light draw near. Closer, it came, until it engulfed her. She closed her burning eyes for a moment, placing her hand over her face as an extra shield, and when she opened them again, she was faced with nothing but the dull fog she had known before. She dropped to the ground, immersed in fatigue and desperation. Her cold fingers curled into the leaves as she crouched in a heap. She cried and called to the trees for help (she assumed they were watching, as where there are leaves there must be trees).

After a short time, when her tears dried and her desperation turned to despair, she felt a warm, firm object underneath her hand. She inspected it and concluded it was a lumpy pebble, not seeing it as the answer to her cries. She left it there and fumbled her way along the ground until she felt the roots of a tree, where she ultimately took refuge. She wrote this all in a letter to her friend and declared that her dreams not only resurfaced memories of her time in the fog forest, but also of why she was there in the first place.

The strangest part is yet to come, Diary.

The lady kept the stone in her pocket, remembering how she came across it and acknowledging it as her only companion, maybe even her saviour, but she couldn't be sure. The residents asked about her time "away", and she showed them the stone as a sort of souvenir; let them hold it, even. Those that held or even touched the stone experienced the most peculiar thing, each in their own unique way. One lady with early onset earthly dementia (for there is an unearthly kind) remembered all of her joyous childhood memories in crystal clear detail. Another man who had lost his voice through careless projection as an opera singer began to sing a melody so beautiful that even the paint on the walls wept. And a small child, who often visited his grandparents at the home, recovered from an illness so evil that the very treatment that promised to save his life was stealing his hair.

The lady's picture was taken as she proudly held the stone to the camera with an open hand, which was posted in the local newspaper. *'Stone belonging to missing mortal makes care home resident's wishes come true.'* The lady quickly became a vulnerable target for thieves and dark witches, and she even had offers of extravagant gifts, money and livestock, which she never accepted. What would you do with a sheep, when you have a stone that could literally *grant* you a sheep, if you so desired? That's what I probably would have thought, anyway. There were no reports of the lady actually using the stone to grant her own wishes, and she must have had a few. Soon after word spread, unrest erupted in the local unearthly towns, with unearthly villagers demanding that the object possessed powers and so belonged to their kind. The Council of the MOTW was non-existent at the time, but a group of unearthly politicians thought it best to remove the stone from the lady's possession, keeping her and the public safe from the possibility that it may fall into the wrong hands, and keeping peace with their kind.

The stone was kept for centuries in an underground vault, caged in steel and bound by powerful spells which only true masters of our craft would be able to unravel. As our technology and science advanced, the stone was examined by the best and brightest, aspiring and expert unearthlies in the field of archaeology. Though they were baffled by the origins and exact workings of its powers, they traced it back as one of the oldest relics of all time, comparable to the bones found of the earliest species, and fourteen years older than the recovered relics belonging to Parisa. They concluded that it must have landed on the earth before our all-mighty sorceress, and some speculated it may have even led her here, as it did for the earthly lady on her voyage. Still, it is a wonder how it came to be and many eager unearthlies and mortals have gone in search for more of the wish-granting rocks.

The stone was transferred to the Musea when the underground vaults began to flood, where it is now showcased behind only a single layer of thick glass. You see, its powers are long expired. One of the archaeologists involved in studying the relic called on it to grant his wish of great fortune. His wish did not come true, and so he asked his colleague to cast a wish for them both. That wish did not come true, either. The Council caught wind of this, imprisoned the archaeologists for misuse of power, and concluded that the stone (once thought to be the most extraordinary object in existence) is now all but a remnant: a reminder of what *was*.

Mrs Magus pre-booked our tickets, so we were able to skip the main queue and wait in another, much smaller one. I was stunned to see none other than our headmaster a few places in front. He seemed to be there alone. I had never seen Mr Goddard outside of the halls of Weyborough High, he gave the impression that he keeps to himself. He absolutely saw us, but awkwardly looked away in the other direction as he whistled and pretended to analyse a painting. I didn't take him for an unearthly admirer. He hurried out of sight after receiving his ticket.

When we got to the desk, we were handed wristbands and briefed about fire safety. We were also given a set of headphones each where a pre-recorded voice spoke when we typed in a number corresponding to a relic or potion, telling us about the history, discovery and supposed powers of that particular artefact. We all sort of wandered off from each other. I kept my eyes on Mel to make sure she didn't drift too far, and I occasionally spotted Mrs Magus staring intently at a display for far longer than the length of the audio. Mr Magus and Cleo presumably skipped a few relics and went ahead of us. I already knew Cleo was less interested in all of this, probably ashamed that he didn't remember any of it from school. I spent a bit of time in the potions and powders section, where a projector beamed against a white wall and explained the processes of some of the concoctions. My favourite was the *'El Du Farus'*, meaning Fairy dust. It was given the name for its baby pink colour. With one sniff of the powder, you are said to fall head over heels in love with your true soulmate. 'Head over Heels'; the image sounds uncomfortable. Surely you would pull a muscle.

I wandered past the diary of Shelby Sparkes, who inspired mama to start keeping her diary, and so inspired me too, I guess. Shelby was a mortal, raised by a widowed sorceress after she was placed outside her front door when she was only three days old, wrapped in a blanket with a note that read:

"Look after my darling girl."

I've heard versions of the story where a box of chocolates was left, too. Imagine that: Here's my daughter who I'd like you to raise for the rest of her life, and for your troubles is a box of chocolates. Whoever it was obviously didn't realise that an unearthly lived there, otherwise they should have at least sourced some lavender cane; a traditional unearthly treat.

The Diary was displayed on a stand, open on a page which was dated *'124 P.E'*. 'P.E'. stood for 'Post-earthly' but is now referred to as the 'Parisa Era'. It's a time when Parisa was suspected to emerge as the first sorceress, and thus begin her long line of unearthly beings. The writing on the page was unclear; it was smudged, and the letters all flowed into one with an impressive cursive font. Apparently, the diary told tales of Shelby's upbringing and her impressive grasp of spells, which she could not perform, of course. But she became a highly regarded teacher; the first to teach both mortals and unearthlies.

Next, I moved on to the oldest artefact collection, where the stone was kept. It had no title, as did the others, which already made it stand out. There was also an extremely brief blurb on a plaque attached to the base of the glass structure. Dated '*245 P.R.E*' (Pre-earthly), it contained little information about the stone:

"Found by a mortal woman, this stone possesses powers to make even the most unbelievable wishes come true."

Of course, not much else could be said. The audio sounded as I entered the item number 11, and pressed play.

"Part of the excitement and terror of the stone lies with the unknown source of its powers. It is one of the very few relics which is left unexplained. And no one (earthlies and unearthlies alike) is comfortable with things that cannot be explained, be it mortal or magic."

I was surprised at just how small it was, Diary, that even I was underwhelmed, which is why I gave you plenty of warning! Just shorter than my thumb, the stone looked desolate in its large casing, and in true dramatic style, a light shone down on it; a metaphor for how it shone down on the lady who discovered it, or who *it* discovered, rather. I was surprised to see her letter to the side of it, though. I could just about make out the words, which were not in such beautiful cursive.

"Dearest Verona," it began. "The strangest dreams have been haunting my sleep…"

It was quite something to actually read her account of it, as opposed to hearing about it through twisted tongues. I stood for a moment, imagining what I would wish for if the relic still possessed its magic. She signed it:

"With warm wishes, Felicity."

I noticed a line of families waiting behind me to get a peek of it. A little boy was stamping his foot and demanding:

"Mummy, I want to see it NOW!"

I get the hint, kid. I moved on to the next display.

After an hour or so of browsing I saw Mel wandering off to the Musea Café. I went to join her, praising the powers of Parisa that she decided to get food, because I was STARVING. All this focusing and using up my brain energy stores took it out of me, and I was craving something sugary. Mrs Magus followed us shortly and ordered a cappuccino.

"Where did you go, Lorrie? I've been exploring the fossils of Scrubtubs."

Peculiar things, Srcubtubs. They were sort of like giant unearthly beetle insects that glowed in the dark and were supposedly highly intelligent. They could understand and communicate with any unearthly beings. They're extinct now.

"I had a look at the stone…"

"Ooh what did you think, I know you were excited about seeing that one?" Mrs Magus inquired.

"Well…"

As I took a breath to answer Mrs Magus and tell her that in fact, I thought the stone was nothing more than a teeny-weeny pea shaped object that could have fooled me for any other pebble in my footpath at home, we heard a shrieking alarm sound and commotion erupted. We placed our hands over our ears to spare them the horror as Mel shouted:

"Is that the fire alarm?"

Before I had a chance to shout back and tell her that we were supposed to go somewhere if there was a fire (although I couldn't remember *where*, exactly), a security guard approached our table, while another approached the table next to us.

"Excuse me, ladies, no need to panic, but we have had an incident and we are having to lockdown the premises. Please sit comfortably until we get this all sorted."

The alarm stopped after ten minutes or so, but it felt like a lifetime. My ears were about to explode, and I could tell from looking at the other visitors that theirs were, too. We were all bonded by our similar facial grimaces.

"What's going on?" Mrs Magus asked a member of staff who passed our table.

"I can't say for sure, mam, but one of our artefacts has… been misplaced."

Mrs Magus turned to us with wide eyes.

"Mel, where are the boys?"

I hadn't even thought about them in all the chaos. Cleo and Mr Magus parted from us over an hour ago.

"I'm not sure, Mama. I'll call Papa." Mel rummaged through her crammed bag for her phone as a guard approached us again:

"Ladies, please collect your personal belongings and follow me."

"Where are we going?" Mrs Magus pleaded.

"Don't worry, mam, please just follow me, and your kids,

too."

After unpacking half her bag to reach her phone, Mel sighed and repacked it all. Mrs Magus was flustered, and I only now realised that we never paid for our drinks, and my doughnut never arrived, how disappointing.

It seemed as though everyone was being ushered to the main hall by the ticket area. I turned to look at the grand glass entrance doors, which were shut closed, and stood in front of them were two stocky uniformed guards. I had a suspicion they were not letting anyone in, or out. What went missing? Was it stolen? Was it a Srcubtub fossil? Surely not a Scrubtub fossil! And where *were* Mr Magus and Cleo? My thoughts were racing faster than my heart, as if they were going for gold! Mrs Magus scanned the room for the rest of her family while Mel was frantically typing a message to Mr Magus, who wasn't answering his phone.

"Excuse me, ladies and gentlemen, earthlies and unearthlies!" A voice boomed through a loudspeaker. "I am the supervisor on duty today. Please quieten down now, I know you are all rushing to get on with your day and as soon as we have retrieved the stone, we will let you do so."

Whispers exploded amongst the crowd.

"The stone?"

"The stone is missing?"

"Mummy, what's the stone?" The little toad that hurried me along with his whining didn't even know what he was so desperate to see. And now it was… missing?

"Please, everyone, let's stay calm. We have notified the unearthly authorities who will be here shortly to review the CCTV footage and take statements, and then you will be on your way. Please accept our apologies for the disturbance."

"Lorrie, weren't you just at the stone?" Mel murmured while I kept my eyes fixed on the guards ahead. "Did you see anything?"

"No. I mean yes I was there, but I didn't see anything." I had a sinking feeling in my stomach. I suddenly felt *guilty*. I wondered if I looked it, too. I tried to picture myself from the outside. A young sorceress (not that you could tell me apart from a mortal) dressed in a cream coat with a pale green scarf. My hair was a little messy, but I thought I did a good job at hiding it in my beanie, which matched my scarf. My brown boots were scuffed, sure, and my backpack had holes in the bottom. It wouldn't be a very good backpack for someone stealing a teeny-weeny pea shaped object, hopefully they see that. I started sweating and I was convinced the taller guard with a stern face and closed fists was staring me up and down.

"Mama, I see them!" Mel stood on her tip toes and pointed out Cleo to Mrs Magus. They were shuffling through the crowd, heading towards us.

"Where have you two been? Do you know what's going on?" Mr Magus was quiet. Cleo was, too.

"Cleo?" I was growing impatient with his sketchiness.

"We were just…" He looked to his papa, who shook his head, as if to signal that Cleo should keep mouth shut. "We were looking for you!"

I'll have to continue this later, I promised Grandmama I'd go through my learnings with her as she didn't set in on our last night. I won't be long; I'll tell you the rest after dinner if I can keep my eyes open.

Chapter 10
Sinthea's ballad

Tuesday 10th September, 9.30 p.m.
My eyes are open, just. I'll have to make this quick.

After we were each interrogated by the police and asked to write down our personal details in case they needed to make further contact with us, we were allowed to leave the building. Upon our exit, we were searched, and the contents of our bags were tipped out onto a tray before they were individually inspected, and a few items confiscated for "evidence". Poor Mel, all she wanted was for her bag to stay packed. They took our cameras, which they explained may help them piece together the puzzle and lead them to any suspects who may have stolen the stone. They informed us they would post them back once they had been browsed and assured us they would take great care of them, which I highly doubt considering I saw one of them basically toss Mel's in a plastic bag before not so gently adding it to a pile of other electronic devices. We left after four hours. By that time, I was ravenous. I mean I could have eaten an entire cow by then. But instead, we stopped for food on the way back to the hotel. We were all a bit miserable after that, so we had an early night.

So that was our weekend, Diary. It was eventful, to say the least. I'll give you a quick summary of school today, and then I'll need to try and get some sleep. I swear the voices of the ancestors are getting louder, I hardly slept a wink last night. I can't work out what they're saying, though, they're all chattering on about different things, which made waking up this morning all the more difficult. When I eventually did, after writing my journal entry I wandered to grandmama's bedroom to say good morning. She looked like she was sleeping more peacefully than I had done in days. I was jealous. She looked pale, though, and still. I lightly shook her on the shoulder and when she murmured in response, I kissed her on the cheek and told her I would be back soon to tell her all about my readings. Miss Michaela was watching me from the door and smiled.

"Come on, Lorelei, you get yourself ready and I'll make your grandmama some lemontwine tea."

Oh Diary, I was *very* disorganised this morning. Mama told me to sort out my bag last night, and I insisted that I didn't have much to sort. Turns out I did... oops. I scrambled to get my things together while carrying my buttered piece of toast between my teeth, and ran out the door to the car, where mama was waiting.

I was roughly fifteen minutes late when I walked into the classroom. Everyone was seated at their desks and our teacher was taking the morning register. With my really good track record (I am hardly *ever* late) Miss Kelpie gave me an informal warning without demanding an explanation and asked me to take my seat. Mel was sitting in her seat, but Cleo's was vacant. I didn't give him much thought, at first.

After the lesson, I made my way to my locker. I had noticed something white peeking through one of the slits, and when I entered my code into the lock and opened it, a small piece of crumpled paper hung from the inside of the locker door. I looked around to see who could have left it, but immediately realised once I examined it. It was a music sheet with *"Sinthea's ballad. One of my favourites"* written in messy handwriting at the top of the page. When I flipped the page, written in smaller text off-centre were the words: *"Thought you might like to try it, think it could do wonders for your triangle!"* He didn't leave his name, but it was clear that the culprit was Dean.

I looked around again, this time with intent. I scanned the corridor in the direction of Dean's locker and caught sight of him. He was laughing with one of his friends, Mareck. I observed him for a moment or three. I had thought about him, while I was on my trip, only once. It was when Mel and Cleo were in a quarrel in the car journey on the way to the Isle. I'm not sure why he popped into my mind, but I thought about the trick I showed him, and seeing his face that day and why he might have been sad. I recalled what he said to me about the spell, how he was amazed by it. And then I wondered what he could be doing at that very moment. Maybe he was working on an engine or listening to a classical composition from the nineties. I sort of wanted to be able to ask him, but I couldn't. I thought I must remind myself to ask him for his phone number when I see him next.

I contemplated whether it was acceptable to ask an earthly for his number. It would be the only one I had, aside from Miss Michaela's. I figured it would be okay since he is my assigned earthly. What if I need to ask him about when our next meeting is (even though we were given printed timetables with the dates already scheduled for the whole term)? Or if he needs to tell me he's running late, like last time? I should have it in case, I thought.

Dean caught me looking at him. He waved. I held up the

sheet and smiled. He smiled back, and for a moment it felt as though we were alone in that corridor, as if everyone else fell away. But then Mareck bashed into him, and everyone came flooding back. I had a strange feeling in my tummy, like butterflies were flying around in there.

"What's that?"

Mel grabbed the sheet from my hand before I had the chance to even compose an answer. I snatched it back and hoped she hadn't read the note.

"Nothing, just some homework from Mr Maguire."

"Oh, I didn't get assigned any music work this week... or did I?" Mel started to panic as she tried to remember something that never happened.

"No, you probably didn't, I think he just gave it to me to practise on my triangle." I was lying through my teeth.

"Oh yeah, I heard about that, Lorrie! Apparently that awkward twange of yours cracked the window," Mel said as she laughed.

"Is there seriously nothing better for people to talk about than my complete lack of triangle skills?" I rolled my eyes.

"Nope" was Mel's response as she smirked.

"Where's your brother, anyway?"

"Cleo... he's taken a day off today."

"Not feeling well. I hope it wasn't the sandstone flakes, mama warned me she mixed up the recipe..."

"No, it's not that. I'm not quite sure to be honest. I went into his room this morning to viciously wake him up like he does to me, and he wasn't there. Bed was made, curtains were open, but no Cleo."

"So, you mean you couldn't find him? You sure he wasn't practising a vanishing trick to mess with you?" I hadn't mastered the trick yet (recall the floating scarf incident) and I'd be surprised if Cleo was even working on that, since he's a couple grades behind me.

"Practising? Cleo? Two words that have never been used in the same sentence, unless when referring to the insults he often tries to perfect! No, Lorrie, no trick! I asked Mama where he was, and she said that him and Papa had taken an unscheduled trip. Fishing I believe…"

"Isn't it odd to take the day off school for fishing? Are they fishing for gold?"

Mel laughed.

"Nope, for disgusting fish. I dunno, boys will be boys I guess."

"Had you seen your Papa this morning?" I was becoming more curious.

Mel shook her head as the bell rang and we started walking towards our next lesson.

"But I heard him in the night," Mel continued. "Whispering to Mama and rummaging through the draws. He was trying to be quiet I guess, but he must have stubbed his toe on something as I heard a thud and an 'ouch'. I must have fallen asleep again because I didn't hear the car leave."

"Hmm, do they normally go off fishing in the night?"

"Sometimes, to catch the rising tide."

It all sounded very dubious, Diary. It was hard to picture Cleo patiently waiting for a fish to gnaw at the bait attached to the string of a rod. I didn't take him for an avid fisherman, but then Cleo does somehow manage to keep surprising me. It was a "sport" that seemed so earthly, so mortal. Although, I once watched the unearthly discovery channel and there was a documentary which followed an unearthly fisherman. He used a spell to make all fish luminescent so he could easily track them and prop his rod in the best place to attract their attention and guarantee a catch. It sounds like cheating, but then would you deprive an earthly hunter for using binoculars to enhance his sight? You would be silly to.

It's strange how the day you go back to school after even a short holiday, feels like it lasts a lifetime. I was hoping to run into Dean again, which would save me from having to make excuses to say hi to him. I didn't, though, but I tried to spot him again so I could. I figured I should thank him for leaving me his music sheet, and make sure he didn't need it for anything. Otherwise, it would be rude, wouldn't it? I saw him in the afternoon, but he was walking in the other direction and Mel was with me chatting away about her run in with Easton.

"Have you seen his new haircut? He is just a piece of artwork, Lorrie! Did you hear that his parents are hosting a birthday party for him on Saturday? I'm invited, obviously, which means you are too!"

I'm not much of a partygoer. Don't get me wrong, I always enjoy jamming as much cake as I can fit into my mouth and party games can be fun. But I'm a tad shy in big crowds, and I struggle to make small talk.

My second cousin, Darius, turned seventeen a few weeks ago. He's a nasty thing, very spoilt and thinks the world of his spell casting abilities. He's not even that great, he shows off with unimpressive Grade 3 spells and throws a full blown two-year-old tantrum if you don't clap and pretend you're in awe. I'm never allowed to show off my spells, grandmama tells me it wouldn't be very nice to embarrass my cousin.

"Second cousin!" I correct her every time.

"Still, Lorelei, blood relative or not, modesty is the best policy!"

Anyway, I spent the whole time sitting with the adults while watching a bunch of unearthly boys, chew with their mouths open and dance (badly) to loud rock music. Ergh, THE worst!

I wasn't sure I had a choice whether or not to go to Easton's birthday party. He invited the whole grade, even the earthlies. Apparently, his parents are very liberal and pride themselves in tackling the divide between the two kinds. His papa even campaigns for earthly rights, and his mama volunteers in a day care centre for earthly children. I used to think it was a bit strange that they did that, *chose* to spend time with earthlies, but after getting on well with Dean recently, and my fondness of Miss Michaela, I understand it a bit better now. They're not too bad, really. They're not as open-minded and their strengths lie in different areas to us, but some of them are pretty nice and interesting in their own way.

"I believe Dean will be there, too. I hope it's not awkward, I would hate a situation where him and Easton were fighting over me at Easton's party!"

The way Mel said it made me think she wouldn't hate it at all, rather the opposite. Mel, unlike me, is a true socialite and flourishes in large crowds. I sometimes wish I could be more like her, but then I notice the slightly irritated faces and eye rolls she receives, and I figure I'm better off in my shy corner.

"Did you say Dean will be there? I haven't seen him out anywhere..."

"Yup, I overheard Mareck talking about it to Sharon who then spoke to Olivia and, unfortunately, Jessica, who said she would only go if Dean went!"

"Jessica? Why does she care about whether or not Dean goes?" I was slightly offended by the idea.

"Not sure, but all the earthly girls seem to flock around him like little moths on a light. It's no wonder he's interested in a strong, independent unearthly like me…"

I decided I would go to the party, and maybe keep an eye out for Dean. Not that I minded about Jessica's apparent attraction to him (which in my view is just bizarre because last time I heard she had a boyfriend), but it would be nice to know someone else there, and maybe Dean would rather spend time with me than with the horrid earthly. I'd be doing him a favour.

For the first time in my life, Diary, I thought about what I should wear.

Chapter 11
Inside voice

Wednesday 11th September, 9.45 p.m.

I had the strangest dream last night. Well, it wasn't a dream per say. I couldn't sleep again (thanks to my dear ancestors) and I had a strong urge to have a go at the *Fortunaes* trick, even though I knew I probably shouldn't. I suppose because we were talking about it yesterday, I was curious about whether Mr Magus and Cleo were set to make their big catch today, if they hadn't already. At least, that's what I *told* myself I was curious about, but part of me also wanted to see whether they did go fishing after all, because for some reason I had a hunch that everything was not as it seemed.

I had faith that the trick would work, because Grandmama *did* have her chicken and pumpkin pie as I predicted. I just hoped I wouldn't see Stumbles doing his thing again. Accepting that it would be a possibility, I closed my eyes, said the words of the spell and placed a drop of fresh dew on my tongue. I thought about the Magus boys and drifted off. I couldn't be sure of how long it took before Cleo entered my dreams, but it was so vivid I almost thought it was real. His dark eyes were the first thing I saw. He had woken up (or I suppose he *is* going to wake up) and started rubbing his eyes. I couldn't tell where he was though, or who he was with. It was dark, but it didn't seem like a tent, which they normally prop up when they go on their trips. It felt bigger than a tent, maybe a camper van, or a small room. As he spoke, the darkness echoed his voice and talked back at him.

"Have you done it, Papa?" were the words he repeated. "Have you?"

A small flicker of light fell upon Cleo's face.

"Not yet, son. I need your help."

I could smell smoke. It was faint, but it was obvious. Cleo sat up, placed his shoes on and tied his laces. He was afraid. His heart was beating fast and I know it sounds crazy, but I knew that he was thinking about how he could get out of this. He grabbed his rucksack — the same one he was carrying when we went to the Isle. He opened the door, and with that the room lit up. It didn't seem like daylight; it wasn't reflecting white, it was shades of orange and bright pink. The room was small, and from what I could tell, square. There was a pile of clothes and a quilt in the corner where Cleo had been sleeping, and another pile lay in the opposite corner. He let out a big sigh and paused before walking forward, crossing the door threshold.

"I don't want to do this."

I could hear the words, as if he was speaking them, but his lips weren't moving. Grandmama told me that with the spell you can even predict people's future thoughts, but it takes many years of practise.

Cleo continued, each step sounding progressively heavier and more reluctant. I could hear the crunch of leaves beneath his feet, and the crackle of a fire became more apparent.

"Son, you know what you have to do." Cleo looked up to his papa and nodded.

Without a response, he placed his bag on the ground. He

knelt down, unzipped the bag, and reached into it, taking something out which was swaddled in a cloth. I could make out a vague shape, but I wasn't sure. Surrounded by a forest, with early beginnings of the sunrise touching the trees, Cleo gently placed the item in the fire. The flames consumed it.

"Good boy."

That was pretty much when I woke up. Stumbles was on the edge of my bed again. I hated leaving it there, I wanted to know what Cleo had burned. I had presumed I was predicting it to happen in the early hours of this morning, so it probably had already. I wondered if I would see him at school today, and whether he would have known somehow that I used the trick on him. I knew if he did, he would probably give me his best impression of evil eyes. It *could* be considered an invasion of privacy, similar to setting in, but it seemed more acceptable as you weren't directly *manipulating* the victim or occupying their mind. I planned not to mention it either way, though. I can never predict how Cleo is going to react. That's one thing about him, that intrigues, but disturbs me.

I ate my breakfast and went to say goodbye to Grandmama, who hadn't left her bedroom for longer than a couple of hours since I got home from the trip. I was really starting to worry about her, but she brushed it off saying she caught a nasty bug and couldn't seem to release it back into the wild (her way of making light of the situation). Mama spent more time with her than she probably has done in her lifetime. I walked past Grandmama's room the other day and even saw them laughing together.

On the way to school, I couldn't help but think about my prediction. What *was* Cleo doing? Where *were* they? As we arrived in the parking lot, I immediately looked around for Mr

Magus's car. It was a red hatchback, shiny and slightly arrogant looking. I couldn't see it there. When I walked into the hall, I spotted Mel by her locker, but no Cleo. I walked up to her.

"Hey, is your brother not in today again?"

"Good morning to you too! Why so curious about Cleo? Have a little crush?" Mel always teased us, but I think it's because she thrives off making people feel extremely awkward (hence the taste of her own medicine trick I played on her with Dean).

"No! Just wondering how much I'll have to catch him up on maths!" Cleo and I are in the same class for maths, and after nearly every lesson I give him a snap summary of what we were taught, which he refuses to listen to most of the time.

"Why are we learning all of this? It's boring. Why will I ever need to know the sum of an obtuse angle?"

"I can't answer that, but if you paid attention maybe you would find out!"

"Nah, I prefer to go through it all again with you, witchy!"

I didn't mind doing it too much, it was all good revision for me, but I wasn't really worrying about that, like I told Mel.

"Umm, well I think he should be coming in after lunch!"

Cleo walked in halfway through maths. Typical. I could tell I would need an extra fifteen minutes to go over today's lesson content with him. It would be a good excuse to catch him and subtly question him about his morning, though, which I totally knew NOTHING about.

"Where have you been?" I asked him as soon as we left the classroom after the lesson.

"Square roots are just ridiculous. Tell me you didn't understand any of that? Surely not!" This is how our

113

conversations generally started after maths, but this time I couldn't help but think he was avoiding the question.

"Well, not really, I mean sort of, but where did you and your papa go?"

"And plotting scatter graphs… we'd be better off leaving that to the earthlies to take care of while we do our important work!" I'm not sure what "work" he was referring to, but I didn't bother asking. I had another agenda.

"Cleo?"

"Lorrie, I can't talk right now." Cleo stopped in his tracks and turned to me, his face looking stern. "I have to go speak to Mr G. Apparently I've missed one too many lessons and I need reminding of how I'm failing my academic potential!" His change in tone took me by surprise a bit, and I knew not to question him further, the way Stumbles knows not to reach for the food scraps when Mama's watching him.

"Okay, good luck," I murmured, feeling timid.

With that, he walked away from me, towards Mr Goddard's office.

"I hadn't realised Mr Goddard was in today?" Mel asked, evidently not knowing that her brother was being reprimanded at that very moment.

Our headmaster hadn't been in School since last week. The last time I saw him was when he scurried away after awkwardly catching sight of us at the Museum. He had taken an extended holiday; we were told by the Deputy.

"Well, I guess he must be. I bet he's trying to put on his tough voice with Cleo as we speak." We laughed, both imagining how Cleo is probably tearing the meagre mortal apart with his back chat and disrespect.

114

"Isn't it strange that he was at the Musea?" I wondered if Mel was as surprised by his choice of tourist attraction as me.

"Yeah, I guess. But then loads of earthlies are interested in our culture. They just don't like to admit it!"

"Yeah, I just didn't think that *he* would be."

"He runs a school where a quarter of his students are unearthly. He's probably just doing some recon on how he can inspire the next generation of Weyborough High."

"You're probably right."

"I know." Mel loved being right.

I didn't see Cleo for the rest of the day. Mel said that Mr Goddard placed him on trash duty. It's the worst punishment, worse than suspension, even (although probably not as bad as Pandymonk community service). It's self-explanatory; with a garbage picker and trash bag you roam the school grounds after the last bell for any litter left behind — mostly by the earthlies, unsurprisingly. Cleo is pretty much an expert at it now, and I must admit he doesn't do a bad job, on the whole. Though last term when he was on duty, one of the snobby earthlies pretended to "accidentally" miss the very large steel bin when discarding their banana peel.

"Oops!" I heard them say. "Garbage mongrel, better pick that up!"

Cleo was biting his tongue, probably because Mr Goddard was supervising him, but he sure gave them a look of pure hatred and the next day he recalled the event to me and Mel.

"Next time use your tiny mortal brain and figure out how to do it yourself!" he said sarcastically, as we were sat in the lunch hall. Mel gave him no sympathy:

"Oh Cleo, get over it. So some earthlies were sassy with

you, what's new!"

"Oops, it just slipped out of my hand," Cleo whined as he threw his banana peel on the floor.

I couldn't help but let out a chuckle, and Mel shot me a look as if to say don't encourage it.

I thought again about my prediction, and that I was probably overthinking it. It was most likely just a piece of coal or some extra bait that Mr Magus and Cleo were getting rid of, or even a ritual they do to mark the end of their trip. Who knows what unearthly males get up to on their papa-son adventures? I also figured that I hadn't practised the spell enough to truly know how Cleo was feeling, and the essence of dread I sensed was surely just an inaccuracy of the spell. As I sat on the steps outside the school entrance waiting for mama, I decided to let it go. I let my mind drift back into reality and spent the next five minutes watching my fellow students running out the gates and disappearing into cars. Most of them were picked up by their mamas, but some of their papas showed up and for a few, mamas and papas collected their children together.

I had these moments, they were fleeting, but they seemed to be getting more frequent, where I wondered what it would be like if I had a papa to pick me up. Would our car journeys be any different? Would we listen to podcasts instead of the radio? Would I be bored to death with talk about sports and cars, instead of conversations about boys and schoolwork? It was hard to imagine, but sometimes I wish I knew.

My attention shifted to an old, banged up pickup truck that was pulled over on the opposite street. I saw a shaggy blonde head floating in the passenger's seat. It remained still, while the man sitting next to him in the driver's seat was waving his hands as though he was swatting flies like Mr Magus does. The man seemed like he was using his outside voice, which mama always tells me I shouldn't do if I'm ever upset about something.

"Inside voice please, Lorelei, I'm not deaf!"

The boy turned his head to look out the window, and I realised that the blonde shaggy head belonged to Dean. Painted across his face was the same expression he had the other day when he was late for our meeting. He didn't see me looking at him, and soon after that the engine roared and the car chugged away. Maybe I'd ask him about it one day. About the cause of his sad faces and his dad's fly swatting. Maybe I'd leave it and convince myself that it wasn't my place to pry, especially not with an earthly. I just may not like the answer. I still wanted his number, though.

When I walked in the door, I noticed that the house was unusually quiet. I couldn't even hear the faint whispers of the ancestors. I immediately knew that something felt off.

"Where's Grandmama?" I asked, before Mama even arrived at the door after unpacking the groceries from the car.

"Oh yes, I meant to tell you. Your grandmama has gone to stay with an old friend of hers for the weekend."

"Who? But it's not the weekend?"

"I meant the rest of the week, and probably the weekend also. So it's just the two of us." Mama smiled with what seemed like an obvious attempt at reassurance.

"She didn't tell me she was going away. We have spells to practise. I have my Grade 6 in less than four months!"

"Lorelei, what have I told you. It's not ALL about magic, and *please*, use your inside voice! And go inside, I can't hold these bags forever!"

It was all very odd. In my whole life, I have never known Grandmama to go *anywhere* for more than a day, let alone a few nights. I also didn't know of anyone who she would visit. I knew of a couple friends she has in another town a few hours away, but she hadn't seen them in *years*! She also writes letters to Darius' grandpapa (her brother) from time to time, but she always tells me that she can't stand him; he's much like his grandson. So I doubt she would be visiting him.

I tried to dig for more information from Mama, but she didn't let on as to Grandmama's whereabouts. Maybe *she* didn't know, herself.

"Oh Lorelei, she's been feeling a bit better and decided to spend some time away with an old friend. That's it!"

Unsatisfied, I decided I would snoop in her desk draws when Mama turned her light out. Later that evening, I crept down the corridor to grandmama's bedroom, guided by a dim light from the torch I keep next to my bed, which was in serious need of some new batteries. The old wooden floorboards were not doing me any favours, they creaked with nearly every tip toe. I heard some movement in mama's room and stopped dead in my tracks, but her light stayed off and I soon arrived at grandmama's room. After searching through her draws, underneath her pillow and emptying her shoe box, I lost hope in discovering any clues of where she had gone. I did discover a medicine box with a handful of small blue tablets inside. I had seen it before; grandmama was ordered by the doctor to take one a day until she felt better from her suspected bug. I hope she didn't need them.

Just as I was about to sneak back to my bedroom, I remembered another hiding spot which Grandmama previously forbid me to search. I knew she stashed her unearthly collectables there, which she had collected from over the years. She once showed me a small handkerchief which she was gifted by a famous sorceress, who was also a family friend, with the initials: SJ. She was so proud of it. I couldn't understand how something used to wipe noses could be so impressive, but I faked my best *'wow'* expression at the time, because I knew it meant a lot to her.

I opened the door to her wardrobe, and on the top shelf sat a medium sized wooden box. It wasn't secured by any lock that I could see; the lid was propped open by the overflowing contents inside. I placed a chair in front of the wardrobe and climbed onto it for extra height. I reached for the box and carefully walked backwards off the chair, clutching it in both hands. It was heavy, and I knew if I dropped it, that would be the end of my night-time scavenger hunt. I carefully laid out the items from the box onto grandmama's bed. I picked up and quickly threw down the handkerchief, being far less careful. There were some intriguing and confusing objects in there, which I would ask Grandmama to tell me about another time. I didn't find anything which could lead me to Grandmama, aside from a small note which read:

"Asteria, we need to talk."

Chapter 12
Little green frog

Thursday 12th September, 7.50 p.m.

"You look tired!" Thanks, Mel. Always so complimentary.

We were waiting for the morning register.

"That's because I am!"

"Not been sleeping much?"

"Nope, although the ancestors were actually quiet for once. Hemlock House just feels different without grandmama."

"Did you find out where she went?" I shook my head. "No, but I did find this note…" I made sure no one was looking before I subtly slid my hand into my bag, pulled it out and unfolded it.

"Asteria, we need to talk." Mel read aloud, loudly.

"Shhh!"

"Sorry… that's weird. Why do our relatives keep disappearing on us without telling us where they're going?"

"I'm not sure, you're wonderful at keeping secrets and I'm not nosey at all!" The sarcasm in my tone was thick.

"Hey, I can keep secrets…" Mel said very seriously. "…when I really, *really* need to!"

I raised my eyebrows at her and it wasn't long before we both burst out into laughter.

"How's that Diary of yours coming along, anyway? Do

you write much in it?"

"Yeah, most nights or sometimes in the morning. I practically fell asleep with it in my hands last night. I woke up and there were some suspicious wet patches on it. Either mine or Stumbles' drool!" Mel screwed up her face.

"Ew, that is *nasty*!"

"Yup!"

"How do you have the patience for it? Don't you get bored?"

"Well…"

"There are so many unearthly TV programmes on at the moment, I'd much prefer to watch those than spend so much time on doing something so… productive! Did you see the one last night about the sorceress who falls in love with a dark wizard?"

"I…"

"Of course you didn't, you were writing in your Diary!"

Sidenote: In seriousness, though, I do have to apologize, Diary. I have become a bit slack and sometimes I've been rushing through my writing. So for any careless spelling mistakes or incorrect grammar, I am sorry! It also doesn't help writing my entries so late at night and running on no more than five hours sleep, so I'm going to try and take more care from now on. And don't pay any attention to Mel's harsh words about you (although I am slightly intrigued about the lady who falls in love with the dark wizard).

Now, back to it. So I wasn't sure about the note. There was no signature on it or any hint as to who it was from. The writing was scruffy, but the paper was white and smooth. It didn't have that yellow tinge or crumpled lines that often accompany old letters. It was just a note, but the strange part

about it was that it was so brief. "Asteria, we need to talk."
Who would write such a cryptic note like that, without even
giving a name? She must have known the person well enough
to recognize their handwriting. And why not call to tell her that
instead, or write it in the note, unless it was absolutely top
secret. So many questions, and Grandmama isn't even here to
ask. Mama didn't talk about her this morning. We sat down at
the table to eat our breakfast and she was merrily chatting
away to Miss Michaela about her new business venture. Mama
wants to start an "earthly pet parlour on wheels". She's always
loved earthly animals: dogs, cats, even bunny rabbits. She had
a hamster when she was my age, who she brings up from time
to time. Grandmama and Grandpapa bought it with the hopes
of bribing her into doing her unearthly studies, and apparently
it did inspire her to recite a quarter of the Laws, but that is not
nearly enough to make it past the Grade 6 test.

"It's going to be the next big thing, Michaela. The earth is
getting busy. Nobody has time to go to the hairdresser these
days, let alone take their animals to get groomed. This way, I
take the grooming to their doorsteps, literally."

Mama seemed to have it all planned out. She saved up
enough money from her shifts at the grocery store (where she
works mostly evenings and weekends) to buy an old van and
had even been in contact with someone who is going to help
her revamp it and turn it into her parlour.

"I've started creating my price list and I even have
pictures of what I think it will look like. Come have a look!" I
sort of zoned out at that point in the conversation, but I think
Miss Michaela said something along the lines of:

"I think it's a wonderful idea! Bambam can be your first
customer!"

Bambam is Miss Michaela's puppy. She rescued it from a shelter not long ago. Don't get me wrong, I don't mind earthly animals, they *can* be cute, but unearthly animals are MUCH more exotic. It's still a mystery how unearthly creatures came to be, per say, but the general expert opinion is that Parisa graced some of the plants and tiny organisms with her powers when she arrived on the earth. Some of them evolved into glorious beings, and others were probably a result of unfortunate mutations or unnatural interbreeding (cough, Chucklebubs, cough cough).

After the register, Mel and I parted ways. She had a science lesson and I had Music. I was building up the courage to speak to Dean. We don't have another meeting scheduled until next Monday, which feels like a while away. I briskly walked to the Music room, anticipating that Dean would be early as usual. I was right; Dean was alone in the room, setting up his tuba. I took a deep breath and walked in.

"Hi, Dean."

He turned to me, paused, and redirected his attention to his instrument. Looking down, he greeted me back:

"Hi."

"Thanks for the music sheet. I'll definitely have to give it a go on my triangle…" I leaned in and whispered… "or maybe I'll just use the spell!"

Silence.

"Well, I thought you could do with the practise."

I nervously laughed but quickly figured out that Dean wasn't joking.

"I could… I'm just hoping I get through this lesson without making a fool of myself."

"You'll be fine."

I was taken aback by Dean's short tone. He seemed mad, and maybe distracted, but definitely a bit dismissive.

"Everything okay?" I walked further towards him and reached out to touch his shoulder. With that, he winced as if he had just encountered a hot flame.

"Please. Just leave me alone, Lorelei. I'm not in the mood to talk about your triangle... again!"

I was lost for words. Dean had been blunt with me before, but he was generally polite. I hadn't seen this side of him before, and I didn't like it much.

I walked away silently and took my seat by my triangle. What was his problem? I didn't ask him to leave the music sheet for me, and I thought he loved making fun of my triangle debacles. And what was with him nearly jumping out of his skin when I touched him, was he *that* disgusted by me? I decided I was annoyed back at Dean, and I gave the back of his head furious looks throughout the rest of the lesson (not that he noticed, he didn't look my way once). I don't want his number any more, I thought. He's a stupid earthly who can't decide whether he wants to be nice or not, and quite frankly I can't be bothered to figure out which way he'll go. I was grumpy for the rest of the day. Mel noticed and tried to get it out of me, but I brushed it off and said that I had started my period. "Bummer" was all she commented and left it at that.

We sat down for lunch and Cleo joined us. He was apparently "studying" in the library for his free period, which Mel and I certainly did not buy.

"You what? Don't make me choke on my broccoli." Mel was as shocked by the idea as I was.

"I did!" he insisted.

"Where is Cleo and what have you done with him?" I

pretended to scan the empty seats at the table.

"Very funny, witchy. I decided to turn over a new leaf and make an attempt to pass this year, so I don't have to do it all over again. I'm also tired of you trying — and failing — to teach me multiplications."

"I am too!" was my reply, while Mel used it as an opportunity to further annoy me:

"Won't you miss your afternoon dates with "witchy" if she doesn't have to help you with maths any more?"

"Mel!" I was not in the mood. Cleo smiled at me, also seeming to enjoy my irritation.

"Nope. I think I'll survive without them! Plus, she doesn't need an excuse to talk to me, do you Lorrie?" Cleo winked.

"You two are NOT funny!" I rolled my eyes, but I sort of felt a bit better and forgot about Dean for a while, and for that I was grateful.

"How was Mr Goddard yesterday? Was he trying to act all intimidating as usual?" Mel changed the subject, probably returning the favour for when I did it the other day so that Cleo didn't find out about Dean's fabricated "crush" on his sister.

"Umm… yeah he was fine."

"Fine? I have never heard you pay such a compliment to Mr Goddard, Cleo." I hadn't.

"Well, obviously he was infuriating as normal, but yeah I've just learned to ignore him I suppose."

"When do you start trash duty?" I asked.

"Not sure, probably sometime next week."

"Strange that you don't have to start now, isn't it? Don't you usually do it from the day of your offence?" Mel pointed out. She was right, that's how it normally worked.

"I would hardly call it an offence, Mel. Papa took *me* out

125

of school so that…" he stopped himself.

"So that you could spend quality time catching stinky fish and not bringing any home?" Mel finished his sentence.

"Exactly!"

Come to think of it, it is bizarre that they didn't bring any fish home. Unless that's what they cooked on the fire. It made sense, catch them and eat them, fresh from the fire.

"I dunno, maybe he's taken pity on me. Or he's scared of the son of the big bad dark wizard!"

"Probably the second!" I teased.

"Oh Lorrie, I forgot to say, I was looking through our pictures from the trip last night." Mel had just swallowed her last bite of her lunch. "There's a good one of us that Mama took. Remember when we posed by the cave marking and held the torches underneath our chins? It's pretty dark but it came out well, it makes us look very spooky!"

"Ooh yeah I forgot about that! I'd like to see it — I'd like to see all the pictures. I even got my camera back in the post the other day!"

"So did I! Surprisingly, it still works. Why don't you come across tomorrow after school and I'll ask papa to set up a slideshow? Cleo — you took loads of pictures. Download them and we can get them up on the screen too. And you, Lorrie!"

"Sure, but I mostly took photos of the caves, so it probably won't be that exciting!"

I love photography, I'm not sure I've mentioned that before. I don't use my camera much, there isn't a whole lot to see around where we live, but I take it everywhere with me on school or family trips. Most of my shots focus on scenery or flora and fauna, so it doesn't appeal to everyone, and I knew it definitely wouldn't appeal to Mel.

"Umm, Cleo, better get yours downloaded in that case!" Mel confirmed my suspicions.

"Ouch," I teased.

After recovering from Mel's brutal insult, we both turned to Cleo, expecting a cheeky remark. He kept his eyes on his tray and continued scooping up large spoonsful of his rice pudding.

"Cleo?" Mel prompted. "You okay to get your photos downloaded?"

Cleo remained silent.

"Earth to the unearthly, can you hear us?" She leaned in and flicked a pea at him.

Cleo dropped his spoon and let out a sigh.

"I lost my camera."

"You lost it?"

"Yeah, I haven't seen it since we got back from the trip."

"But I saw it on the kitchen counter the other—"

"No, you didn't, Mel. That was probably Mama's."

"Umm, nope, pretty sure it was yours. It had that green frog sticker on it that I keep teasing you about."

"Green frog sticker?" I asked. I hadn't noticed it before.

"Yeah, it has this random sticker on it which I think our uncle gave him once for being a "good little wizard". Isn't that right, Cleo?"

"It wasn't mine Mel, DROP IT!" Cleo banged his tray on the table as eager eyes of students in nearby chairs swarmed him with looks of disdain. I do have *some* sympathy for him at times, but Cleo does a good job of reinforcing his reputation.

Cleo stood up and walked away from the table as Mel and I stared at each other, not knowing what the other had done to make him so upset.

"I only said it was an odd sticker! He's been in such a foul mood lately. More so than usual."

"Hasn't everyone!" I muttered under my breath, mostly for my own benefit.

"What was that?"

"Oh nothing, he does seem to be more irritable than normal, though." I agreed.

Mel and I finished our lunch and figured that Cleo had probably wandered off alone somewhere in the school grounds.

"Well, I better go looking for him. Want to come, Lorrie?"

"I would, but I need to pop to the library and get a few books out. Now that Grandmama's… somewhere… I need to do some self-directed study for my spells."

"Okay, well wish me luck!"

I wished Mel good luck, she needed it. It was one thing *finding* Cleo (he had some really good hiding spots) but it was another convincing him to come back to class. I'd tried it before myself. But maybe with this "new leaf" of his, it'll be easier.

I made my way to the library and thought about the little green frog sticker some more. I started to think I had seen it before, or at least one similar to it, but I couldn't remember *where*. I didn't think I saw it on the camera, I had a feeling it was somewhere else. Maybe in an old sticker book belonging to Darius' younger sister, Helena, who is an avid sticker collector (her bedroom door is COVERED in the things). Hmm… nope, not that. She doesn't tend to go for slimy toads, she's more of a princess girl. It played on my mind the entire walk to the library, but then as I was browsing the spell books in the unearthly section, it came back to me like a gust of wind, coming from nowhere, and nearly knocking me off my feet: It was in my fortune.

I *had* seen it but hadn't thought anything of it at the time — why *would* I? I remember it so clearly, even thinking back on it now. Cleo pulled something from his bag, it was dark and solid, but a small — almost microscopic — green frog sticker was illuminated in the light of the fire, before it was hidden by a cloth. It's as if my mind kept it locked away, and I had just found the key. The overwhelming sense of dread came flooding back and almost drowned me (okay, so I'm being a tad dramatic, but I really did feel it all over again).

Could it really be? Was Cleo burning his *camera*? I couldn't tell that by the shape, and the cloth was hiding its colour, but the size certainly matched that of his camera. And if it was his camera, then *why* was he burning it?

"Excuse me… EXCUSE me, can I please get past?" An impatient whisper interrupted my epiphany. They had plenty of space.

"Sure, sorry." I moved in closer to the shelf, practically hugging it.

Why was he burning it? He had told Mel he lost it, but he *lied*. He had it even after the trip. Could it be that he had taken a picture of the stone, or that his camera held some other evidence that would have led the police to suspect him and Mr Magus? I pondered over the possibility that I may have gotten it wrong, going back to the whole cause and effect thing I explained earlier. Did I just pin the sticker into my memory because we had been talking about it at lunch? No. I am not very confident about a lot of my spells, but with this one, I knew I was right.

My heart was racing. I bolted out of the library to find Mel. Our next lesson was about to start, I lost track of time. I raced towards the classroom, not because I was worried about my third late arrival, but because I *needed* to speak to Mel, NOW. I arrived at the classroom and caught my breath for a moment. I peeped into the window and saw Mel sitting at her desk. Cleo's was empty, she obviously hadn't found him or convinced him to return. Some "new leaf." I waved my arms around, getting the hang of the fly swatting gesture, as I tried to attract Mel's attention. After a minute or two she looked in my direction, prompted by other students who had noticed me first. It was like the most unsuccessful game of charades ever. Mel glared at me for a moment, before realising that I was calling her. She raised her hand and asked to go to the toilet. The teachers *hate* it when we ask them that.

"Why don't you go before the lesson" or "You've just had a whole hour of lunch" is the typical response. They have a point, but if you gotta go, you gotta go. And if you need to get out of the lesson, it's a great excuse. You can't punish a weak bladder, after all!

Mel walked out the door, gently closing it behind her before asking:

"What?"

I pulled her arm and led her away from the door in a panic, making sure no one would overhear what I was about to say.

"Ouch. Lorrie, what's wrong?"

"Mel."

"Lorrie...?"

"Did the guards send Cleo his camera back?"

"What? What are you talking about?"

130

"At the *Musea*, did the guards give Cleo his camera back, after they searched it for evidence on the missing stone?"

"Is this really what you've called me out of class for? Not that I don't welcome the escape, Mrs Kelpie was banging on about some or other famous artist from the sixties."

"Mel, listen to me PLEASE. Did Cleo get his—"

"I'm not sure, Lorrie. I didn't even see him give it to them in the first place! Now can we get back to the lesson? I can only imaginary pee for so long and you're late, again!"

I suddenly realised the gravity of my discovery. I stood, frozen in my place.

"Lorrie, are you okay?"

"Mel. There's something I need to tell you. It's about Cleo."

Chapter 13
Where the sun don't shine

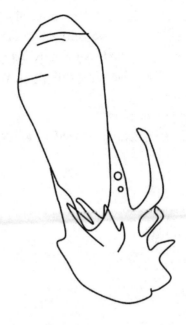

Friday 13th September, 8.00 p.m.

Of course, I am superstitious. What unearthly wouldn't be? The earth is full of bad (and good) voodoo. This Friday the 13th felt far more ominous than others. I wondered whether Mel would speak to me or not. After using her outside voice for a good twenty-five minutes she started giving me the silent treatment. Mel and I have had arguments, mostly over stupid things like who copied who when we both got the same pendant as a Parismas gift.

The chain was sterling silver, and the charm hanging from it was an Emerald (which, in our culture, symbolises healing and restoration of beauty). Crush it up into a fine powder and, along with other important elements, you can make a potion that, with one sip or a tiny drop on a wound, you will be healed. To this day, Mel honestly believes that I heard her talking about her Parismas wish list and stole the idea. If that *was* the case, why would I show up to school after the holiday's displaying it proudly around my neck? It was a bit awkward... Have you ever shown up to a party and found that you were wearing the same dress as someone else? Or, in your case, Diary, ever been in a store where all the other Diaries were encased by the same brown faux leather? Well anyway we were both told to take our necklaces off and settle the dispute outside of school. Mr Goddard felt that, at a glance, the sparkling green around our necks could pass for an earthly collar. "Unearthlies wear strictly blue". Parisa forbid we tamper with the divide!

The fight we had yesterday was a little more vicious. I explained to Mel that I practised my trick on Cleo, and that I saw the little green frog on his camera before he fed it to the fire, following his papa's instructions. I also tried to describe the feeling I had, the feeling that *Cleo* had.

"It was terrifying, Mel, it felt like there was a weight on top of me and my insides were about to burst open under the pressure!"

Mel was mortified that I "had the nerve" to perform the spell on her brother:

"I can't BELIEVE you did that! How *could* you? It's a TOTAL invasion of privacy!"

133

"I know Mel, it was wrong, and I shouldn't have done it but—"

"But? But WHAT?"

"But you're not seeing the point…"

"The point about my papa and my brother being *thieves*?"

"Well no… yes… I don't know Mel but you can't deny they were both acting very shifty all weekend with your dad taking random phone calls and Cleo not handing his camera in…"

Mel's eyes were filling with tears and her cheeks were bright red.

"You, of all uneathlies, Lorrie. I thought you were better than them. It turns out you're just the same." Mel wiped her tears and walked away, leaving me alone in the empty corridor.

It's going to take a lot to get over this one. For all our silly fights and falling outs, Mel had never looked at me the way she did just then. Betrayal. I wasn't sure she would ever forgive me for it, and that scared me, because she was the one person I always had on my side. Even when Easton, the love of her life, made fun of my pigtails in our first year, Mel slammed him for it.

"Don't you dare say nasty things about Lorrie, or you'll have me to answer to! Oh and also, I really like your bag!" Although Mel's position of defence quickly turned into flattery, she stood up for me, which continued in the years to come.

I tried to do the same for her when whispers in the halls told tales of her papa's dark magic. I was never any good at it, not like Mel. I wasn't quick at thinking on my feet and nobody ever seemed even the slightest bit afraid of me.

"You couldn't intimidate a goldfish if you tried, Lorrie."

Mel would laugh, but I could tell she appreciated it when I *did* try.

One time, I told Jessica to "shove it where the sun don't shine". She was spreading rumours about Mel kissing Caleb; a disgusting unearthly who grew up a few houses away from her. He was nice enough, but he picked his nose and scratched his bum when he thought no one was looking.

"Where exactly is that?" Jessica sneered back at me.

"Well... you don't want to know, so shush about it or..."

"Or...?"

Let's just leave it at that. Nine times out of ten, my efforts at defending Mel resulted in Mel having to defend me defending her, and I loved her for it. In that moment, and as I write this, I feel a crushing sense of regret. I can't lose Mel, I *need* her. We have been inseparable our entire unearthly lives and, to tell you the truth, as much as she nearly drives me to the brink of insanity at times, losing her would be like losing a limb. I need my limbs! I need Mel! And I'm petrified of what I've discovered. I tried to find her at the end of the day to apologise and tell her we can leave it all behind, if she wanted. But as soon as she saw me coming, she practically sprinted in the opposite direction. Cleo came up to me before the last bell while I was packing away some books from my locker, seemingly not knowing about the fall out and about my dangerous suspicions of him.

"You seen Mel?" he asked. "I heard she was looking for me. Sorry for my outburst earlier, it was a bit uncalled for."

Before I had the chance to reply, and I wasn't sure what I would have said, Mel yelled at him from the other side of the hallway.

"Cleo, come here NOW!"

"Okay, okay. *Sheesh* what's up with her? Seeya, witchy!"

"Bye," I mouthed, with no words coming out. "I'm sorry, Mel," I whispered as she turned her back and walked out the doors.

I sent Mel a dozen messages last night, and Mama let me use the home phone to ring theirs, in the hopes she wouldn't know it was me calling and pick up. I had a speech prepared. My tactic was to use sweet talk and tell her I would beg on my knees, if that's what it took. I plan to bring up my discovery again, of course. I can't exactly *let it go*. If Cleo and Mr Magus *have* stolen the stone, I need to do *something*. But I want Mel's forgiveness first, and I figure it's best to wait for grandmama to return so I can seek her guidance. She will know what to do. So, after dinner I dialled the Magus' number. Mrs Magus answered and told me that Mel was in bed with a fever and couldn't come to the phone. I obviously knew that wasn't the case, but I said, "I hope she feels better" and hung up the call. I went to sleep begging the powers of Parisa that Mel would talk to me today.

I obviously didn't beg hard enough because she avoided me all day. Cleo didn't speak to me, either. I think he knew he wasn't supposed to, but I got the feeling he didn't know why, because he waved at me from a distance when Mel wasn't looking. I decided it was best to give her some space and hope she cools off. I also assumed that our slideshow night was off. I wonder whether Mel will talk to me at Easton's party tomorrow. I don't even want to go now. We hadn't spoken about how we would get there, but it was pretty much a given that Mel and I would go together. I was hoping mama wouldn't agree to take me so that I would have an excuse to bail, but she was over the moon that I was going to a party, and not just *any* party, but a party where unearthlies were *encouraged* to socialise with earthlies. Mama was ALL for it. Great, I guess I'm going. Who knows, maybe Easton will shut the door in my face if he catches wind of mine and Mel's fight. Although, something that's always been in the back of my mind but that I've never dared voice is the possibility that Easton doesn't feel the same about Mel. I've never actually *seen* him talk to her much at school. He says hi when he passes her in the halls, and he did help her with her books that time, but I wasn't so sure the love affair was completely... reciprocal.

I picked out an outfit for tomorrow, Diary. You can't see it, but it's laying out on my bed. I'm never sure of how to dress for these things, so I always play it on the safe side and stick with casual. I'd much prefer to be underdressed than overdressed and knowing that Mel is the opposite means that there's no chance we'll have any wardrobe similarities — that would just be the worst possible sandstone flake topping on the cake. So, I'm going in faded blue skinny jeans with a pale pink plain top, and a brown jacket. I'll get my scuffed brown boots out too, for the occasion. I haven't bought Easton a gift, I wouldn't have the slightest idea of what to get him, but mama picked out a card for me when she was at work.

'Howdy there. Hope you have a cow-TASTIC birthday!' it reads, with a cartoon image of a cow wearing a birthday hat.

It seriously looks like it was designed for a four-year-old. Mama stood over my shoulder while I wrote in it, telling me to take my time and "write neatly, do it neatly!" But I have absolutely zero intentions of giving it to him. Mel said she was planning on buying him a poster of a film they watched in an

English lesson before summer. Apparently, they spoke all throughout the film, mocking the actors for their horrific portrayal of their characters and finding plot holes in the storyline.

"I can't WAIT to give it to him. It's like our little inside joke." Mel shrieked. I wasn't sure he would get it…

I didn't tell Mama why Mel hated my guts, but she could tell I was upset. She tried to reassure me that "whatever it is, you two will get over it", and suggested we do some baking to take my mind off it. Mama and I used to bake together a lot. It was one of the few things we did, just us two, when I was growing up. But then I started learning harder tricks and working towards higher Grades, and I just didn't have time for it any more. In place of flour and sugar, my focus shifted towards unearthly ingredients, and I started to mix potions instead of cookie batter. There were moments where I realised that I missed it; licking the bowl, smelling the freshly baked cookies… but mostly I missed doing something with mama.

"That's a great idea, Mama!" We decided to make triple chocolate brownies.

"You get the recipe out, and I'll start weighing the ingredients!" Mama instructed, "But not before I put on our famous mama-daughter music medley!"

"Oh no, Mama, not the music medley!" I cringed as I covered my face with my hands in anticipation of the terrible seventies pop tunes. 'Shiny red broomstick' by 'The Charmz' features as the third track, to give you a sense. It was part of the baking tradition though, and the only time we ever got the CD player out.

After a few mishaps (Mama dropping an egg on the floor, Stumbles treading flour EVERYWHERE and some frantic mixture splatter from the wild electric whisk) we popped the brownies in the oven and sat down with some hot chocolate in front of the TV. About halfway through the 'method' section, once we felt satisfied that we at least *tried* to honour our tradition, we both gladly agreed to turn the CD player off and switch to my playlist. Mama said she was pleasantly surprised by some of the classical songs and even turned the laptop up at one point. It was nice to share that part of myself with her.

Fifteen minutes later, after we devoured our hot chocolate, the timer went off and the brownies were smelling IN-CRED-IBLE. Mama took them out to cool and told me to find a "nice earthly movie", emphasis on 'earthly'. But I was going to anyway. I was happy to take a break from magic and all the recent trouble it brought me. We ate our brownies with some ice cream, and it melted into a gooey delight. The flavours exploded in my mouth as I sat there wrapped up in a blanket with mama, singing along to a cheesy musical and having the best time I've had in a while. I told mama I wanted to do this again with her, soon. She smiled and didn't need to tell me how much that meant to her.

Lessons learned from today:

1. When Mel hates your guts, leave her alone.
2. Mama buys terrible cards which must be destroyed.
3. Stumbles gets in the way, always.
4. Flour is very hard to get out of the carpet.
5. Earthly activities are fun, after all.

So, another Friday the 13th has come and gone. I'm letting myself forget about the stone and my row with Mel. I'd like to be my two-percent mortal, even if only for tonight. Tomorrow, I'll be unearthly again.

Chapter 14
Skittles

Saturday 14th September, 8.10 p.m.

The party started at one p.m. I allowed myself to have a small lie in (or rather, Stumbles allowed me to) and snoozed my alarm at nine a.m. I didn't actually get out of bed until nine forty-five though, I was thinking about all of the events of the past few days and replaying my prediction in my head. You know how dreams usually fade over time? Well, this one seemed to become more vibrant and detailed. It's almost like the inside of a window clouded by mist and every day it clears a little bit more, making the outside world visible. This time, I saw Mr Magus. His son was looking up at him, silently pleading to get out of this place.

"Son, you know what you have to do." His face was expressionless, but it emitted a trace of compassion.

When I had the dream, I woke up immediately after the flames engulfed the camera. But now, a few more moments emerged in the aftermath.

"Papa, do we really need to do this?"

Mr Magus nodded.

"If they come looking for the camera, they'll see the pictures of the stone, and if they see the pictures, it'll lead them right to us."

I knew I was right. And suddenly, I cared a bit less that

Mel was still upset with me. I had bigger problems.

Although I set myself plenty of time to get ready, I somehow managed to procrastinate which led me to rush up to the last second. I asked Mama in the car when Grandmama would be back, I desperately need to talk to her.

"I'm not sure, Lorelei. I haven't heard from her, but I'm assuming it will be tomorrow or Monday."

"I miss her." I commented.

"You know, I do too!" Mama agreed.

I smiled, touched by her rare, loving attitude towards her mama. I pictured all three of us baking triple chocolate brownies together, when grandmama returns. I hope she will join us in our earthly inspired activity — we really did have a lot of fun.

Mama parked on the street opposite Easton's house. I wasn't sure what to expect. I knew there would be earthlies there, party snacks were a given and music was sure to be blaring, but would there be any party games? I love them but I'm no good, and I wasn't sure if we were too old for that. Fourteen is a difficult age. We kind of want to be cool and act grown up, but secretly we all just want to be kids and make fools of ourselves. If there are party games, pass the parcel is a personal favourite of mine. I'm the only one who seems to prefer getting the small candy in between the layers to the main prize in the last box (which is normally a glorified bar of soap).

As I hurriedly got out the car, after purposefully "forgetting" the birthday card Mama bought for Easton, I told Mama goodbye and said:

"Don't forget to pick me up at four!"

I thought I had gotten away with it, but as I closed the door and looked left and right to cross the street, Mama rolled down the passenger side window.

"Lorelei, don't forget the card!"

While my back was facing Mama, I closed my eyes and sighed, before turning around and thanking Mama for reminding me. I took the card from her hand and walked up to Easton's house.

There were green and blue balloons attached to the hanging plants on either side of his front door — no doubt as a statement that both kinds are welcome. I saw a few other kids who I recognised from school (and some who I didn't) getting out of cars and walking towards the house. As I got to the door, I rang the bell before I could change my mind and chase after mama's car which had now turned a corner and faded out of sight. I could hear some quiet music and loud chatter, and I noticed movement in the windows. I remembered I was holding the card, and right before Easton's papa opened the door, I stuffed it behind one of the neatly trimmed bushes. No one will know.

"Hello, and welcome to Easton's fourteenth birthday party!"

"Papa, you don't have to say that to everyone, they know it's my party!" Easton shoved his papa out the way.

This was the moment, the potential door slamming in my face.

"Hi, Lorelei!" He grinned. "Come on in, I think Mel's in here somewhere."

Gulp. As I followed Easton through his house, he gave me a brief guided tour:

"This is the lounge; we'll probably be in there later. I know it's lame, but my mama set up pass the parcel…"

(Bingo!)

"...and this is the kitchen, feel free to help yourself to some snacks, although don't get too excited about them, my ten-year-old sister helped with the brownies..."

(I bet mine and mama's brownies were better)

"...and this is the garden, where we'll probably spend most of our time, if the weather holds."

Easton looked up to the sky and I followed. Thick, grey clouds were forming, and I wasn't sure they would be kind to us. I looked around the garden. There were probably a dozen or so people, with more piling in. I noticed a music station on a fold out table positioned near the corner of the wooden fence, and there were some adults setting up a barbeque. On the grass, some outdoor party games had been laid out. I saw some hoola hoops lying next to buckets of water on the ground, and a willing victim who was standing behind a big wooden board with their face peeking through, about to be smacked by a flying wet sponge.

I looked around to see if I could pick out anyone I knew. The number of my friends who I would have to avoid was growing. Mel, Cleo, Dean... And then of course there were the other earthlies who I didn't particularly care to spend time with (namely Jessica who would apparently be here if Dean was, which is still *beyond* me). I couldn't spot any of them, and was slightly relieved, until I realised that it meant I would have to find someone else to socialise with. It's not something I'm particularly good at. My confidence is low; people don't find me especially funny when I crack jokes (probably because I always mess up the punchline) and I don't really understand the purpose of "small talk". Is an uncomfortable silence really worse than agreeing over the state of the weather? Apparently so. I wandered around awkwardly for a while, contemplating who seemed friendly enough to approach. I picked out a couple of unearthlies who I had shared some classes with and had spoken to before. I decided on one of them: a girl who lent me her pen once when mine ran out of ink. She wasn't playing with the sponges, which was a bonus because I didn't fancy a wet blob of soap exploding in my face. I started to walk towards her when I noticed a light tap on my shoulder. Dean.

"Mr Good Boy," I said sarcastically, hoping he would infer from my attitude just how "good" I did <u>not</u> think he was.

"Hi, Lorrie." I stared blankly at him, not having much to say and striving to make him feel as uncomfortable as I could.

"How are you?" he sheepishly asked after scratching his head.

"Me? Fine."

"Oh… that's good." Small talk. If Dean was trying to say sorry, he was failing, and I couldn't be bothered to watch him.

"Well, enjoy the party, I'll see you around!" I spun around and prepared to walk away from him, very assertively, I might add.

"Lorrie, wait!"

I showed off another loud sigh and faced him once again.

"I'm sorry, okay. I acted like a—"

"A jerk?"

"Yeah." He looked down.

"Dean, I'm tired of you bouncing around like a yoyo not being able to decide whether you like me or whether you don't!"

He was quiet.

"I do like you, Lorrie, more than I thought I would — more than I wanted to!"

He looked up and held my eyes. I couldn't figure out if I

still wanted to be mad at him. He did seem genuinely sorry.

"Then why do you act like you do sometimes? I thought we were friends, and I was going to ask you for your number, even."

"Oh. I wanted to ask you the same…"

"Really?" I could feel the butterflies waking up again.

"Yeah! I don't mean to take it out on you. There's some stuff going on, some things that are happening to my family, and… it's not anything to do with you, so I shouldn't take it out on you. I am sorry."

After Dean explained what was upsetting him so much and talked about the argument he had with his dad in the car, I accepted his apology and gave him my phone number. In short, he told me that his papa's mechanic business is falling apart, and that they are in some financial trouble as a result. He blamed lack of customers but said that his papa is mad at him because he doesn't spend more time helping him out after school.

"You spend too much time on your music, and you're great at it, son, but it won't put dinner on the table!"

He talked about how he feels torn between his passion for his tuba and his duty as a son. He also has a younger brother, Charlie, and he desperately wants to be a good role model for him. It sounded complicated, and I felt terrible for him. Then, we spoke for a while, about other things. I told Dean that I had listened to Sinthea's Ballad, and that I liked it a lot. He gave me the names of a few more to listen to, and we laughed over the 'Shiny red broomstick' song. He said he wanted to try the brownies Mama and I made, and I promised him that next time he pretended to feel unwell, I would make him a fresh batch.

"Good incentive to be fake sick!" He remarked with a wink.

After a while of talking, Dean asked me if I would like to challenge him at the giant skittles, warning me that he's a champion at it when he plays with his brother, and usually knocks over all nine of them with only one roll of the small wooden ball. I laughed and asked him whether it was a fair fight with a five-year-old, and he chirped that it most definitely was.

"Challenge accepted!" I proclaimed.

We walked over and I picked up a ball while Dean set the skittles in their position.

"Unearthlies first!" He declared as he stepped aside. "No cheating though, I'm watching!"

I didn't cheat, of course, and I knocked over eight on my first go! Dean went next, and let's just say I beat him fairly quickly.

"Whole different ball game when you're playing with someone your own size!" I teased.

"Ha, ha, ha," he sarcastically snickered. "Not very graceful in victory I see!"

It was the first time I felt like I was truly natural with Dean, which is not something I thought possible with an earthly. I suppose because all of the other earthlies at the party were mixing with the unearthlies, it didn't feel so unusual. I did catch Jessica shooting me a look of total disgust though, but I didn't even mind that.

Dean announced that he needed some party food to cheer him up after his defeat. He asked me if I'd like anything, and I initially said no, but then called after him and said, "I'll try a brownie, just to compare!"

Just as he disappeared through Easton's back door, Mel submerged. She instantly caught my eye, and me being my awkward self, I looked away quickly and pretended I hadn't seen her. Quick, act like you're busy... I picked up one of the skittles and pretended I was inspecting it. I wasn't sure if I was a good actress or not, but I went with it and committed, holding it up to my eye and rotating it at different angles. I could see Mel walking straight towards me, despite my performance. My heart was racing and my cheeks burned. What was she going to say? Was she going to throw her plate of food in my face? Or worse, yet — knock me on the head with a skittle? With that thought, I irrationally hid the skittle behind my back and looked up. I couldn't deny that I had seen her now; she stopped right in front of me.

"Lorrie. Can we talk?"

Mel spoke softly, which caught me off guard. I was ready for a fight, or rather I was ready for *her* to fight, and me to stand there like an ineffective scarecrow on a mission to deter a flock of birds.

"Umm, yeah sure." I was hopeful, but I tried not to show it on my face.

I thought it would be better to have the first say and apologise to Mel so that she knew I acknowledged my wrongdoing. Before she could open her mouth, I opened mine:

"Mel I'm so sorry, I should never have done that to Cleo and I'm—"

"Lorrie, I found something in Papa's office..." The look on Mel's face resembled Cleo's when he was kneeling in the face of the fire.

"Was it the stone?" I asked, perhaps more bluntly than I

should have.

"No, but I think you need to see this." Mel was carrying a small bag with a long handle which was hanging from her shoulder. She made sure no one was watching and pulled out a folded piece of paper.

"I think it's best if I show this to you somewhere else."

Mel and I walked into the kitchen, where Easton's mama was decorating his cake with candles.

"Mel, let's wait for the cake."

"I had the same idea!" Mel and I often floated on the same wavelength.

When Easton's mama called everyone inside to sing happy birthday to her son, Mel and I slowly wandered off from the crowd and scouted the hallway for an empty room.

"In here," Mel gestured.

There was a desk set up with a computer screen, and piles of paper neatly piled beside the keyboard. It became apparent that it was an office room. Mel switched on a small lamp which sat on the desk as I shut the door, as quietly as I could. We could hear the ending of the song followed by three chants of "hip, hip, HORRAAAAY!"

"Cake time!" Easton's voice bellowed.

I knew we would be safe in here, for now. I looked again at Mel, who was unfolding the paper. I was afraid of what she was going to show me, so I waited a few moments before drawing closer to her. When I eventually did, I peered over Mel's shoulder as she lay the crumpled paper out under the light on the desk.

"What is it?" I could make out faint pen marks on the page, but I wasn't sure what they meant.

"It's a map, Lorrie, of the Musea… and there's an 'x'

where the stone was on display."

Shock. Was this proof? I could see it so clearly now.

Mr Magus had even gone to the trouble of labelling all the exits in the building, with a big red circle around the words: *'fire escape'*.

"Mel, where did you find this?"

"Well, I was really mad at you at first, Lorrie. I was furious. But then when I started to think about it, Papa had taken quite a few business calls..." Mel gestured inverted commas in the air with her fingers. "And we hadn't seen them for such a long time that day... anyway, I decided to go looking through Papa's draws in his study when everyone was asleep, kind of like you did with your grandmama. I figured that if you found something in her hiding place, then maybe I would find something in Papa's."

"Does he know you took it?"

"I'm not sure. He didn't say anything to me this morning, and it was buried underneath other papers that looked like work documents, so I'm not sure how long it will take him to notice. I suppose he should have burned it in the fire, too." Mel nervously laughed. "Too soon to joke?" she asked, judging by my lack of response.

"Probably," I sympathetically smiled.

Mel and I debated what we should do next. We decided against going to the unearthly authorities for fear of what they could do to Mr Magus and Cleo. I suggested we go to Grandmama, but Mel didn't want to in case *she* took it upon herself to report them. Grandmama thought herself a law-abiding unearthly citizen: very committed to the Laws and the council of the MOTW. We also figured we probably don't know the whole story, and Mel is so desperate for there to be

149

a perfectly reasonable explanation as to why they stole such a powerful and potentially dangerous object (although I must admit, I'm not so sure there is). The only thing we could think of was to ask Cleo himself. We hatched a plan to confront him, and we needed to do it, soon.

"He's here, Lorrie. He came with me to the party. If we don't do it now, who knows what will happen." Mel's sense of urgency coaxed mine.

"Okay, let's do it."

Mel took a deep breath and wrapped her arms around her tummy, which presumably felt a lot lousier than mine.

"I'm afraid, Lorrie."

"I know, Mel."

Chapter 15
Butterflies

Monday 14th October, 12.05 a.m.

Sorry that you haven't seen me for a while, Diary. It's not that I don't love a good cliff-hanger (I do), but the events that unfolded over the next few days kept me from writing my entries. Partly, I was concerned that you would fall into the wrong hands. Also, to be perfectly frank, you were the last thing on my mind. I even needed reminding to pee, in amongst all the turmoil (thanks, Cleo).

It has been precisely one month since I last wrote in you, so there is a LOT I need to catch you up on. I think what I'll do is write my entries in chronological order, retrospectively, so it's easier for you to follow. But be prepared, things get a little… crazy.

I'll start where I left off. Where was that again? Oh, yes, Easton's party.

Saturday 14th September

Mel and I agreed that we needed to speak to Cleo, and it couldn't wait. Mel opened the door and peeked through, making sure no one would see her coming out of Easton's papa's office. She closed it behind her and left me in the dim lit room. I glanced around and inspected the bookshelves to keep myself occupied and distract me from the butterflies (the nasty kind) in my tummy. His papa kept loads of books, mostly political writings from what I could gather. I pulled one out, and a cloud of dust followed. I brushed the hard cover with my hand, and the title was revealed:

'The trials and tribulations of Earthly people: How to bridge the divide with the mortal kind.'

The book was obviously aimed at unearthlies, but I hadn't ever heard of its existence, so it must either be old or modest. I thought perhaps one day I would read it if I could remember its name. Becoming closer to Dean over the past two weeks has sparked something in me, something I never thought possible: a curiosity about the earthlies. In that moment, an unexpected thought entered my mind, without seeking permission or even giving a warning. It was of my papa.

I imagined an alternate life, one with Papa in it, reading me bedtime stories and teaching me how to ride a bike. If our kinds were more accepting of each other, and learned to be inquisitive instead of avoidant, would everything be totally different? Maybe "apa wouldn't have had to leave us, and we would all three live in our own house, a smaller house, with a humble garden and a tree house. I always wanted a tree house. Maybe I would have a brother or a sister, and mama would have taught me spells and embraced her powers, instead of resisting them. I reckon Papa would have liked Dean; a fellow earthly to talk about car stuff with. We could have had a nice life together. Make no mistake, I loved spending my childhood learning from Grandmama and Hemlock House is my home. But — and it hurts even writing it down — I could finally understand Mama's hatred of the Lore, it ripped away her husband and denied me the chance to grow up with a papa.

I almost welcomed the opening of the door.

"Where are you taking me?"

"Shhhh," Mel hissed.

"Oh, hi little witch. Are you two speaking again, then?"

I stared at Cleo and I was sad. Although I sometimes find him deeply frustrating, he *is* one of my closest friends. I mean I spend nearly *all* my time with him, even if that is mostly a result of being Mel's brother. And I was about to accuse him of committing treason and breaking the code of the Lore (which, lucky for him, I was not best pleased with at this moment in time).

"Hi, Cleo," I said, solemnly.

"You're in a mood!" Cleo taunted.

I held onto that moment with the three of us, just for a second, as I knew that everything was about to change.

"Cleo…" Mel began. "We need to ask you something…"

"What's up?" Cleo asked, realising the sombre mood and conforming to it. "Well?" His eyes shifted between the two of us.

"Cleo…" I interjected, after appreciating that Mel was too choked up to speak. "There's something we need to talk about, and just know that we will always be here for you, and you can tell us anything…"

"What? Do I have something in my teeth? I swear it isn't a brownie!" He joked, but I could tell he was anxious.

"There's no easy way to say this, Cleo." Mel continued as she fought back her tears.

"Come out with it then, you're scaring me!"

I walked closer to him, conscious not to speak too loudly.

"We know you stole the stone."

Cleo was silent.

"I—"

153

"Before you say anything, we have proof." Mel pleaded with her brother not to make any excuses; it would make it harder for us all.

Cleo tilted his head down and, without saying anything, he walked towards the desk. He seemed to accept that he wasn't getting out of this one, which was a first for Cleo. I wonder, looking back on it now, whether he was almost grateful to have somebody to tell. Turning away from us, he began his testimony.

"If I tell you, you won't believe me."

"Try us!" I said, trying to sound more encouraging.

"If you really want to know, I'll have to start from the beginning. But I warn you, once you know the truth, you'll wish you didn't."

Basically, the conversation we had was utterly mind blowing. I would go through it, sentence by sentence, but we would be here a while. In summary, Mel and I had no idea what can of worms we had opened. And it was a very stinky can. The stone had been stolen, and Cleo knew who did it. Sort of.

A couple of weeks ago, Mr Magus received a tip off from an informant while he was at work. The Council of Sorcery and Enchantment, otherwise known as 'CSE', received hundreds of them a week, but this one was particularly threatening because it involved the dark sorceress, Sereia (remember, the one who wanted to turn earthly blood into poison). Sereia was hatching a plan to escape from Soulas Lossesta, harnessing the powers of the stone to wish herself freedom and incredible might, and finally fulfilling her promise of bringing carnage and ruin to the earth. All that the informant knew was that the stone would be stolen by someone who worked for Sereia, and soon. So, Mr Magus planned a trip to the Ilse of Dominia where he and his family would visit the Musea de Potin ela Charmus. Yikes, that did sound threatening. The informant, who Mr Magus knows personally, asked him to promise not to divulge the information to anyone else; it was of utmost sensitivity.

I'm not so sure who would have confessed such a thing to a suspected dark wizard, but Mr Magus managed to keep it confidential until his son found the very same museum map that his daughter would later find (Mr Magus isn't too good at hiding things, I've concluded). Confronted by Cleo — who was beside himself that his papa may after all be the dark wizard that everyone accused him of — Mr Magus explained everything. Cleo bravely offered to help his papa steal the stone to prevent it from falling into the wrong hands.

"Shouldn't you have told the Council of the Mother of the Wand?" Mel interrogated Cleo for the entire conversation.

"You can't trust them, Mel. Apparently Sereia has someone working on the inside, someone high up in the Council!"

"Well then, shouldn't you have told the unearthly authorities, at least?"

"No go!" sighed Cleo.

"If Sereia has someone in the Council, what makes you think she wouldn't have someone in the authorities? She's been hatching this plan for years, who knows how many unearthlies she has on her side. They could be a neighbour, a family member, even the postman could be implicated! Nobody can be trusted."

"Not even us?" Mel whimpered; I could tell she was hurt that her papa and brother kept this from her.

"I'm sorry, Mel. I wanted to tell you, but the fate of the earth is at stake here!"

"Who was the informant?" I asked, with anticipation.

"Papa wouldn't say, just that they are an old friend of his who has recently started working for the CSE as a field agent."

"Who has the stone, now?" Mel tried to set aside her hurt feelings.

"We're not sure — whoever Sereia ordered to steal it!"

"So YOU obviously didn't succeed, then!" Mel said, cynically; her hurt feelings still very much there.

Cleo shook his head. "We got there too late."

Mel asked Cleo what their plans were once they stole the stone; he didn't really have an answer.

"I'm not sure. I guess Papa had a plan, or he didn't, who knows. I didn't question it, there wasn't time!"

Mel then said what was playing on my mind this whole time, and I was so grateful she did.

"Cleo… did you ever think that Papa could… that he could be the—" He didn't let her finish the sentence.

"Of course not, Mel. You know Papa as well as I do. He isn't guilty, never was!"

I had to take Cleo's word for it, it's not like I could ask Mr Magus himself: "Are you a dark wizard, Mr Magus?" "Yes, you caught me!" The conversation would almost certainly NOT go like that.

"So, you were just planning on stealing the stone, just like that? Would it really have been *that* easy?" Cleo nodded in response to my question.

"It was a big deal and all when it was discovered by that earthly, but since it no longer shows its powers, well, there's probably a hundred other relics in there that could do more damage."

"So, what does Sereia want with it then? It doesn't have any powers!"

"Or it does, Lorrie, and she's figured out how to use them. Then she could do anything, wish anything. Endless dark possibilities!"

"So, let me get this straight…" I recapped, making sure I had all the details I needed to confirm Cleo's innocence. "Your papa was told that Sereia had a plan to steal the stone and conquer the world…"

"Correct!"

"And your papa thought that the only way to stop her was to steal the stone himself…"

"Yup."

"He didn't want to tell anyone in case they were working for her, and he also didn't know what he would do with the stone once he had it…"

"Umm that about sums it up."

I was satisfied that Cleo was telling the truth, but something didn't add up… How did the Council of the MOTW not know about this, and how did Sereia convince what sounded like an orchestra of unearthlies to do her dirty work? Promises of fortune, perhaps? Or maybe she brainwashed them by twisting the word of Parisa. It wasn't relevant, but it did intrigue me. What can make someone so evil, so full of hatred? Maybe *they* need to read Easton's papa's book!

"How did you find out about it, anyway?" Cleo asked after a prolonged silence as Mel and I were digesting it all.

He had obviously been trying to work it out in his head. He knew we had the map, but I guess he suspected that there was more to the story.

Gulp.

Now was the time, I hadn't lost Mel, but I might lose Cleo, and the thought of that was almost as hard to stomach. Perhaps I should explain a little more about my friendship with him...

Mel and I hit it off from the start, and by 'hit it off' I mean we first held each other's hands when we were eight months old, shared an ice cream at five and had our first sleepover at seven. Cleo didn't really do any of that stuff with us, but he was always *there*. Sometimes he stole our teddy bears and cut their ears off or trampled on our sandcastles which made us cry. But he also jumped into leaf piles with us and we threw popcorn at each other while watching terrible movies. He was also one of the few people that somehow managed to distract me from feeling sad by making me angry instead. Although his humour was controversial and he annoyed the life out of me at times, Cleo is also my best friend, come to think of it. The idea of telling him the truth was as scary as it was with Mel, probably even *more* so, because it was *him* who I ultimately betrayed by entering his future and, knowing Cleo, I wasn't hopeful that he would take it well.

I held my breath as I thought about how to tell him, and just as I opened my mouth, Mel opened hers, too.

"We found the map and I remembered how shifty Papa was and how you didn't hand in your camera to the guards, and just kind of pieced it all together. I asked Lorrie to help me confront you as I wasn't sure how you would react..." Mel, always defending me.

She caught my eye and nodded, as if to grant me permission to keep the damaging truth to myself.

"Oh..." Cleo almost looked ashamed of the prospect of his sister being afraid to approach him. "You can ask me anything, Mel, *anything*! I'm sorry that I've sometimes reacted... badly, but I'll try harder."

Mel smiled, and it was a touching moment between the two of them, that I let them have for a few seconds before I sought answers to my own questions.

"Cleo? What *did* you do with your camera?"

Please don't lie, please don't lie, please... don't lie!

"Umm, well, Papa told me to get rid of it because I had taken a few close ups of the latch. I didn't want to, I had this awful feeling that we needed to tell someone, but I did it anyway."

Thank you, Cleo, now I can trust you.

"How were you going to steal it, anyway?" was Mel's next question.

I hadn't thought about it, but I was interested as to how two unearthlies, one who is basically a glorified toddler, were planning on stealing the most prized and well secured possession of the Musea.

"Our plan was always to set the alarm off..." Cleo began. "And we managed that by jamming the door of the security room. You know, where they have their CCTV screens and defence controls. It was the best idea, really, cause the majority of the guards couldn't get out for a solid ten minutes. Then, while everyone gathered in the main hall and the guards tried to figure out why they had been barricaded, we snuck into the display and planned to unpick the bolt, which is hidden underneath the title plaque. But, when we got there, it had already been taken."

"And you said you don't know who did it? Did you notice anything unusual about anyone?" I was becoming more unsettled, and the urgency of the matter was growing, rapidly.

"No idea, that's the worst part. Before we burned the camera, Papa and I looked at the pictures over and over again, hoping to see *something*, SOMEONE, who could give us a clue as to who it might have been. But we saw nothing." Cleo looked at the ground again, possibly reliving his disappointment.

Once Cleo had told us everything, Mel walked up to him and embraced him. I felt the urge to do the same thing. I was so relieved that it wasn't him who stole the stone, and even though he planned to, it was for the right reasons. I was incredibly impressed at just how right the reasons were. I was also very glad that I didn't have to tell him about the *Fortunaes* trick, although I had Mel to thank for that.

I didn't give it much thought and I spontaneously wrapped my arms around Cleo once Mel stepped aside. He was a bit stunned and stumbled back a bit, before slowly closing his arms around me, too. It was nice. The last time we hugged was when Mrs Magus prompted Cleo to say thank you to me for last year's birthday present, which was a pair of woollen socks that boasted pictures of monkeys and splattered the words "Go bananas!" (also, a mortifying purchase of mama's!). It was an unpleasant experience; very awkward and he smelled like sweat. But this time, perhaps because we meant it (and because we were all going through a roller coaster of emotions) it felt comforting.

We may have stood together for a bit *too* long because Mel faked a cough a few times as an unsubtle cue to bring our attention back to the room. We hurriedly parted from each other and re-assumed our familiar awkwardness.

"Okay, so that was weird," Mel commented, acknowledging that we all experienced a particularly uncomfortable moment.

"So, what do we do now?" (I was half wanting to save the world and half wanting to distract us all from the tense atmosphere).

"I'm not sure, but we need to do *something.*" Mel offered.

"There's one more thing…" The words churned a knot in my stomach.

"What is it, Cleo?"

"Papa made me swear that I wouldn't get involved any more. He didn't tell me why, but I found this letter in his jacket pocket when I was helping him look for his car keys…" (I changed my mind, Mr Magus is TERRIBLE at hiding things.)

Cleo held out an all-too-familiar looking crumpled note which read:

'Tell him to stop, she can't know yet.'

"Lorrie, is that…" Mel was thinking the same thing I was, and it shook me to the core. Staring at the note, I replied:

"Yes, it's the same writing as in Grandmama's note."

Chapter 16
Crazy, evil sorceress

Sunday 15th September

We heard everyone start to disperse from the kitchen after the cake had been cut and dished out.

"We can't talk here any more, it's not safe."

Cleo wanted to be vigilant, so we agreed to meet the next day. I offered my house as a base for the meeting; Mama had a rare early shift at the store and, provided Grandmama didn't come home, we wouldn't be disturbed (aside from the postman, who Cleo suggested might be an evil Sereia minion in disguise). One by one, we filed out of the office. Pretty soon after that, Mama picked me up and grilled me about the party. It became apparent that she was interested in the unearthly/earthly dynamic.

"Did you speak to any earthlies? Did everyone seem to get along all right?"

I told her about Dean, only a little bit, though.

"Yeah, I spoke to one boy. He's my assigned earthly…"

"Oh yeah?"

"He's really nice, his name is Dean. We just chatted for a bit and played some Skittles… I won, obviously!" I teased.

"Oh Lorelei, I'm so glad you had fun and got to speak to some earthlies. And this boy, Dean, he sounds nice!" Mama wasn't even trying to hide her investigative schemes.

"Yup, he is." I kept it brief, hoping she would be satisfied with my clear attempt at halting the discussion.

When I got home, I investigated the note I found in Grandmama's bedroom and held it next to the one Cleo found, comparing the two. The stroke of the 't's were the same, and even the spacing between the words were comparable. Was I overthinking it? Was it just a coincidence? I wasn't sure, but I had a funny feeling that it *could* have been penned by the same writer. If it was, what did that *mean*? These were all questions which we were going to discuss and attempt to answer the next day.

I couldn't sleep that night; my mind was a spinning wheel, and the ancestors were screeching at me. I was so close to screaming back and begging for clarity as to what they were so desperate for me to know.

"Patience, my darling, you will hear when you are ready!" That was always grandmama's reply when I complained about the voices. What did that even mean? What would I hear and when would I be ready?

"In time, you will find out." How unsatisfying was that answer!

Time is a strange construct that never offered you ANY precision. It could mean seconds, minutes, days, weeks, months or even *years*.

I woke up on that Sunday with a throbbing headache after what was probably a little shy of four hours sleep. Mama was already at work by the time I forced myself out of bed. I showered, grabbed a muffin and sat down at my desk to make some scribble notes on your last page, which you probably noticed, Diary. I have since regretfully torn the page out, but it

163

went a little something like this:

Things to consider when plotting to save the earth:

1. Should we really be doing this? Aren't we a little in over our heads? ~~Probably~~ definitely.

2. Who knows about this? — Myself, Cleo, Mel, Mr Magus and the secret informant.

3. What would happen if we <u>didn't</u> do something? — Sereia could use the stone to take over the earth and then... doomsday!

4. What would happen if we <u>did</u> do something? — We may stop Sereia from using the stone to take over the earth, but we may also make everything worse and end up doing community service in the pandymonk enclosure.

5. What "something" do we need to do? — Not entirely certain. Finding out who took the stone would be a good place to start.

6. How would we find the stone? — Also not certain. Hoping Mel and Cleo will shed some light.

7. Do we actually know what the stone does? — Ish — it was used to grant wishes.

Overall Pro's	*Overall Con's*
Saving everyone from earth domination	*We may be imprisoned or killed in the process (that's probably the worst one)*
	If we aren't killed, we'll probably get into a whole lot of trouble for not telling anyone
	I could be grounded for the rest of my unearthly life
	Probably a load more...

After writing it all out, it seemed like a no brainer, stay out of it! But I couldn't shake the feeling that if we did nothing, who else would? I showed it to Mel and Cleo when they arrived. It turns out they had made their own pros and cons list, and while Cleo and I regrettably agreed that the pros outweigh the cons, Mel wasn't so sure.

"I do NOT think that we should do this. Who's to say we *could* even do it?" Mel insisted.

"We have to, Mel! If we don't, who will?"

"What about papa? Isn't he still involved in it all?"

"He's acting like a wounded puppy; he keeps telling me it's too late and to keep out of it!"

"What if he's right?"

"He's not! The choice is literally between life or death, so how could the side of death be right?"

They argued, and all the while I was studying my own list, trying to make up my mind. On the one hand, saving the earth would be pretty good. I could finally live up to my prophecy of Orenda line redemption (even though it's probably all just nonsense), and the earthlies would see that we could do good too, not only bad. On the other hand, I didn't like the idea of getting killed, imprisoned or, similarly, grounded. While I pondered, I noticed a pause and when I lifted my head, Mel and Cleo were both staring at me.

"Lorrie? Your call."

"Aww I HATE it when you make me make the decision! I guess we'll have to find the stone, then."

We started off by brainstorming who could have taken it. Cleo said that he saw a lady who was hanging around the display, looking particularly dubious. Mel had also seen an

165

older man who was wearing sunglasses and a hat, potentially as a disguise of his identity. He, too, had inspected the stone. I could only really offer the annoying child that kept crying at his mama while I was trying to read the blurb, but we quickly disregarded him as a suspect. Since Cleo had disposed of his camera, Mel and I searched through the pictures on ours, hoping for a clue. It was like a more intense, gloomy version of the slideshow we had planned. We couldn't find anything, of course, and some of the pictures had been wiped by the unearthly authorities before the camera's had been posted back to us.

"What are we gonna do? We've gotten NOWHERE!" Mel whined.

"I guess, if we can't figure out who it was for sure, we could maybe try and come up with the most *likely* suspect?"

I wasn't sure what Cleo meant by that, but after some explanation we started jotting down likely characteristics of someone who could secretly be working for a crazy, evil sorceress.

"Unearthly or earthly?" I asked, pen in my hand.

"Hmmm, unearthly!" Cleo confidently asserted.

"Yeah, I reckon so. Why would an earthly be helping to bring upon their own demise?" Mel agreed.

"Okay…" I wasn't sure, but I wrote it down with a question mark in the margin.

I let Mel and Cleo continue their suggestions.

"Probably someone… unsuspecting."

"Yup, maybe someone who had a family with them."

"I reckon they could have been disguised as a guard, even. Papa and I thought about doing that ourselves!"

We sat together for a full two hours, deliberating over who

could have been involved and creating a profile for the perfect candidate: Unearthly, unsuspecting like a papa or mama with their children, maybe disguised as a guard, maybe as a tourist, looking a bit nervous and hanging around the displays for longer than they should have (like the Scrubtub display, where spending anything more than five minutes would warrant suspicion). Overall, we had ZERO success with it, and all had different ideas of who it could have been. In truth, it could have been anyone!

When that didn't work, we tried to draw out a timeline of *when* the stone could have been taken. That way, maybe we could pinpoint how they escaped, and what spells they may have used to assist them. We quickly discovered that this exercise was useless, but here was the reasoning: If they used a Grade 3 trick, we could assume they were a rookie and maybe a bit younger. That was highly unlikely to be the case, as we concluded that Sereia is mastermind enough to recruit more skilful criminals to her team. So, they were probably a Grade 8/9, or higher. Also, if their escape was particularly challenging (say when the entire building went into immediate lockdown) there may have even been *more* than one thief! We knew one thing for sure: the stone had been taken in between the time I saw the display and the time when Cleo and Mr Magus returned to it once they jammed the security door. That was roughly a seventy-five-minute window; ten or so of which occurred during the alarm and the immediate shutting of the doors. It was more likely than not that the suspect escaped just before then, which would put it sometime between 10.40 and 11.45 a.m.

From Mr Magus and Cleo's research, they knew all the blind spots where the CCTV wouldn't have been able to capture them, such as in the fire escape stairwell (we were studying it on the map as we debated). They also knew that the guards had a coffee break (don't ask me how) at eleven a.m., which meant the suspect would have less eyes on them at this time and should have been able to navigate through the main hall and make their break to the stairs. It made sense as a viable escape route. If they *did* flee down the stairs, it didn't tell us whether they used advanced trickery. So, with that in mind, we were no further in our efforts to unmask the offender. We took a break and sure enough mama's car pulled into the drive.

"She's early!" Panic.

We scrambled to pack our drawings and notes away, much as Cleo did when he toppled over after his clash with Dean. Mama was pleased to see who I had as company:

"I'm glad you two worked things out," she said as Mel and Cleo walked out the door to go home.

We arranged to meet again at lunchtime in the forest the next day. Cleo said he would finally show us his hiding place. That in itself would be quite the revelation.

I asked Mama if we could eat dinner early. I said I was feeling tired and wanted to get an early night before school. That was a lie. I wanted to practise one of my spells. I had been neglecting them and they were sure to be my main weapon in the fight against dark magic.

I opened my spell book to the first page of the Grade 6 section. I flicked through spells; some I had fond memories of some I still needed to learn. I stopped at the *Instramalus Vocus* spell that I showed Dean and took a momentary pause to locate my phone. I don't think I mentioned this, Diary, but he messaged me earlier today, mid-way through our detective work:

"Hi there. Is this the right number for the Ultimate Vormera Skittle Champion?"

I had seen it and while it wasn't my top priority, it came a close second. I typed, deleted and re-typed a message, never quite finding the courage to hit 'send'. I wanted to be funny, though I wasn't sure why; it wasn't my strength. I also didn't want to seem like I was trying *too* hard. I initially wrote out: "Nope, try again", with a winky face after. But then I was worried he would think he did have the wrong number and delete it. I then typed: "Hey stranger, this is she", because I heard a character say it once in a TV programme and she sounded pretty smooth (which was what I was aiming for). BUT I didn't like *that* because I had used the wrong pronoun and he wasn't a stranger. DELETE! I settled on: "Yep, are you the head of my fan club?" with a simple, unassuming smiley.

I shut my eyes while I sent the message, and immediately threw my phone down on my bed. I returned my attention to my spell book, promising myself I wouldn't check my phone for a reply for at least ten minutes. I uttered words of self-encouragement, followed by instant regret and overthinking. Come on, Lorrie, there's more important things to worry about than whether Dean replies to your ridiculous message. Seriously, "are you the head of my fan club", who even says that? Okay, focus.

I turned the page again and noticed the vanishing trick. *'Vanish Aries'* — Vanish into the air. I laughed, again remembering the floating scarf. I also gazed over *'Rootus Sprowus Treus'* — Root sprouting to tree (that was the one I was meant to learn but went to the Isle of Dominia instead, and just as well!) and one that had always captured my attention: *'Masquer'*. It means 'Masquerade'. Do it right and your facial features change shape and size, to the point where you look nothing like yourself, but only to those who set their eyes upon you. So, my ears won't physically go any bigger (if that's even possible), my eyes wouldn't change colour and my hair would remain the same length, but anyone who looked at me would see them all transform, until the spell wore off.

Masquer is one of the few spells that doesn't require a long list of casting essentials. The only element it asks for is a tiny quantity of crystal infused water. I had some of it left over from another spell, and I keep it in a jar on my top shelf. If you're picturing my bedroom as a shrine for all things magic, you would be wrong, Diary. I like to think it's… understated. I only have a few potions and one or two other relics, aside from a stack of unearthly books, of which there is an abundance.

I reached for the jar, unscrewed the lid and dipped two fingers in. I gently placed it back on the shelf and sat down on my carpet. While reciting the words to the spell in my head before saying them out loud, I ran my wet fingers along my face; from my forehead, down my nose and to my chin, and then from one ear to the other, across my closed eyelids.

"Masquer faschi conceal, Masquer faschi conceal…"

I repeated the words five times, while focusing my energies to my head and visualising my morphed features. I opened my eyes, hoping I performed the spell correctly. Though, I soon realised that I hadn't even considered how I would know if I did. Grandmama told me I would still see myself — the way I *actually* look — in a mirror, because why would I need to disguise me from… well… me. Maybe I could recruit Stumbles; I heard him scratching at my door.

Sure enough, when I opened it, he was there. Stumbles

170

paid no more attention to me than he usually does, which is just about at the zero mark, unless he's waking me up in bed. Disappointed, I crawled under the covers and shut the lights out. I assumed that by the morning, the spell would have worn off anyway, whether it worked or not. I shut my eyes and my mind drifted in and out of consciousness. It was at the point when everything went silent that I heard a voice, or a few voices, clear as the crystal water that was drying on my face, which echoed:

"Look to the caves, young one."

I was ready.

Chapter 17
Culprit

Monday 16th September

I thought about our trip to the caves and remembered the marking that I was consumed with. The two cloaked figures and the ambiguous mark. The tour guide wasn't particularly helpful so when we went back to school, I found a book on the caves in the library. There are different interpretations of the drawing. An unearthly artist who specialises in life drawings believes the marking to be an expression of Parisa's loneliness in the caves, and how she longed for a companion. A philosopher draws the conclusion that Parisa assumes the role of the larger figure, while the smaller figure in her trail is to be the next great sorceress. I also read an extract from an Astrologist, who understands that the figures are lining up to face a great power that will prevail upon the earth sometime in 2051. None of the explanations mentioned the small mark at their feet, so maybe it was part of another drawing or a meaningless, irrelevant blemish. I sensed it though, that whatever the marking was, it was important. The voices and every fibre in my unearthly being were telling me so. But I didn't have time to think about it, I needed to focus on our mission. We still had no clue who took the stone, and even less of a clue where it was. For all we knew, Sereia could have it already.

I watched the clock for the entirety of my morning lessons that day. I had packed a sandwich, knowing I would be skipping the hit-and-miss meal offering in the lunch hall. When the bell rang, I wasted no time in shoving my books in my bag and being the first one out the classroom.

"Lorrie?" I heard a voice calling my name just as I shut my locker. "It's the head of your fan club, wanting an autograph, if you would be so kind!"

Dean.

How I wished in that moment that I had all the time in the earth to talk to my assigned earthly. One glance at him and, without hesitation, I decided I could spare a few minutes to pass witty remarks. What's a few minutes in the grand scheme of things? Surely the end of the earth could wait.

"Very funny! I can give it to you, but you'd have to pay a small price."

"There's always a price." He rolled his eyes. "How are you doing?" he asked, cheerfully.

"I'm okay, just a lot on my mind at the moment... How's everything with your family?"

"Eh, it's okay I suppose. What's on your mind?"

"Oh, you know, just the norm, figuring out who stole a potentially deadly relic so that an evil sorceress doesn't get her hands on it and terrorise us all!"

It was nice to say it out loud, and I was fairly confident that Dean wouldn't think I was being serious. He chuckled, confirming that he didn't.

"Oh, really? That's tough, need any help?"

"Well, if *you* were going to recruit someone to steal said relic, who would it be?"

"Hmm probably someone you wouldn't see coming!"

"Yep."

"And… maybe someone who has connections…"

"Uh huh."

"I'd go for someone in a respected position, personally, and maybe someone who also seems a bit wimpish. That way no one would ever suspect them."

"Would they be in a disguise?"

"Nope, I reckon they wouldn't need to. Their disguise would simply be that they were themselves."

"Hmm, I think you're on to something." I was mostly joking; Dean's profile for Sereia's recruit was quite different to ours.

"So, if I said to you right now, name someone who could have done it, who would be your guess?"

"Hmm my first guess would be Jessica; she's definitely got a hidden agenda…"

I was glad he realised that.

"Although Morton also looks a bit suspect when he's roaming the halls after the bell."

"Interesting… so you're going for an earthly?"

"Oh, definitely!"

"Why definitely?"

"Cause us earthlies are useful to you unearthlies. We're almost always underestimated, which makes us the ideal recruit."

Dean continued picking out people who he thought it could be, but I suddenly started to consider what he had said. An earthly who we never saw coming, who has connections, is maybe in a respected position, doesn't need a disguise… who was there that day at the Musea who would fit that profile? I had an uneasy feeling, and I started sweating, knowing that I was on the precipice of profound realisation.

Think, Lorrie, *think*! I could see Dean's lips moving but his voice was mute. I was in a silent hall that was slowly submerging into darkness, and I focused all my energy into this one thought. You were there, Lorrie. You saw something, or someone, and you know who it is. Unexpected, not in disguise, earthly... COME ON, Lorrie! I closed my eyes for a few seconds and opened them to see a distorted queue of tourists standing in front of me, waiting for their tickets. I looked to my side and observed a sign on a pole:

'*Pre-booked tickets.*'

I was in the Musea. Did I muddle the *Fortunaes* trick, and jump *back* in time, or was this just a memory, so strong in my mind that it felt real? I wasn't sure, but I kept looking forward. I was waiting for someone: the culprit. Children ahead of me were laughing, and Mel and Cleo exchanged insults behind me. Mr Magus was there, too, while Mrs Magus had re-joined us after her trip to the toilet. I even felt the weight of my backpack, realising that later I would obsess over whether the guards standing at the doors thought it could transport a tiny pea-shaped object. I stared at the floor, at the ceiling, at the families standing behind and in front of me, and then I saw him. As the answer exploded in my mind, my surroundings came back to life, and Dean was standing where I left him.

"You know who I think it could be, Lorrie, who I think would make for an interesting villain..."

My heart stopped, and I couldn't help but notice that time did, too.

"Mr Goddard." I uttered the words and from that moment on there was no going back.

"You got it, he's your guy!"

I told Dean I had to go, without any explanation. Before he had the chance to reply, I was off. He probably thought I was very rude, but if he knew what he had just unintentionally helped me to unearth, I'm sure he would appreciate my hurry. It didn't even cross my mind that I could be wrong. I KNEW it was Mr Goddard.

I headed for the forest and as I pushed through the main doors, I saw him. Our Headmaster was getting out of his car and I realised it was the first time I had seen him since the trip. I was torn. I wanted to watch him, but I wanted to stop him even more. And to do that, I needed to find Mel and Cleo. My previous self would have stood there and mocked his spotty tie and scruffy hair. True, we *never* would have suspected him, but what unearthly would take one look at Mr Goddard and think: "Hmm, he looks like the perfect earthly to carry out a dangerous heist and lead my dark army into earth domination." I did NOT understand Sereia's logic here. I allowed myself the satisfaction of giving him a furious glare while his back was turned, and then I peeled my eyes off the culprit. Later, I would contemplate how on earth we missed this.

The forest was at the back of the Weyborough High, separated from the main building by the field. Once upon a time the land proudly boasted nothing but trees, and then the introduction of competitive sports to the school poisoned it. Some lunchtimes the football team have their practice, and we were hoping they would that day so that we could go unnoticed (it was the only time I had hoped to see hooligans chasing a ball on a patch of grass, and they didn't show. Typical.) I saw Mel and Cleo from the other side of the field. Cleo was crouching down but I couldn't tell what he was doing, and Mel was standing with her arms folded, chatting away at him. I scanned the field for any bystanders, and cautiously waved to Mel when she saw me. I scurried across the grass with purpose, and any passers-by would swear I was hunting someone down if they paid attention to my frantic arms and the forward lean of my upper torso. I got the impression Mel certainly thought I was.

"You okay, Lorrie? You look like you've joined the marching band!"

"Yeah, she just has that 'let's save the earth' look!" Cleo chirped.

"Cleo, take us to your hiding place!" I demanded. I *was* on a mission, after all.

Cleo walked us deeper and deeper into the forest. I didn't realise it extended quite that far; Mel and I never ventured any further than Morton's patch of replenishing leaves. We climbed over a couple of fallen branches, and I used my arms to ram some of the hanging branches out of my way. Cleo "accidentally" catapulted a small branch backwards as it flicked off his shoulder, which hit Mel straight in the face.

"Oi!"

"Oops. Sorry Mel, did that get you?"

She looked back at me and rolled her eyes without responding.

"Are we there yet?" I was growing impatient.

"Just about!"

Cleo led us through a tunnel-like arrangement of trees, which opened out to a small clearing. It was quite beautiful. The sunlight was peeking through a thin layer of branches and there was even a small plot of grass which was slightly indented, probably from the weight of Cleo's bum that occupies it every day. So peaceful — no wonder he keeps it a secret. I could picture myself joining him there, the three of us telling stories and practising spells after visiting Morton. An image of bliss. It's a shame I had to go and ruin it with talk of our villain.

"So, I had a think last night and I reckon Sereia escaped and stole the stone herself, it's the only explanation!"

"Mel keeps rambling on about this. I *told* her, there's no way Sereia could escape, not without having the stone in her grubby hands first!"

"How do *you* know? She's an almighty evil sorceress, Cleo!"

"Because I have a little something called LOGIC!"

"Well, I don't see YOU coming up with any brilliant ideas!"

"I know who did it." I spoke softly, at first, not quite believing my own words.

"I'm *trying*, but it's hard to think with you jabbering away!"

"I know who did it." I raised my voice.

"Well SO-RRY, maybe if you listened the first time I wouldn't have to jabber away!"

"I KNOW WHO DID IT!"

Birds must have fled their nests, horrified by my shriek. Cleo and Mel stopped arguing and turned to me.

"What?" Mel asked, while Cleo remained silent.

"I said…" I sighed as I sat down next to what I later discovered was a thorn bush, which I didn't notice at the time because my legs felt like they were melting, and I was becoming lightheaded just thinking about the gravity of the situation. "…I know who it was."

They were both silent. It was an unusual phenomenon when it came to Mel and Cleo, but it happened then, and I would have enjoyed it a lot more had it not been for the circumstances.

"Who?"

I could tell Cleo dreaded the answer but dared to ask for it anyway, while Mel joined me on the grass. She obviously noticed the thorn bush because she carefully lowered herself far away enough from it, and didn't suffer a subsequent rash, like I did, which hurt like a thousand paper cuts (if you can imagine that, Diary. You have enough of it to know!).

"Who is the one earthly you saw that day who you didn't expect to?" I wanted them to figure it out, too, so I wouldn't be alone in my shock and misjudgement.

They pondered it for a while, and Cleo surprised me with his restraint at not shouting out random names.

"Did you say... earthly?" Mel clarified.

"I did. We had it wrong; it was never an unearthly and they were never in disguise..."

"It can't be him..." Cleo got it first.

"Who? Someone just tell me already!"

"Lorrie, there's no way..."

"I know it sounds crazy, but I *know* it's him, I can *feel* it!"

"I can, too."

"Um, HELLOOO?"

Cleo replied to Mel but held my gaze.

"It's Mr G."

(*Phew*! I was glad we were thinking of the same earthly, otherwise *that* would have been problematic).

Mel spun her head between the two of us.

"Whaaaaat? No! How could it be *him*? He's so... PUNY!"

179

"Which is exactly why he's the perfect candidate, isn't it, Lorrie?"

I nodded. We all took a while to digest it, and then Mel asked me how I found out. I explained that I spoke to someone about the perfect crime and asked them who they would accuse of being Sereia's minion (purposefully withholding Dean's identity).

"You didn't tell him, did you, Lorrie?"

"No, Cleo, of course not."

(That was a white lie. I told Dean *exactly* what was happening, he just didn't believe me so it's basically the same thing as not saying anything, right?)

"Good! Carry on…"

I paraphrased Dean's logic and then described what may or may not have been an inadvertent spell where I had a flashback to the Musea and saw Mr Goddard's face, staring straight at me, tauntingly.

"I swear I even saw him smile, a creepy smile, which I can say with one hundred percent certainty he did NOT do when we were there in real life. It's like I saw through his cloak, and I would bet Stumbles' life on it!"

"I also had a funny feeling about him, maybe that's why we've never got on."

"It's not, Cleo. You never got on because you can't go a day without getting yourself into trouble!" Mel mocked.

"Yeah, yeah whatever, but I definitely have a feeling about him *now!*"

"What do we do now?" We kind of all asked each other, in different ways.

"Well, we need to get our hands on that stone!" We kind of all told each other, in different ways.

180

We took the entirety of lunchtime to plot our retrieval of the stone. I even forgot to eat my sandwich. Cleo proposed that Mr Goddard had already given the stone to Sereia, and Mel thought that if he hadn't, he would hide it somewhere far, FAR away from here (which, if he had any sense, he would. But then he didn't know the one thing we did; we were on to him). I wasn't sure either way, but I knew we had more work to do:

"I don't know if he still has it or not, but he's our only lead, and we need to find out more…"

The only place we all have access to is his office at Weyborough High. It was a long shot. Any evidence he had he surely would have been ordered by Sereia to destroy. But maybe, just *maybe,* being the careless earthly he is, he would leave us some breadcrumbs. After all, he wasn't all that subtle when he ran away from us at the Musea which, although it took us a while to realise, if that doesn't scream guilty, I don't know what does.

So, there we were, entrenched in the forest behind the school building, acting as witness, judge and jury, and devising our plan to gather evidence that we could give to the Council of the MOTW. That way, even if there *was* someone on the inside (as the informant claimed) there was no way they could argue this as a hoax.

After the final bell rings tomorrow, the three of us would return to the forest while we waited for Morton to do a ground sweep and lock the doors, then sneak back into the building when we could be sure no one was around. Cleo knew of another way in; a door leading out onto the field from the changing rooms. I bet it stunk of sweat and misguided popularity — I would find out soon enough. Before our final lessons, we would send a message to our mama's. I would tell mine that I was going to Fickle House for dinner with Mel and Cleo, and they would tell Mrs Magus that they would be spending the evening with me. We relied on our mamas not speaking directly to each other, otherwise it was game over, but it was a risk we had to take.

"Okay, so meet back here at four p.m. tomorrow?" Cleo checked his watch.

"If I can find 'here' again, then sure!"

"We'll come together, Mel, I think I remember the way!"

"Just walk into another branch and you'll find it soon enough!" Cleo snickered, before we all parted ways and returned to our lessons.

"Oh, and another thing, little witch. Well done for your detective work, just don't go telling your boyfriend any more, all right?"

Chapter 18
'Somewhere to Hide'

Monday 16th September (continued)
I should have warned you, Diary, a few entries are needed to explain everything that happened that day. My eyes go blurry and my hands get tired after a while, so bear with me — it's only the beginning.

Mondays normally took it out of me, but this one was especially trying. After Mel incessantly quizzed me about who my "boyfriend" was that Cleo referred to (to which I declared absolute ignorance) we took a seat at our desks for lunchtime registration. I liked Dean, and my tummy fluttered when I was with him, but he wasn't my *boyfriend*. I wasn't sure I wanted one of those, and an earthly one would certainly complicate things.

"Like mother, like daughter." I could almost hear the gossip erupt once word spread. I wasn't even sure if I should advertise my friendship with him. Mama would no doubt approve, but Grandmama had suffered through enough turmoil from her daughter's disapproving affiliation. It doesn't have to stop me from imagining it, though; passing quick remarks and spending my weekends performing Sinthea's ballad for him (the spell version), and it was a nice image, one that I would keep to myself. I liked the idea of that: keeping it to myself. It was delicate and I wanted to keep it safe, so that it would never be spoiled by the stain of reality. Unless, of course, Cleo starts spreading rumours. How did he know, anyway? Was he spying on me?

"Melusine Magus?"

"Here!"

A few more names were called to confirm their presence in the classroom.

"Lorelei Orenda?"

"Here!"

"Thank you for showing up on time, Lorelei. I realise that has been a recent shortcoming of yours…" Mrs Mapleton had it out for me. If only she knew I was trying to save her and everyone else from impending doom, maybe then she would be kinder to me.

Speaking of Mrs Mapleton, I hadn't had the pleasure of seeing her recently. My next meeting with Dean wasn't until the Wednesday of that week, and the one scheduled for that day had been cancelled as we had an impromptu assembly, which doesn't happen a lot. It usually means that there is an important school announcement or award ceremony for the sports teams. I normally try to guess, but that day it didn't occur to me, for obvious reasons.

When we filed into the assembly hall, the atmosphere was foreign. It was unusually quiet, and what must have been the entire staff team were standing at the front. There's only ever been fifty, maybe sixty of them in attendance, max. But all eighty-two were mushed together in a bundle of authority.

"What's this all about?" Mel also sensed the strange mood.

"Who knows!" I whispered as I shrugged. "Maybe Morton's cat died?"

Ozzy was a ginger, ratty looking thing. He had stuck by Morton's side ever since I started at Weyborough High. I've never been sure if he is actually Morton's cat or not, but he's hardly friendly to anyone else, especially not me and Mel. Perhaps he knows of our tricks against his earthly friend. I would be sad if he had died though, I almost felt comforted that Morton had a companion by his side; I hoped it meant that he wasn't lonely.

"Shhhh," the teachers reinforced the silence as we took our seats.

"There is an important announcement to be made. Please everyone, take your seats as quickly and quietly as you can." Mr Johnston, the deputy head announced, less enthusiastically than his teachings of erosion.

Once everyone had been accounted for, Mr Goddard (who usually leads the assembly) took his seat in the front corner of the room. My anxiety levels threatened to blow the ceiling off just by his presence. What was he still doing here? In joining Sereia's army, surely his duties as a High School Headmaster would be sacrificed in the process. I didn't doubt my premonition, though. He *was* our guy.

Mr Johnston began by updating us on the exam schedule, which was still months away. I had been so focused on my unearthly studies that I hadn't paid much attention to my schoolwork. He then did the usual spiel about how we all need to play a part in looking after our earth by throwing away our litter and making use of the recycling bins.

"Now let's not be litterbugs, kids!"

Cleo would be out of job if everyone paid attention (not that he would be too devastated). Although I joke, it is an important issue. I'll have you know that I was the chair of the

Earth Protection Society (EPS) at school all of last year, which didn't do much for my social status. Funny that, I thought to myself. If we manage to save the earth from a crazy, evil sorceress, our popularity will soar. But if we save it by keeping plastic out of the oceans and taking the bus every once in a while, that somehow doesn't equate to the same level of respect. How can it be uncool not to poison the very ground we walk on? And the earthlies are the worst, they call us the toxic intruders of the land, but they are the real garbage dump trucks. I would continue to fight that war after fighting the one that lay ahead if I survived it.

Once he had said his final words on the matter, Mr Johnston took a pause.

"Now, there is some regretful news I have to share with you all…" He paused again, for dramatic effect. "Our Headmaster who has dedicated some twenty-one years to the school has decided to take an early retirement with immediate effect."

A wave of gasps and chatter ricocheted off the walls, sounding much like my ancestors.

"We wanted to take this opportunity to thank Mr Goddard for all of his hard work in making Weyborough High the flourishing community it is today."

I spotted Cleo in the crowd. Although we didn't *need* confirmation of our suspicions, it did reaffirm Mr Goddard's guilt. We must have been the only three in that hall that weren't surprised by the news, and the only ones who were terrified by it.

"Tomorrow will be his last day, so please take some time out of your day to wish our headmaster well in his journey."

WISH HIM WELL IN HIS JOURNEY OF

DESTROYING THE EARTH?

The announcement elevated the urgency of our heist. He leaves tomorrow, and no doubt he will take any evidence with him.

Mr Goddard stood to address us, but he kept his head down the whole time.

"It is with great sadness that I announce my departure from my position as your headmaster. Thank you to all my students and colleagues over the years for your support. I wish you all the very best in your future endeavours."

With that, he returned to his seat.

Cleo caught up to us after all of the students piled out of the assembly hall.

"Do you know what this means?"

"Yes, Cleo, obviously it means he's running away to join the Sereia circus!" Mel snapped.

"It means we need to do this tonight. We need to do it now." I spoke with trepidation *and* fortitude.

Cleo nodded. We had twelve minutes before the end of the school day.

"Quick, message Mama, tell her we're going to Lorrie's!" Mel instructed Cleo, as I took my phone out for the same purpose.

We didn't have time to make it to the fields; there were far too many teachers and students buzzing around. Everyone was collecting their books from their lockers and some had even spotted their mama's and papa's who arrived early, waiting outside for them.

"What do we do?" Mel was rattled, and so was Cleo.

"I'm not sure, but we need to figure it out, fast."

We needed a place to hide, but where? Where could we

go that Morton would <u>not</u>?

"I have an idea!" I offered. "Follow me." I wasn't certain it would work, but it was our only option at that point.

I led Mel and Cleo to the music room where I knew Mr Maguire would have packed away his instruments already. He was very protective of them all, so he usually wiped and put them away immediately after the lesson. I had also noticed that he wasn't in the assembly, and I saw him walking out of the gate at around the same time I saw Mr Goddard emerge from his car, so I figured he had probably left early, for whatever reason.

"You think this will work, Lorrie?" Cleo was sounding doubtful, which didn't instil confidence.

"Not in the slightest." I couldn't lie.

"Great!" Mel said, sarcastically.

"I know he has a key to his cupboard somewhere in here. It's where he keeps the larger instruments. It'll be a squeeze, but we can fit." I pointed in the direction of the cupboard, which was built into the walls.

"Does Morton check inside, witchy?"

"Honestly, I don't know. But knowing Mr Maguire, I doubt he would let ANYONE have access to it without him around."

"Well, it's our best bet. Let's find the key. Lorrie, check the desk, would ya? I'll look in between the benches."

"I'll keep a look out for anyone headed this way…"

While Cleo and I rummaged through the draws and under the benches, Mel stared out into the hall through the tiny glass window of the door.

"Anything?" Mel asked.

"Nope."

"Anything now?"

"Still nope."

"How about NOW?"

"Mel, we haven't found it yet, would you just be patient we're TRYING here!" Cleo barked, and I was grateful he did otherwise I was going to, and our friendship had had a rocky couple of days.

"Fine, just hurry!"

"Anyone out there, Mel?" I was cautious that it was nearing the time of Morton's checks.

"Not that I can see, just a couple of earthlies wondering out of the toilets."

We were starting to become frenzied in our search for the key. Cleo peeked through the keyhole to see if he could wedge something in there and unpick the lock.

"Guys… I can see Morton!" Mel spoke slowly and fearfully.

"Is he coming this way, Mel?" Cleo now had a paperclip fixed in the lock.

"He's checking all the classrooms, one by one. He has four… three more to go before ours!" Time was running out.

"Two…"

"Anything, Lorrie?" Cleo abandoned the paperclip and guessed the words to an unlocking spell that we had been taught for our Grade 3 test but could barely remember. It didn't work.

"One more…" Cleo was now using his full force to pull at the doors.

"I got it!" I found the key on the windowsill, behind the closed blinds. Sometimes hiding things in the most obvious places makes them the most well-hidden.

"Quick, Lorrie, open it!"

We crowded around the door and my hands were shaking uncontrollably. I couldn't get it open.

"Lorrie…" Mel's voice was desperate.

In that moment, one of two things could have happened. Morton could find us there and demand an explanation for why we were trying to unlock the music cupboard. We could plead with him not to tell Mr Goddard and say that Mr Maguire gave me permission to retrieve my triangle from the cupboard so that I could take it home to practise. I could hope that Morton would never know how impossible a situation that would be, as Mr Maguire would *never* agree to such a thing. Morton could either report us, and risk Mr Goddard finding out that we were on to his plan or leave us alone. In the former possibility, I could compel him to forget ever seeing us, and he would carry on with his duties paying no mind to what he had just witnessed. But in our panic, we somehow forgot that we have the power to do that. The other thing that could have happened is that I would guide my hands to calmly twist the key and unlock the cupboard, so that we could all hide and avoid the other potential consequences of Morton finding us. Which do you think happened?

Neither. The footsteps grew louder, and the doorknob squeaked as it turned. Someone entered the room, but it wasn't our beloved groundskeeper. It was Dean.

"Dean? What are you doing here?"

"What are *you* doing here, Lorrie?"

"What are you doing here, earthly?" Cleo demanded.

"Can we all just stop asking each other what we're all doing here?" Mel rolled her eyes but spoke with relief that it wasn't Morton who discovered us. She then leaned into me and said, a little too loudly:

"Do you think he's following me?"

We all heard her, and Dean had a blank expression on his face. What would he do if he knew that Mel thought he had a massive crush on her, and that it was all my fault?

"I saw you three wondering off after assembly and I wanted to check everything was all right..." Dean must have been conscious of Cleo's death stare, as he kept an eye on him while he walked up to me. "You seemed a bit stressed out earlier, and I wondered if you were okay..."

"How noble of you." Cleo growled.

Surprisingly, Dean mustered up some courage and turned to face Cleo, directing his next question to him.

"Now my question, what are *you* doing here?"

"Can I have a word with you, Lorelei?" I wasn't sure if Cleo had ever said my full name before. "And you, Mel!" He pulled us aside as we turned our backs on Dean.

"Well done, witchy, now what do we do?"

"I'm... I'm not sure, I—"

"Well, you got us into this, so you get us out!"

"What is he talking about, Lorrie?" Mel was none the wiser.

"Actually, Cleo, I think you'll find that *you* got us into this!" My patience was wearing thin with his attitude.

"How did *I* get us into this?"

"Well, for starters, you found out that a very powerful relic was going to be stolen and didn't TELL anyone..."

"Look where TELLING people has gotten us, Lorelei. Do you really think that that would have been a good idea?"

"Better than THIS one!"

We both took a breath as we tried to calm down.

191

"There's only one solution."

"What?"

"You won't like it…"

"Well, spit it out!"

"You're going to have to wipe his memories!"

"WHAT? I am NOT doing that, Cleo. He is my friend!"

"Then I will…"

"No, you will absolutely NOT. I won't let you!"

The tensions were high, and I was readying myself for a fight. The first thought I had was to use a shielding spell on Dean, which would render him temporarily immune to enchantment. If I had to, I would consider sticking Cleo to the wall with an attachment spell, too.

"Guys?"

"What Mel?" We yelled, in near perfect unison.

"I'm pretty sure he can hear *everything* you're saying…"

Mel nodded her head in the direction of Dean. The three of us slowly swivelled around and were confronted with a nervous looking boy who had his hands in his pockets and was staring at us with a timid smile.

"Well, that's just fantastic! You can be the one to ruin the entire mission and then the blood of everyone will be on *your* hands, Lorelei!"

I glared at Cleo and exhaled loudly, hoping to make it obvious that he was driving me crazy.

"Go on then, tell him. It's not like it matters much now!"

I approached Dean after a brief staring battle with Cleo. He started backing away from me.

"I'm not sure what's going on but please don't do anything to my memories… "

I immediately halted my feet. I don't think I will ever get

over how frightened Dean looked that day, and it was *me* he was afraid of. It made me doubt whether we would ever be able to be friends after all of this.

In that tragic moment I realised that no matter how much I tried to protect it, our friendship was maybe a little *too* delicate for me to keep. I could mourn him later, but I had a job to do.

"Dean, this is going to be a lot to take in…"

Chapter 19
About 'Thyme'

Monday 16th September (continued again)
I told Dean everything.

You might be wondering why I didn't take away his memories. Well, something changed in how I felt. I can't pinpoint exactly *when* it happened, and I'm not even sure what it meant. If you had asked me two weeks ago, I would not have paid much thought to an earthly, as wrong as that sounds in hindsight. But the idea of using my magic on Dean... well, it was a betrayal I could never inflict on him. It could be argued that it would have been a kindness to shield him from the evil of our kind, but it would not have been *right*. He deserves to know the truth about us, about what we're capable of. The good and the bad. I was fairly certain he would never want to see me again, but there was no turning back once I revealed Sereia's scheme.

"Are you okay, Dean?" He looked like he was frozen in time. "Does any of that make sense to you?"

"Course it doesn't, he's an earthly. They can barely fathom a shooting star!"

"Would you shut up, Cleo?" Mel was also irritated with her brother.

"That doesn't even make sense!"

"Dean, I know it's a lot and—"

"Just give me a minute."

He walked away from me and positioned himself facing the wall; his hand out to steady himself. I knew he wouldn't tell on us, but I was getting ready for him to leave.

"I understand if you want to go, Dean. This isn't your problem."

I could hear Mel talking in the background, still confused about it all.

"So... is he *not* here to see me, then?" Cleo didn't even validate that with a response.

"I'm sorry, I won't bother you again and—"

"Lorelei." He swung his body, which made me jump. "What's the plan?"

I was utterly astonished. Dean wanted to help us, and I was told never to deny an offer of help. "Unearthlies need unearthlies, we're collective beings!" Grandmama had always preached, but I was learning fast that unearthlies needed earthlies just as much.

Mel and I explained what little of a plan we had to Dean. Cleo looked like he was eating sour sweets the whole time, but he tolerated Dean's presence, which was all I could ask for, at that point in time.

"So, Morton finishes his rounds at roughly four-twenty-five p.m. That's when we head to Mr G's office."

"And when we get there?"

"Keep up, Mr Good Boy. We look for evidence!"

"Gotcha! What exactly are we expecting to find?"

"Who knows… something."

That must have been the most words the two exchanged with each other, ever.

When the clock struck four-twenty, I peeked out the door and signalled to the others that it was safe to leave the hall. It seemed that Morton totally skipped the music room, to our fortune. I think he got distracted by Ozzy, cause Mel swore she heard him say: "Good boy, let's get you all cleaned up", with an intonation that you would use to talk to a child, right before Dean walked in.

With our backs flush against the walls, we crept around every turn in the corridor.

"What's the plan when we get there? Do you have a key?" Dean was thinking ahead, which was one thing we hadn't done.

"Umm… I guess we'll try the unlocking trick?"

"Well, it seems I can't do it, little witch, so that leaves you!"

"Hey, I can do it!" Mel was shrouded in offence as we approached his office.

'Mr Goddard, Headmaster' was carved on a plaque in two lines. Cleo laughed as he dared her:

"Go on then."

Mel closed her eyes and asked us to remain quiet.

I'm not going to lie, I wasn't expecting her to manage it, but she did, and without much effort it seemed. We were all stunned at first, when we heard the latch click, Dean probably more so than us. Had he ever seen another magic trick, other than the one I showed him? I would ask him one day, if he decided to speak to me again.

"*Why* didn't you do that when we needed to get into the *cupboard?*" Cleo demanded.

"Cause you put me on *guard duty!*"

I realised that we should give Mel her due credit. She could be a bit boisterous at times, but that was mostly because she absorbed all the excitement in the air, and there always was, when she was around.

"Nice one, Mel!" I said with a grin, hoping she felt valued.

One by one, we entered the office. We began by searching the draws, as frantically as when we were in the music room. This time, we put Cleo on guard duty. Call it… payback. The first place I searched was the windowsill, not totally sure of what I was expecting to find.

"There's nothing in the draws!" Dean announced.

"He's probably packed them away already!" Mel had her hands tangled in the roots of her hair, signalling her distress.

After probably ten minutes or so, we were all feeling a bit forlorn. Mel especially, her voice began to crack as she spoke:

"There's nothing here."

"I have another idea!" I had to second guess who said that, and I was slightly astonished that it was Dean.

197

"What's that, earthly?" Cleo was ready to dismiss him.

"Well… Mr Goddard's PA, Miss Flint, she's got a cabinet that I've seen, where he keeps some of his documents. Could there be any evidence in there?"

"Well, she *could* be involved, I suppose." I tried to sound convinced.

Cleo suggested that Mel and Dean go have a look in her office, which was the room next to Mr Goddard's.

"Why *me*?" I suspect Mel was still convinced that Dean only wanted to get close to her, and it made her uncomfortable.

"Because it makes sense for another boy to go with you, and Lorrie's already busy flicking through piles of paperwork!"

"I can protect myself you know; I don't need a boy. Certainly not an earthly one!"

"I think he's right, Mel, it makes sense. Plus, I need you to get me into the door with your impressive spell!" Could Mel really be blushing at that? Yep.

This was the first time the boys were agreeing with each other. Before he left, Dean placed his arm gently on my shoulder, with the kind of tenderness that made me think he didn't hate my guts after all.

"I'll be next door, if you need anything."

"She'll be just fine, earthly. Lorelei can handle herself!"

Cleo peered out the door of Mr Goddard's office and told Mel and Dean that it was safe to leave. They walked out, with Mel in front, and a few moments later I could hear a faint commotion through the shared wall. It wasn't the first thing on my agenda, but I wanted to know why Cleo despised Dean so much.

"What's your problem with him, anyway?"

"I don't have a problem with *him*, per say. It's all the earthlies, they just seem so… underwhelming!"

"Well, if you gave them a chance, you might feel differently."

"Maybe, or I'd feel exactly the same."

I decided to steer away from the topic. We would probably never see eye to eye on the matter. I wondered why Cleo felt so averse to earthlies when it was his own kind that ostracised his whole family. Maybe it was pride, maybe ignorance. Probably a mixture of the two.

"I don't think Mr Goddard left any evidence here." Cleo sighed as he stared out into the hall.

"Hopefully, they find something next door!"

Suddenly, the lights all went out and I heard myself gasp.

"It's probably Morton finishing his search." Cleo spoke softly, sensing my panic and attempting to reassure me. But then we saw a torch light dancing in the hallway.

"Is anybody here?" A deep voice beckoned.

"Cleo, that isn't Morton!"

The room next to us also hushed.

"If you're here, make yourselves known!" I recognised the familiar tone.

Mr Goddard was making his way down the hall, and his personal assistant's office was closer to him than his own. You know the expression: "my heart was in my mouth"? It describes total fear and anxiety. That's what I felt, and not for us, but for Dean and Mel. I heard a door creak, and Mr Goddard entered his PA's room. Muted voices had never felt so dangerous. I didn't know what was said at the time, but the other day Dean opened up about it. Mr Goddard caught him and Mel, red handed, rummaging through the filing cabinet.

"What are you doing here?" The interrogation began.

Mel couldn't find the words, and Dean could only be honest like he always is, to his detriment, even.

"We know what you're up to!"

"What am I up to?"

"I don't really understand it, I'm still a bit confused, but you're up to no good. And we're going to stop you!"

I admired him for saying that, misguided as he was. Dean had more valour than all of us put together.

"I need to help them!" Cleo was about to storm out of the office without any flicker of a plan. I caught his arm and pulled him back.

"Cleo, no!" I think I knew it was too late. "You can't help them if he catches you, too!"

We stayed as quiet as we could, huddling together mostly to support each other's weight. If Cleo hadn't been there, I fear I might have sunk into the floor in a slump of anguish. It had been silent for a few minutes, and I couldn't hold Cleo back any more. He opened the door and thrust his head out. I followed.

"Who else is with you, who else knows about this?"

"Umm…" I was reassured to hear Mel's voice, even though it was momentary.

"No one, sir, just us," Dean asserted.

"Well then, you made a mistake, kids. You shouldn't have done this."

We heard some more muffled conversation and Mr Goddard walked Mel and Dean out into the corridor.

"You leave me no choice. You're coming with me."

I caught Dean's eye as he walked out into the hallway and looked towards Mr Goddard's office. They were walking away

200

from us, towards the exit. He shook his head, as if to tell me not to leap forward, but I ignored him. This time, Cleo held *me* back.

"Remember what you said, witchy. We can't help them if he catches us too!"

Mel, use your magic, was all I could think! But Mel seemed a little... weary. She was slouched on Dean's shoulder as they walked towards the main doors, followed by Mr Goddard. Cleo and I watched them, helplessly, as they were ushered out of the building. We stared at each other for a while, numbed by the immense shock. My eyes were filling with tears, and Cleo placed his arms around me. There was a complete absence of sound in that moment. We were bonded by the shared agony we were experiencing. His sister and my best friend, along with my nearly best friend, had been captured by a villain whose intentions were uncertain, but definitely dark. They sacrificed themselves, for us.

"Lorrie, we'll get them back. I promise."

I couldn't speak, my mouth was dry, and the words were stuck in my throat. So instead, I placed my head on Cleo's shoulder and surrendered to the reality that we may not survive this. I didn't have time or energy to decipher how they had been captured. Mel was powerful, more than we all knew, and she could have easily defended her and Dean against Mr Goddard. Their capture was the one part of it all that Dean couldn't bring himself to tell me about. When he did, only the other day, he told me he felt ashamed that he couldn't protect her, and guilty. She was the unearthly, but he was the one who suggested they search that room in the first place. We cried together, recalling the events following that night, and I made sure Dean knew that none of it was his fault. So, after a while, he let me in on his suffering as he recollected the events of the sixteenth of September. A date which none of us will ever forget.

Dean explained that Mr Goddard was soaked in thyme infused water. We assume he had taken a bath in the stuff. Remember how I said it was the one thing that could prove deadly for an unearthly to ingest? Well, just being in its mere presence has the potential to cause extreme fatigue and disorientation, especially in large doses. None of us realised it at the time, but Mr Goddard had also caked the doorknob of his PA's office door, and the filing cabinet that Dean and Mel rummaged through, in thyme powder. Which meant they were on to something and he knew it. We were naïve to think we didn't raise his suspicions, on reflection. Mr Goddard didn't strike us as a criminal mastermind, but the unearthly he was working for *was* one. The thyme powder that Mel breathed in, together with Mr Goddard's odour, rendered her helpless and unable to conjure any of her energies. Dean said he had taken a swing at Mr Goddard, but that our headmaster threatened him with thyme infused gas which would be released by the mere push of a button. The gas would consume the room and certainly be the death of Mel. Dean wasn't sure whether Mr Goddard was bluffing or not, but he couldn't take that chance.

Just as well he didn't. The unearthly investigators have since inspected the office and it turns out there *were* packages of thyme gas in the vents, which were attached to wires that would cause them to explode when given the signal by a small device with an unoriginal big red button, which Mr Goddard was holding in his hand that night.

"Are you okay to keep talking?" Dean took a gulp of his warm cup of tea, and I could tell his hands were trembling as he relived the events.

"Yeah."

He took a breath and explained that Mr Goddard directed them to a car, which wasn't his own, as Dean tried to carry the bulk of Mel's weight. Her feet were dragging, and her breathing was shallow. I have shivers just thinking about how lousy and weak she must have felt. Mr Goddard kept telling him to "keep going, hurry", as Dean struggled to lift his feet. When they got to a grey car with a couple dents in the side, Mr Goddard instructed him to help Mel into the back seat. Once he had, Mr Goddard tied his wrists together with thin, black rope. Dean pulled up his sleeves and showed me the scars. I had noticed them before.

Mel was barely awake, so Mr Goddard didn't bother blindfolding her. He placed a scarf around Dean's eyes and assisted him into the car (similar to the way I assist Stumbles to the ground when he climbs on my bed). Dean shuddered when he described the car journey. Mel's head flopped onto his shoulder, and he wanted to hold her hand, but he couldn't. He said that he whispered to her, telling her everything was going to be all right. He couldn't be sure if she was even awake enough to hear it, but he wanted her to believe that they were going to be okay, even if it was a lie, so at least one of them could feel comforted. The ride was bumpy and dark, and although it felt like an eternity had passed, Dean assumed it was roughly an hour before the car stopped. In reality, Mr Goddard had taken them to a small, timber cabin in a woodland just seventeen miles from the school. Dean couldn't believe that when he heard the cabin's location.

Mr Goddard pulled Mel's limp body out first, and a short while later he opened the door next to Dean and yanked his arm. Dean fell to the ground and inhaled some dust.

"Sorry, kid. I didn't mean to be so forceful. Help me out here, I'll pull your arms and you lift your feet."

He walked Dean into a dusty square room, much like the one I had seen Cleo and Mr Magus in during the *Fortunaes* spell. He guided Dean to a chair and instructed him to sit. He then tied Dean's ankles to the legs of the chair, ensuring he couldn't run. Dean said he tried to shift in the chair a little, but it felt like it was bolted to the ground because it didn't budge. He assumed that the reason Mr Goddard never taped his mouth shut was because no one would have heard him if he screamed, which led him to believe that they must have been somewhere secluded. Once his legs were tied, Mr Goddard took his blindfold off. Dean immediately looked for Mel, who he saw slumped in a chair some two or three metres away from his. She looked pale and sweaty. He was worried about her.

"What have you done to her? Will she be okay?"

Mr Goddard ignored his questions at first as he rummaged through a large bag.

"Please, just tell me if she'll be okay!" he pleaded. "PLEASE!" Waiting for an answer was torture for him.

Cleo and I were probably on our way home at the very same time. We knew we needed to save them; we just didn't know how.

"Cleo, we need to tell someone. We can't do this alone. It's bigger than us both." I took Cleo's silence as agreement.

"Is your Grandmama back yet?"

"I'm not sure."

"My papa's home, so let's go there first and tell him what happened. We'll get them back, Lorrie."

I knew that he said that for himself too, to keep him from

losing his mind.

"I know, Cleo." I smiled and squeezed his hand.

We walked home, which took about half an hour. The night was still, and deceivingly peaceful. As we approached his house, Cleo paused and, without realising, I walked on ahead. When I noticed that he was no longer beside me, a few steps later, I turned back. I wanted to be discreet. It was getting late and from what we had just been through, I was practically waiting for another one of Sereia's minions to jump out at us. I reversed my steps and stopped in front of Cleo.

"Are you okay?" It was a hopeless question.

"How am I going to tell Mama and Papa?"

If you asked me to describe Cleo's face, I couldn't put it into words. I just knew that his heart was broken and he was terrified, like me.

Chapter 20
Secret Society

Monday 16th September (...and again)

The door was locked. It was nearing six p.m., but there were no lights on in Fickle House. Strange. Cleo walked around the side and found the spare key which was camouflaged inside a pot plant.

"Hmm, it's nice to have a key for a change!" Cleo unlocked the door, walked in and called out for his mama and papa. His mama's car was on the drive and Cleo was convinced that they were both due to be in all night. "Mama? Papa? Hellooo, anyone home?" It was eerie inside. Cleo flicked the light switch on in the hall. The coat rack was scarce, and Cleo's calls were met with echoes of his own voice, which suggested that no one was home.

"Maybe they went out for dinner or something, and took your papa's car..."

"Yeah, maybe." He didn't sound satisfied with the proposed explanation.

"Would you like something to drink?" I had just remembered that I hadn't eaten or drunk pretty much anything all day, and my stomach was hit with a pang of hunger, which came from nowhere.

"Yeah, water would be great, thanks!"

We drifted into the kitchen and Cleo took out two glasses

from the mounted cabinet. We sat in silence and it got to the point where neither of us were quite sure how to break it. An hour had passed, then two. Quarter to eight and we were becoming restless. Cleo was pacing up and down next to the kitchen counter, and I was fidgeting with my sleeves and tapping my foot nearly constantly. Cleo made us each a cheese and peppadew sandwich. The bread was a tad stale, and the cheese was verging on mouldy, but I was hungry enough to eat my own fist, so I wasn't about to complain. Cleo tried to call both his mama and papa separately and sent them each a message reading:

"Urgent, please call me."

"They normally pick up, Lorrie. What if something has happened to them? What if Sereia found out that Papa knew what she was doing and she took them, like she did Mel?" Cleo was spiralling and I didn't blame him.

It reminded me that I should check my phone. I was glad I did; I saw a message from Mama, which she sent half an hour ago.

"What time will you be home, love?"

I had come closer than ever to telling her what was going on, but I was terrified that if she found out, she too could be a target of Sereia's.

"Hi, Mama. Not sure yet, will keep you posted. Oh, and is Grandmama home yet?"

If Grandmama *was* home, I needed to know. If anyone could help us right now, it was her.

"What do we do if they don't come home, Cleo? I'm afraid that… I'm afraid that we're running out of time."

Cleo took a seat on the sofa. He leaned forward, placing his head in his hands.

"I just want to know if Mel's okay."

It took me a while to consider what he was saying until I swiftly remembered that I could find out.

"Of course!"

"What?" He lifted his head.

"Cleo, this whole time, in amongst all the chaos, we've forgotten that we're unearthlies!"

"What do you mean?"

"The setting in spell, I can do that to Mel! I can find out if they're okay, and maybe even where they are!"

He jumped up as if he'd just felt the pierce of a pin on his bottom.

"Lorrie, that's brilliant! Do it now!"

Was I afraid of what I might see? Of course. But I was more afraid of what I might *not*. Cleo struggled to remain quiet and he started pacing again, invigorated by the prospect that we might be able to find them. So, I decided to go to another room. I drifted into the lounge and sat down on the carpet where I searched my brain for the right words. Cleo gave me a picture of Mel, which wasn't needed for the spell, but it made it easier to focus. To enter her mind, I needed to connect with her. I should have explained before, but to *connect* with someone, you need to trace a reciprocal moment in their minds — an experience you bonded over and shared mutual feelings towards. To explain it better, do you remember when Grandmama set into me when I was reading (or pretending to read) the Laws on the Magus family trip? Well, I asked her what she thought about, and she said that she focused her energies on the time when my first tooth fell out. I couldn't stop crying. I was absolutely devastated because I thought that one of my teeth had "died" and I felt bad that I let it, like a pot plant I neglected to water. In that moment, she said she felt sad for me, too, because she loathed to see me so upset. It was the sadness that we shared, and she channelled it to connect with me, allowing her to set in.

When I tried to connect with Mel, I thought about the very first time she stood up for me. We were in the local playground, which has really deteriorated since we were kids, and we must have been seven or eight years old. Mel and I were taking turns at pushing each other on a swing, and it was Mel's turn first. A snotty nosed earthly boy ran across and demanded that we let him have the swing.

"It's my swing!" he kept shouting.

"Well, we got here first!" Mel insisted, as she continued to push me.

The boy, obviously upset and probably not used to being challenged, pushed Mel out the way and stopped the swing so suddenly that I jolted forward and fell flat on my face. I was wailing, mostly at seeing the blood gushing from my nose. Mel stood up, brushed the dust off herself and kicked him so hard in the left knee that he fell to the ground. I don't know how she did it, but to really teach him a lesson, she conjured a water patch which appeared in his jeans, making it look like he'd wet himself. He ran home and never tried to steal a swing from us again. Mel knelt beside me and asked me if I was okay. I told her I would be fine and gave her a great big hug, before she helped me up. I didn't even care about my nose at that point, or the scrapes on my arms, we just started howling. I hadn't laughed so hard in my life. I told Mel it was the nicest thing anyone had ever done for me and she made a promise to make people look like they'd wet themselves if they ever tried to steal our swing again.

It was a tricky one to pick, in hindsight. There was a mix of emotions involved. From pain to embarrassment, to hilarity and then to triumphant. For that reason, though, I thought it would be the perfect experience to connect with Mel. I placed her photograph in front of me, uttered the words of the spell and dived into the memory of the swing. I recalled it so accurately and was hit by a wave of feelings. From pain to embarrassment, hilarity to triumphant. I could feel it working, I was so close. Everything went dark before I opened my eyes a few moments later, expecting to see what Mel was seeing. Instead, I was faced by the same photograph of Mel, smiling at the camera like she was having the best time of her life. Cleo opened the door ever so slightly, and whispered through:

"Did it work?" I was stunned that it hadn't, I had practised it so many times before.

"No."

"It's okay Lorrie, you tried your best." Cleo tried, but he couldn't hide his disappointment.

"What do we do now?" he asked. "Any other tricks up your sleeve?"

"I need time to think, I don't really know. I'm feeling a bit overwhelmed and I can't think straight…"

"What about Dean?"

"What about him?" Please don't make this into another earthly/unearthly debate, was all I could think.

"Try set into him!"

"I don't know, Cleo, I'm struggling with the spell and you know what the Council is like with setting into earthlies…"

"I think they'll make an exception on this one, Lorrie." He crouched next to me. "Please, give it a shot. It's meant to be easier to set into earthlies, their minds aren't as resilient as ours."

I sighed. "Okay, I'll try, but I can't promise it'll work."

"Thank you." While Cleo's hope reignited, mine did not.

"But you need to leave again, you're distracting me."

"Consider me gone!" he said, as he bolted out the room and slammed the door shut.

What moment could I use to connect with Dean? There were certainly less than I had with Mel, but they were somehow just as poignant. I considered the time I showed him the *Fortunaes* trick, or when the butterflies visited my belly after I found Sinthea's ballad in my locker. I settled on the Skittles. It was the first time I could tell we were both comfortable — no, more than that — we were both *happy* to be with each other, knowing that there were other people around (earthlies and unearthlies) who may have noticed. For some reason, that was very important to me. When I mentioned our friendship being delicate, that was the one time it had felt strong. Strong enough to withstand a war, even. It was strange to think that our Skittle competition was only two days ago — so much had happened since then. I so longed to be back there with him, which made it easy to connect. I closed my eyes, recited the spell, and fell into Dean's mind.

This time, when I opened my eyes, I saw a pair of scuffed up shoes. When he looked up, I could see Mr Goddard sitting on the ground opposite Dean. He was staring at a piece of paper and muttering something to himself. Dean looked down again, this time into his lap. His hands were tied and the fabric covering his knees was lathered in dirt stains.

"I'm sorry, Dean." His head jolted up.

"Lorrie?" I couldn't tell if he said my name out loud, or if he just thought it. Either way, I heard him.

"I'm here. Don't say anything else, just *think* it."

We were still.

"Are you okay?"

"I'm all right. Mel's not doing too good, though." He turned his eyes to Mel, and my body tensed when I saw her.

"What happened?"

"Thyme. He had the place covered in it."

"And now?"

"I'm not sure, but I can smell it in the air. Maybe it's on the floor, maybe it's coming from a vent. I don't know. Will she be okay?"

"It depends how much of it she's ingested. Where are you?"

"I don't know, he blindfolded us."

"I'm so sorry, Dean, I wish I never involved you in this!"

"I involved myself, Lorrie."

I could hear a door opening, and was surprised to find out that Dean could, too.

"What's that?" He asked.

"It's the front door, I think someone's come home…"

"Please don't leave me." Dean was terrified, and the thought of it nearly destroyed me.

"I'll be back, I promise."

With that, I pulled myself out of the spell and returned to the lounge. I heard chatter in the kitchen and a voice belonging to Mrs Magus. When I walked in, she was talking to her son, but diverted her attention when she saw me.

"Oh, hi Lorrie. What's going on?" She could tell Cleo was in a bad state — he had given up pretending otherwise since we arrived at his house.

"I need to tell you something, Mama."

My heart broke for Mrs Magus. She was about to find out that her daughter was kidnapped by an earthly working for the most horrifying dark sorceress of all time, and that her son and her husband were at risk of the same thing.

"Is it Mel?" She guessed it. Call it mother's tuition, or so I thought at the time.

Cleo didn't respond.

"Cleo, tell me now, what happened to Mel?" She looked at me, hoping for an answer.

"Mrs Magus, I—"

Before I could finish my sentence, she broke down in tears. Cleo flashed me a look of confusion before he walked over to his mama and put his arm around her shoulders.

"Mama, I'm sorry, I tried to protect her but—"

"It's my fault, son," she interrupted.

"No, I don't think you understand…"

"Where has he taken her?"

She did understand. It turns out that Mrs Magus knew everything, before we did, even. And her part in it was far bigger than ours.

We sat there in disbelief as Mrs Magus explained to us how she helped Mr Goddard to seize the stone. In fact, it was her who orchestrated the whole thing! And, unlike her husband, she stole it for the bad side… Sereia's side.

"I don't understand." Cleo repeated on a loop, while I remained still, wishing I could melt into the wall. I *hate* conflict, which is ironic since I involved myself in the biggest one yet.

Mrs Magus explained that she stole the stone before we had even entered the Musea and replaced it with a replica (which meant I was staring at a fake for far too long).

"When you went to the toilet?" I caught on before Cleo did.

Mrs Magus nodded.

"The toilet is directly behind the stone, separated only by a thin plaster wall. I passed through with a phasing spell, took the stone and re-joined you in the queue."

"Did you know that Papa and I were planning on stealing it?"

"No, but a messenger for Sereia warned me that someone would."

"But you were sitting with us, Mrs Magus, and the guards searched you?"

"Yes, Lorelei. I had given the stone to Mr Goddard who had left some three minutes before the alarm sounded."

"How did they find out about the stone then, Mama, if it was a replica?" Cleo's eyes burned with deep betrayal.

"I'm not sure on that one, perhaps the guard checked the displays and noticed the obscurities of the replica..."

After we gained sufficient information to satisfy our curiosity, Cleo wanted a justification.

"Why did you do it, Mama?" He avoided meeting her eyes.

"I'll tell you everything, son. Just know, I didn't realise it was Sereia who was in charge of it all..."

We were hanging on to every word. Mrs Magus told us that she had been contacted by an anonymous unearthly who offered her sympathy at the community's cruel gossip and rejection of her family. She said that she was promised redemption of her husband if she joined a secret society formed to protect unearthlies from false accusations of dark magic.

"It was the perfect opportunity, I thought, to make this whole mess go away!"

Mrs Magus jumped at the chance to join the society. At first, she was asked to provide seemingly insignificant information, such as the names of her husband's work colleagues and associates. Then, she was instructed to meet Mr Goddard, "an earthly ally", at an abandoned warehouse. Before she knew it, she was being directed to gather more information on behalf of the anonymous leader of the group (which turned out to be Sereia), relating to the powers of the mystery stone.

Mrs Magus eventually realised that things were probably not as they seemed, and when she decided to leave the society, it was too late. Sereia had already made her complicit in so many illegal acts and threatened to reveal them if she did not cooperate. She didn't know a way out, and so she continued to follow the secret society's instructions, which led to stealing the stone from the Musea. Coincidentally, Mr Magus had suggested a trip to the Isle of Dominia for the same purpose of stealing the stone, unbeknown to her. It was so convenient.

While Mrs Magus wasn't sure of why the stone was needed, she had hoped that the secret society would use it for good, maybe even for cases where injustice could be challenged, such as her husband's unfounded allegations. She convinced herself of that, in fact, in order to follow through with it. But after she stole the stone, Mr Magus confided in her about the informant, and she soon became aware of a much bigger threat. With that, Mrs Magus hid the stone and cut all communications with the secret society, and Mr Magus immediately drove to the Council headquarters (where he is now) to hand over all of this information, concerned that his telephone communications could be compromised.

Mrs Magus took Cleo's hand and apologised again. He pulled it away and turned his back on her.

"Where is it, the stone?"

"Cleo, please just—"

"WERE IS IT?" He yelled.

"I'll show you, but first tell me where your sister is?"

"Mr Goddard has her, Mrs Magus."

The room fell quiet as Mrs Magus softly sobbed into a tissue. Cleo was furious, and I wasn't sure how to feel. Mrs Magus soon composed herself and stood from the chair she was sitting in.

"They're tracking me, so Mr Goddard would know I was coming…"

"So we'll go!" Cleo stated.

"You won't save her that way, son. There's only one way to put an end to this all…"

"Tell us, Mrs Magus, what is it?" I impatiently asked. We didn't have time for any more dramatic pauses.

"You need to deliver the stone to its Keeper. That is the only way Sereia can be stopped and your sister can be saved."

Chapter 21
Furry little forgetting friend

Monday 16th September (... last one)

"What do you mean, it's Keeper?" Cleo and I had never heard of the stone having a 'Keeper'.

"I mean it's protector, it's guardian."

"I don't understand, Mrs Magus. When I've read about the stone it hasn't mentioned anything about a Keeper?"

"That's because no one knows about it, not even the Council."

"How do *you* know then, mama?"

"Lorelei's Grandmama." Mrs Magus glanced at me and smiled. "She figured it out."

"*My* grandmama?"

"Yes. You see, the informant contacted her through an '*Inkus apparus*' spell."

I should explain, Diary. *Inkus apparus* is used to send secret messages, usually containing highly confidential information. It avoids the risk of sending a physical letter or text message that may be intercepted by the wrong people. The Council of the MOTW use it as their main form of communication. With a special type of ink (which is not easy to produce for its substances are highly exclusive) and a spell which is personalised to incorporate the recipient's address in its words, any letters you write on a piece of paper will appear somewhere, most likely also on paper, in the recipient's house. There are stories of it appearing on walls, though, and even windows.

"Upon receiving the note, your grandmama travelled to an undisclosed location to meet with the informant. Together, they located the daughter of the last Keeper: the nurse who found the stone in the forest. Her daughter had a library full of information, documenting what her mama came to learn about the stone through visions and research, and about her role as its protector."

"I don't understand, she was an earthly?"

"No, son. She was a sorceress. You have to remember that sixty odd years ago, unearthlies were completely segregated from earthlies. The lady was desperate to lead a life dedicated to helping others, and she believed that she could make more of a difference as a nurse for earthlies than as a sorceress. So, she denied her unearthly identity."

"Do we know who the informant is, Mrs Magus?"

"I believe your grandmama does, and so does your papa, Cleo, but he hasn't shared the identity of the informant with me, for their own safety."

"Okay, so about this Keeper... what did Lorrie's grandmama find out?"

"Well, when the Keeper has served their duty to the stone — the exact "when" for which is determined by the stone itself — a new Keeper is assigned. It is assumed that the stone selects its protector for their innate protective qualities."

"So, what happens when the stone is reunited with its Keeper? And what happens if it isn't?" Cleo was asking the questions now — I was more preoccupied with who the informant could be. Someone I didn't know, probably, and someone I may never know.

"Well, we aren't sure of what it all means but we do know one thing: only with its Keeper is the stone safe from Sereia's hands, and so we need to find her, before Sereia finds us."

"Her? Do you know who the Keeper is, Mama?"

"Well, it's a shot in the dark, but we *think* we do."

Mrs Magus explained that Grandmama suspected that the old neighbour who had gone missing a few weeks ago (the one who most people thought Mr Magus meddled with when she witnessed what she thought was dark magic) had wandered into the fog forest — the very same one that lured the Keeper before her. Possessed by an invisible force that compels her to search for the stone, the lady is all but a slave to her mission.

"If my grandmama is wrong, and it isn't her, then..." I didn't need to finish the sentence.

"Yes, Lorrie. Then I'm afraid our fate is in Sereia's hands."

"So... where exactly *is* the fog forest?"

I was hoping that Mrs Magus wouldn't run out of answers. If we had even the *slightest* hope of finding the Keeper and reuniting them with the stone, we *needed* them, and time was running out. There is only so long that even an unearthly can go without food or water, after all. If we didn't hurry, the Keeper would be lost to the trees forever, and Sereia was presumably already devising a plan to make sure that that very thing happened. In fact, I wouldn't be surprised if there wasn't already a whole fleet of her army dispatched to recover the stone, which they would find with us.

"That is the one thing we don't know."

"Great."

"But I know how you can find out... the archive of hidden

maps."

"The what of hidden what's?"

"The archive of hidden maps, son. It stores thousands of maps revealing hidden locations that have been camouflaged by powerful spells of Parisa herself. It is stored in a small chamber in the unearthly Town Hall."

"The unearthly town hall... as in where the Council of the Mother of the Wand congregate? Mrs Magus, that place has to be one of the most guarded of all unearthly buildings!"

"Lorrie's right, Mama. There's round the clock security, it's near impossible to get in even when you have a pass!"

"Luckily, your papa has one of those! How do you think he got his hands on the Musea map?"

"He found that in the archive of hidden maps?"

"No, son, in a different one, but in the same section of the hall. He worked out all the logistics, too. The guards change duty every four hours, so next time they're scheduled to do their swap is at eleven thirty." Mrs Magus looked at her watch. "Which gives you forty-five minutes from now."

"Oh... okay." Cleo stumbled through his words. This was all a LOT to take in.

"Listen carefully. You will have a ten-minute window where you'll be able to slip around the back and enter through the side door which the employees use. It is left unattended during the swap. You will need the pass — here."

Mrs Magus handed us a small, plastic card with a picture of Mr Magus printed above his name and title:

'Mr Arion Magus, Secretary for the CSE'.

"And when we get inside?"

"Follow the signs to the archive. In a fortified building such as the town hall, the need to be discrete in the signage has

220

been somewhat… overlooked."

"Perhaps they need to change that."

"Perhaps you're right, Lorrie. Now go, before it's too late."

Mrs Magus insisted that this was the safest way. If Sereia thought that *she* had the stone, Fickle House is the first place she would visit. It didn't make it any less terrifying, especially not for Cleo. Mrs Magus held us each in a prolonged embrace before Cleo grabbed his backpack, replenished with food and water supplies, and we made our way to the front door.

"Wait, you will need this."

I turned around and reached out my hand to take the stone from Mrs Magus.

"Be careful."

The street was quiet, only a few dim lights were peeking through windows of lethargic houses. It had just passed eleven and the walk was at least twenty minutes. Cleo and I didn't say a word to each other for the first ten. We were both contemplating the events of the last eight hours. I looked at him a few times, waiting for him to break down, and I could feel his eyes on me for the same purpose.

"How long do you reckon we have left, little witch?"

"Well, we just passed the Florence Inn, so I'd say we're probably over halfway there!"

Cleo sighed.

"So, what are the odds that we'll survive this?"

"Wow, Mr optimistic over here!" I pretended to laugh, assuming he was doing his thing of picking the worst moment to crack a joke.

"I'm serious, Lorrie." He grabbed a hold of my hand to

stop me in my place. "Will we survive this?"

I smiled, betraying my strongest internal emotions.

"We're going to try our best."

"Shhh." Cleo stopped in front of me as we approached the hedge in front of the unearthly town hall. There were three guards positioned at the top of the grandiose stairs leading to the front entrance of the building, and another at the bottom.

"Okay, so according to my watch we have just under five minutes until the guards change. That's our moment!"

"Cleo, your mama said we had a small window. As soon as they leave their stations, we need to be ready."

"My thoughts exactly."

That was a painful four minutes. My heart was now practically on a racetrack, and my nasty butterflies were in a swarm. The guards were dressed in black and must have been qualified to at least Grade 10 to have secured their roles. Magic was their main weapon, should they need to use it, ranging from a simple locking up spell where your legs become swaddled in rope and you fall flat on your back (if you're lucky enough not to fall flat on your face). Or, if you attempt to fight back, a '*Frozay*' spell would certainly stop you in your tracks. That's where your entire body freezes as if you've fallen into an ice lake, just without the arctic cold sensation to go along with it. It doesn't cause any long-term health damage, but I hear the headache afterwards is the worst! Call it: *brain frozay*.

"All right, we're coming up to eleven thirty. You ready, Cleo?"

"Yup, now or never!"

We were leaning forward from the hedge, ready to pounce when the time came for the guards to swap over. We would then need to make our way around the side of the building, briefly stepping out in front of it to meander around the hedge. Mrs Magus assured us that the guards would be distracted during their handover of keys and wouldn't notice us if we moved fast enough. Remember how I mentioned before that I despised organised sports? Well, I didn't really join in that much, naturally, which meant I had the fitness of a door-knob. I was relying on the adrenaline souring throughout my body to give me a bit of a boost, should I have needed it.

Eleven thirty passed. Then eleven thirty-two... three... eleven thirty-six and the guards hadn't moved an inch.

"Lorrie, why aren't they swapping? I swear my watch isn't fast..."

I checked mine to compare.

"Nope, eleven thirty-seven."

By eleven forty-two we were becoming twitchy.

"Let's give it five more minutes, Cleo."

"And then?"

"And then plan B."

"I didn't realise we had a plan B?"

"We don't."

I watched the big hand tick six more times around the dial, passing through the numbers with what seemed like ruthless mockery. When it turned eleven fifty, and the guards hadn't budged, I decided we couldn't hang around forever. Mrs Magus must have got the times wrong, or the shift patterns of the guards had changed. In either case, we needed to think of another way in.

"Do you know '*Memoir Erase*'?"

"Do I look like I know *Memoir Erase*?" Cleo took offence at my question. "I couldn't even open the lock in the music room, never mind erase someone's memory."

"Well, you threatened to do it on Dean!"

"I was bluffing, I hoped you would do it first!"

"I don't know it well enough to perform it on three people simultaneously… What about the '*Phasus throw*' one that your mama used in the Musea?"

Cleo stared at me, somewhat indignant.

"I take that as a no… how about—"

"Lorrie, these are all grade 8 spells at the very least. You don't even know them well enough, surely you don't think that I would?"

I sighed in hopeless acceptance as I looked around in search of a solution.

"I guess you're right, the guards probably have a shielding spell guarding them from unearthly magic, anyway."

"We may as well go home; we are clearly NOT destined to save the earth and everyone we love…" Cleo kicked the ground in frustration.

"I have an idea." I was aware that the *Zoo of Unearthly Creatures* was right around the corner from the town hall; I kept seeing it labelled in the street signs with an arrow steered in the same direction. I smiled at Cleo, knowing how brilliant it was. "Pandymonks!"

What was one more place to break into, it would be good practise, I thought to myself in justification of my actions. No pandymonks would be hurt in the process.

"Lorrie, you are a genius!" Cleo momentarily forgot his caution and raised his voice a little too much.

"Shhh,"

"Oh, sorry… You're a genius witchy! Let's get us a furry little forgetting friend!"

We made our way to the Zoo and snuck in through a gap in the fence. I won't bore you with the details, but let's just say a few scrapes later (Cleo tripped over a bowl of suspicious looking brown sludge) and an episode of Chucklebub induced hilarity, we arrived at the Pandymonk enclosure.

"Okay, so one of us goes in and the other stays back a safe distance to provide constant reminders on what it is we're doing. Sound like a plan?" It wouldn't have been any good if we *both* couldn't recall where we were headed, and why.

"Are you volunteering, witchy?" I suppose I was.

"I heard they're friendly, right?"

"Well, if that's what you heard…"

"Come on, Cleo…"

"What?" He laughed. "I'm sure they aren't going to bite your face off, if that's what you're asking."

"A little reassurance never hurt anyone!" I rolled my eyes as I walked through the gate.

I wish I could watch it back: Cleo reminding me over and over again why I was holding a Pandymonk (of all things) in my arms.

"But *why* a Pandymonk, and why are you so far behind me?"

"Keep walking, witchy. I'll remind you again in seven seconds."

It turns out my Pandymonk was very friendly; I grew quite attached to him.

"I think I'll name him Bob."

"Why Bob?"

"Why not Bob?"

Cleo wasn't so fond of my name.

"She looks more like a Pauline."

"I am not naming Bob Pauline! And 'she' is clearly a 'he'!"

It was a debate not worth having, but we needed a bit of humour to lighten the mood.

"So, as I've explained a thousand times already, we're going to make a run to the side of that building over there and you need to get just close enough for the Pandymonk charms to work on the guards and make them forget we were ever here. Got it?"

"Sorry, what was that?"

"Oh, this is useless, just follow me!"

It's all a bit hazy because of the Pandymonk situation but I think Cleo ran ahead and I must have chased after him.

"Come on, witchy!" he shouted, knowing that the guards had already spotted us both.

"Keep running!" I couldn't keep the pace (remember, fitness of a door-knob) and fell behind pretty quickly. Cornered by four guards, I gripped onto Bob.

All I remember thinking is that I was doomed. But the next thing I knew, Cleo grabbed onto my arm and pulled me in between two of the guards as they rubbed their heads in confusion, contemplating why they had left their stations.

"Good job, Pauline!"

"It's Bob!"

"How can you possibly remember his name but forget that an evil sorceress is plotting to take over the earth?"

"It's the important things." I teased.

When we approached the side door, Cleo held up Mr Magus' pass to a small device attached to the wall, which flashed green and beeped at us before it let us through.

"We're in!"

"In where?"

"Oh witchy, as soon as we find that archive Pauline needs to go!"

I handed my Pandymonk over to Cleo after we grumbled over who would be the better navigator.

"Cleo, I did a six-week apprenticeship here a few summers ago, so I know the passages better than you!"

"Fine." Cleo relinquished and scrunched up his face while holding Bob at arm's length.

My turn to do the finding and reminding (quite a catchphrase!).

I could see how it might have been *slightly* annoying for Cleo, in even a short space of time I must have told him the same thing fifteen times.

"We are going to the archives to get the fog forest map to find the lady", which was shortened to: "archives, map, lady", when I became lazy. On our way through the corridor, we passed a supply closet where I left Bob with a little biscuit and a few drops of water, which I deliberately spilled on the floor. I promised him we would be back and hoped that between the two of us we would remember that he was there. We eventually arrived at the door labelled:

"Archive of Hidden Maps"

They really need to up their security, I thought. It's like telling a robber exactly where all the bank notes are kept and giving him the secret code!

"After you, witchy." Cleo once again held up his papa's pass to the door, and followed me in.

Chapter 22
Little Wizard

Tuesday 17th September (a few of these, too)
Cleo closed the door behind him.

"Okay, so where do we start?"

"Good question. I guess we pick any one of the fifteen or so filing cabinets." I had roughly counted them, trying to work out in my head how long we would be here. Until morning, I concluded.

It was twelve thirty and I was tired, but we couldn't stop.

"Your plan worked, witchy. I'm impressed!"

"Which plan?" Cleo frowned at me. "Kidding." I smirked.

Cleo approached the first cabinet and no surprise it was unlocked.

"Right then, I'll start here. Do you think they're in alphabetical order?"

"Maybe?"

I made my way to a larger cabinet and quickly discovered that the maps were not in alphabetical order. It wouldn't have helped much, anyway, we weren't exactly sure that the fog forest would have held that name sixty years ago when it was first recorded.

"Cleo, I think they're grouped by category…"

I realised as I was browsing through maps of hidden road systems that unearthlies can travel along to reach exclusive locations, mostly for private holidaying. I had never travelled on hidden roads, not that I can remember, anyway. I suspect Grandmama has, and maybe even Mama.

"Hidden forests, got it!"

Cleo abandoned his search through maps of hidden gateways for teleportation (which I would love to explore after all of this if we make it out alive) and joined me as I flicked through tons of folders.

"Dancing forest, Forest of dreams, Wild tree forest, Felicities' Forest... that's it!"

"Who's Felicity?"

"The Keeper; the one who found the stone in the Fog Forest, or should I say, 'Felicities forest'. I thought it might have had a different name back then."

I pulled the file and slid the map out as my heart sank.

"Cleo, it's blank..."

"What do you mean it's blank?" He snatched it from my hand as I felt my shoulders concave with the weight of disappointment.

"This is UNBELIEVABLE!" Cleo kicked the cabinet which produced a loud metal clunk. It's a wonder how he hasn't broken his big toe by now.

"Cleo! Do you want to get us caught? Shh! Just give me a minute to think..."

Cleo started nervously tapping his foot, which I had to try my best to zone out.

"Grandmama told me about hidden maps, I'm sure she did..." Tap, tap, tap. "What did she say..."

"Lorrie let's just—"

"Shh! I'm thinking..."

I recalled a conversation I had with grandmama a couple

229

months ago. We were watching an episode of something I can't remember the name of on the unearthly discovery channel. It basically followed an unearthly who was going around exploring hidden locations around the earth. I think it was a travel show mixed in with a bit of magic and cuisine. He discovered all sorts of places with their own habitats and, in some cases, their own *communities*. The general understanding is that Parisa herself cast a series of mysterious spells which either created, or separated, areas from the realms of the physical. In some cases, for protection, in others for amusement. They exist in our world, but are hidden in plain sight, feel, smell and all the other senses, entered only with a '*Paraphysicale*' spell, the words for which are unique to every location and are documented in Parisa's earlier writings.

To explain it better, Diary. Imagine if you drew an outline of the earth, as it is, and then drew another outline of a different earth on tracing paper and lay it on top. The two earths are different, yet one in the same. That analogy always had me wondering whether Parisa created the other realm with the intention that unearthlies would inhabit it. What if she never intended for unearthlies to stay in the physical and live alongside mortals, but we just got stuck somehow? These were the kind of profound questions we cover in unearthly Philosophy. Anyway, while no unearthly has the power or means to create such a location within this realm, explorers such as the unearthly on TV have entered them and even spent years trying to discover their intricacies. They made maps to remember the locations, and some even chose to remain there, for they can be wonderful. I was half listening to the man on the TV when I asked Gandmama if she had a map for a hidden location in amongst her box of collectibles.

"No, darling. Even if I did, you probably wouldn't be able to read it because…"

In that cold, narrow closet, I couldn't for the unearthly life of me remember why Grandmama said I may not be able to read the map.

"Think, Lorrie, think!"

"Think, witchy, think!" Cleo echoed, like my very own Parrot.

We heard some commotion outside, and it sounded close.

"I swear I have a vague memory of two kids making a run across the front of the building." One man spoke with a gruff voice.

"I sort of remember it, too. Call for back up."

I looked at Cleo and the terror on his face was a mirror of mine.

"We need to get out of here, before whatever back up they're calling arrives!"

I nodded, crumpling the map as I tensed my hand.

"I'll take it with me, in case I remember."

The voices were meandering away from us, and we knew if we didn't try and make our escape, we may never get the chance. Cleo pulled on the rusty door handle slowly, prolonging the creaking sound of the grinding metal. He opened the door enough to poke his head out, like he did at the school a few hours prior. He waited a moment before announcing:

"It's clear. Do you know the way back, witchy?" I was fairly confident that I did.

I led the way through the corridors as I had done before, but in reverse. I hesitated around every corner. So far so good, I thought. We were so close to the exit when I misjudged the same gruff voice belonging to the guard, thinking it was further than it was, and nearly marched straight into his path. I was swiftly pulled back by Cleo, with my back crashing into his chest. I felt his warm breath brushing my ear as he covered my mouth with his hand, pre-empting my gasp at the whiplash. He walked us backwards into a creek in the wall, where we waited until the guards disappeared around the corner. When they were out of sight and earshot, I spun around to face Cleo. I could smell the Peppadew from our earlier sandwiches as he spoke:

"Don't sue me for shoulder pain after all this, witchy. I'm only trying to keep you from getting caught, although you seem pretty intent on it." He smiled.

I felt a strange sense of safety in that moment, despite not being safe at all.

"Let's keep going, we're nearly there."

I caught sight of the side door and was half surprised that I'd managed to find my way back. We were actually going to make it, until it dawned on me.

"Cleo, are we forgetting something?" He gazed at me, confused at first, but we realised what it was at almost the same moment.

"Bob!" "Pauline!" we said, in unison.

We didn't even need to have the discussion; I knew I was going back for him.

"Lorrie, wait!" Cleo tried to get me to slow down, but I didn't care. I made a promise, and I nearly always keep my promises. I thrust open the supply cupboard door, and there was my Pandymonk sitting next to a pile of cookie crumbs, looking ever so timid. I basically launched him at a stunned Cleo when he caught up to me before I rushed on ahead, pulling at his sleeve to follow. I hoped we could outrun Bob's forgetful charms.

You'll be proud of me, Diary, I managed to sustain my breath and we made it out in probably half the time we made it in.

"Let's get this little guy home."

I said goodbye to Bob and thanked him for his service.

"I'll see you again, buddy. Thanks for your help today."

He seemed relieved to be back in his enclosure and I was slightly hurt at the pace with which he bolted out of my arms, not even turning to have one last look at me. Could I blame him? We had probably traumatised the little guy. The next thing that Cleo did, surprised me. He placed his arm around my shoulder and said:

"He'll be okay, witchy."

It's not that Cleo wasn't sympathetic, when it came to the big stuff, but he wasn't normally so *gentle* with it. I was glad I hadn't lost him as a friend (although I was reminded again of the intense guilt I felt at casting the *Fortunaes* spell). Maybe one day I would tell him, or he would find out. I would live in fear of that day.

"So, any luck remembering?" Cleo asked me after he emerged from the hole in the fence surrounding the Zoo.

"Little bits are coming back to me. I know grandmama said something about there being a spell, one that hides the marks on the maps…"

"Let me get this straight, a spell that hides the marks on the maps… which led to locations… which are hidden by a spell? Sheesh, this magic stuff is *not* easy to wrap your head around, no wonder the earthlies can't comprehend it!"

I couldn't deny that it was all pretty complicated.

"There's only one thing we can do, but I can't guarantee it'll work."

"Let's hear it?"

"Everything that is uttered in Hemlock House is witnessed. The ancestors are practically writing it all down, nosey as they are! If we have any hope of figuring out how to reveal the map, we need their help."

Cleo and I nearly inhaled a pack of sugar-coated jelly sweet to give us the boost we needed for yet another journey on foot. This time, our pace was slower, and we had less urgency in our stride. Not because there *was* less urgency, but because our feet felt like they were attached to anchors, and we had both already given up a little bit of hope, though neither of us wanted to admit it for each other's sake, as well as our own. I got the impression Cleo wanted a distraction from it all. To pretend for a moment that he was living his old, simple life of sarcasm and wit. I was happy to oblige.

"Hey witchy, do you like the theatre?"

"It's not bad, I guess. I enjoy the music. Do you?"

"Well, I didn't think so, but then papa took us all to see one about an unearthly kid losing his powers and taking up karate. It was quite clever, really. Typical underdog story. He found out that the real magic was *him*."

"Oh yeah, what happens in the end?"

"Well, no one expects him to, but he wins the big fight — spoiler — and settles for an earthly life. Happy ever after."

I couldn't be sure, but I thought I sensed a sort of yearning in the way Cleo described the play. Like it made him sad, almost, so I tried to lighten the mood.

"Oh, you'd have hated that then! Imagine being an

earthly. Would you loathe yourself as much as you do them?" I jarred him in the side with my flexed elbow in a taunting manner, but he remained quiet. "Cleo?"

"I'm not sure I would hate it, to be honest."

"Really? But you're always on about earthlies being weak and unsophisticated and all that…"

"Yeah but…" His walls that he spent so long building were there in that moment crumbling down. I had suspected them, of course, but never dared to employ a sledgehammer.

"It'd be easy, in a way, don't you think? Less to worry about, less to learn and fail at…"

"Cleo, you aren't failing at anything. Besides getting a girl to like you, maybe!" My teasing was met with more silence. This wasn't the time for joking around, Lorrie.

"Think about it though. We see these earthlies every day and they seem pretty happy. Their lives aren't nearly as complicated, and they're all tucked up in bed right now snoring away while we're out here on a rampage not to mess up, which we keep doing, by the way."

It finally made sense, at least some of it did. Cleo's displeasure towards the earthlies was not because he felt they should be jealous of him, it's because *he* felt jealous of *them*.

"Cleo, they're no different to us, in some ways."

"Oh, is that what your boyfriend taught you?"

I ignored the 'boyfriend' part of the question.

"They have the same problems we do, and yeah maybe a little less pressure…"

"A little?" Cleo raised his eyebrows at me, demanding I correct myself.

"Okay, a lot. But they also don't get to feel the things we do, Cleo. They don't experience the kind of energy we have, the sights we get to see. Take the maps, for example. Can you imagine what it would be like to see an invisible waterfall bursting with the colour of rose gold? You don't have to because we *can*. But they... they will never be able to experience that!"

"I guess. I just think sometimes, I don't know, it's tough having all these expectations. With great power comes... great disappointment. You saw what I did in there, how I couldn't even unlock the cupboard, and Mel got it in a couple seconds!"

I knew Cleo was conscious of his... shortcomings, but I didn't realise he felt so down about them. I always assumed he didn't care; he certainly didn't act like he did. That was his wall.

"Hey." I stopped at the front of the long driveway leading to Hemlock House. "*You* figured out your dad's plan and helped him find a way to steal a valuable relic from a guarded museum..."

"A not very well guarded museum!"

"*And* you must have saved me at *least* five times tonight from certain captivity..."

"True."

"AND you're my best friend. Who cares if you can't do an unlocking spell, you can practise that! You can't practise being there for someone. You either are or you aren't, and you *always* are."

"Thanks, Lorrie."

"You just need to stop being so hard on yourself and show up to a lesson every once in a while. You're smart, I know you are. You can't hide from me, little wizard!"

I was glad we had the conversation, even in the most inopportune of times — I had been wanting to get it off my chest for a few days now. Cleo must have been too; he laughed with a lot less woe.

"You're right, I should probably do my homework, eh? New leaf and all!"

I laughed as I nodded.

"And by the way, I'll have you know that I am a catch with the ladies! Just the other day Larissa asked me to go bowling with her!"

"Larrisa Fisk?"

"Yup!"

"Ooh, I am impressed. Just don't mess it up." I winked at him, before I spotted three figures standing in the window of the living room.

"Didn't know you were having company, Lorrie?"

"Neither did I."

As I approached the front steps the voices grew louder. They hushed as I opened the door, which had already been left carelessly ajar. I looked behind me and caught Cleo's expression, again reflecting my own. Mama rushed to meet me before I had even taken off my shoes.

"I'm okay, Mama!" She flung her arms around me and held me so tight I could feel the air escaping my lungs.

"Lorelei, we need to talk." She barely acknowledged Cleo's presence.

"I know, there's so much I need to—"

I hadn't finished my sentence before Grandmama walked through, followed by a tall man with a short beard, scruffy hair and a perky nose. I recognised him immediately from the pictures. I stared at him while directing my question to mama.

"What's going on, Mama?" I could tell she wanted to answer me, but she couldn't get the words out.

"Lorelei, dear…"

"Grandmama, where were you? What's happening?"

I had a premonition that my entire unearthly life was about to change. Grandmama walked towards me and grabbed my hand, while the man staring at me through the doorway reached for Mama's.

"We didn't mean for it to happen like this, dear, but we now don't have a choice. Do you know who this man is?"

Perhaps she thought she would spare herself the pain of revealing the man's identity by allowing me to guess.

Chapter 23
Night Owl

Tuesday 17th September

I had realised the man standing in the hallway was my papa, but at the very same time it dawned on me that he could be the informant, too. Call it a hunch. My skin went cold and my limbs stiff, as if I was the subject of a *frozay* spell. It was probably my mind's way of telling my body: This is all too much for us to handle, we're going to sleep now, bye. I looked over at the man as grandmama's hands were still wrapped around mine. They were warm, but they felt lighter than usual. Although grandmama didn't take my hand very often, I had always thought of hers as proud and strong, but now they seemed fragile. Somehow, I was focused more on that than on the massive event that had occurred (or series of massive events, I couldn't quite decide which would win a competition for the most enormous, colossal, life-altering event).

"Lorrie?" Mama repeated after I hadn't responded to the first few name calls.

I transferred my gaze from Grandmama's hands to the man in the doorway: my papa. I was surprised by how familiar and strange he seemed, all at the same time. He took a step forward, approaching me as cautiously as an earthly mouse who had trespassed in Stumble's territory.

"Hello, Lorelei. I'm... I'm Paul."

He had a name. His eyes and his mouth both smiled as he held out his hand to greet me. I stared at it as if it could cause me harm, and so he quickly pulled it back. Paul's voice was deep and kind, with a trace of nervousness that he tried to hide but became obvious when he cleared his throat.

"It's nice to finally…" He looked to Mama before finishing his sentence and she gave him a reassuring nod. "It's nice to meet you."

Stunned, I felt my feet moving me in another direction, as if they were on autopilot. My head bobbed as I walked upstairs, taking each progressive step slower than the one before. Four sets of eyes were fixed on me. I walked into my bedroom, stood in front of my bed, rotated one hundred and eighty degrees and let my body fall back, without any apprehension of the impact. I lay there a while, staring at the ceiling. It was a relief to have the weight of my body supported as I heard chatter downstairs.

"Just give her a moment, Fiona. The poor thing has had a lot to take in over the past few hours…"

"She'll come around, Paul. She just needs some time." Mama said before she asked Cleo whether she could get him anything to eat or drink.

"No thank you, Miss O."

I could imagine the awkwardness of everyone gathered in the hallway, not knowing what to say or do with themselves. I was glad I had a moment to myself, but I wanted someone to join me.

So, I closed my eyes and connected with Dean. He was still in his chair, but this time there was an empty space in front of him, where Mr Goddard was crouched before. It was quiet and I couldn't feel our headmaster's presence, so I presumed he wasn't in the room.

"Dean, it's me."

"Lorrie? Where have you been? Are you okay?"

I was reassured by the sound of his voice, even though I knew it was all in my mind; he wasn't actually *speaking*, but more like *thinking* the words.

"I'm okay, how are you? How is Mel, can I see her?"

"I'm not sure you want to, Lorrie, she's not looking too good." He kept his head forward, looking straight at the textured brown wall ahead.

"Please, Dean. I need to see her."

With reluctance, he showed her to me. Mel was still on her chair next to his, but her body had slumped forward even more. Her nose was suspended above her knee, and her hair fell forward to cover most of her face. I could see her right cheek though, its grey-white pigmentation stood out.

Dean was struck by my panic which caused him to shut his eyes and turn his head.

"I'm sorry, you didn't need to see that."

Grandmama warned me that setting in was a two-way process; I could see through Dean's eyes, hear his thoughts and feel his physical and emotional state, and while he couldn't for some reason see what I saw, he was able to hear and *feel* what I did.

"It's okay. Is she…" I really did not want to ask this. "…Is she… alive?"

"I can hear her breathing, but it's faint. I tried to reach for her but my hands…"

He looked down at his wrists, which were stained with patches of both dry and wet blood. At that moment, my own wrists were burning. I could almost feel every individual string digging into me, like tiny arrows piercing my skin.

"It hurts! You're hurting so much, Dean." The thought of it was agony.

"It's not that bad, Lorrie." He didn't know that it was too late to deny the pain.

"Remember, I'm in your head. I can tell when you're lying."

"Right… any idea how we can get out of this, Lorrie?"

"We're trying. Cleo and I… we think we have a way, it's just been a bit of a crazy night."

Dean chuckled.

"You can say that again! Wait till I get back to school and tell my earthly friends what I've been up to, and on a school night!" He still had his humour, at least.

"Tell me about your night, to distract me from all this. If just for a moment."

I couldn't be happier that he asked.

"Where to begin… So, we found out that Mrs Magus helped Mr Goddard steal the stone, which by the way has it's on Keeper, then we kidnapped a Pandymonk who I named Bob, used him to make the guards at the unearthly town hall forget they ever saw us, stole a map that reveals a secret forests location, although we haven't quite figured out a spell to expose it… oh, and I just met my papa who I believe is also working with Mr Magus to bring Sereia down, though that hasn't been confirmed."

I inhaled a full two lungs of air, forgetting that these were all thoughts, and I didn't actually need to restore my breath because I hadn't been talking. I sensed I was holding it anyway, though.

"Wow, Lorrie. That is quite the night. Wait, did you say

— or even think — that you met your papa?"

"Yup."

"That's big, Lorrie. What's he like?"

"Tall. Scruffy. He has my nose."

"Lucky him, I like your nose."

"You do?" I felt myself blush, which was an inconsequential, two percent mortal reaction, given the circumstances. But I couldn't help it.

I told Dean that, speaking of my papa, I thought I had better go and meet him — properly — and find out how to stop Sereia, if that was still even a possibility.

"Will you come back, Lorrie? It's just that, if I don't see you again, I wanted to tell you that-"

"Dean, you will see me again, in your mind and in real life too, once this is all over."

"Do you really believe it will be?"

"Yes." No.

He didn't believe me, I felt it in both of our guts and, worse, I could feel him giving up hope.

"There's one thing before I go that I wanted you to hear, Dean."

His mood lifted ever so slightly. Without further explanation I mustered up the energy for the *Instramalus Vocus* spell. The instruments in my room danced. I only had a ukulele that mama bought me for a previous birthday, a violin that I got at a second-hand store with great ambitions to master, and a tuba that caught my eye outside an unearthlies house the other day, with a 'for free' sign scribbled on a scrap piece of weathered cardboard. I had planned to give it to him when we had our next meeting — a peace offering for my Skittles victory. You might think that it sounds like an odd ensemble of instruments, Diary, and it is. But the spell twists and interweaves the sounds, and they sounded as beautiful as ever. Can you guess what they played?

Dean did.

"Sinthea's ballad? Lorrie, it's beautiful."

Tears were filling our eyes, mine twice; once with his and once with mine. Thinking back on it, I wondered what everyone downstairs was thinking in that moment, when they heard an array of sounds radiating from my bedroom.

"What an odd time to listen to music." I could picture grandmama saying.

"At least she's playing the ukulele I bought her" was probably what mama was thinking.

"I've just met my daughter and she'd rather listen to a song?" was perhaps what papa — I mean Paul — was pondering, and

"Witchy, come downstairs and save me from this cringeworthy family reunion", was likely Cleo's desire.

"Remember this, Dean. If you promise me you won't give up, I promise I'll play it for you every day, if you ask me to. Deal?"

"Deal."

Our mutual feeling of pure joy kept me going that night, fleeting as it was.

I sat still on the end of my bed for a moment before returning to my reality. When I felt as ready as I could be, I opened my door and made my way to the staircase. Gripping the rails unnecessarily, I gradually descended and was met with the same four pairs of eyes, still floating in the hall. Immediately before my entrance, Mama and Paul were in conversation, Grandmama was leaning against a wall fiddling with her precious (lucky) stones, and Cleo had his hands in his pocket while he tried to avoid meeting anyone's gaze. The atmosphere was infused with relief that I had returned, and then suspense.

"Paul, can I speak to you in private, please?" He nodded and followed me into the lounge.

Eager eyes upon us were abruptly shunned as I closed the door. Perhaps one day I'll tell you about our conversation, Diary; the very first time I ever spoke to my papa (that I could remember, anyway). I had many questions for him. Some remained unanswered, and some changed everything. But this entry has a different purpose.

After we spoke, we emerged into the hall where Mama, Grandmama and Cleo were still drifting.

"Grandmama, we need to know how to read the map." She smiled, as if expecting me to ask that question.

"Let's get to it, then."

Grandmama reminded me of the spell, and although I begged her to perform it, she insisted that I hover my hands above the map as she talked me through it.

"I'm not strong enough, Lorrie. You need to do it."

What did she mean by that? Grandmama was the strongest sorceress I knew. I'd ask her when — if — we returned from the fog forest. Together, we uncovered the sparse traces on the desolate map. They appeared slowly and gently, like condensation forming on a window.

"There!" Cleo waltzed up behind me. "There's the fog forest!"

I asked Grandmama if she was coming, but I already knew the answer. Mama hugged me again and stroked my hair.

"I can't, Lorrie. If Sereia finds your grandmama and

your... Paul... I need to stay behind to protect them."

Mama hadn't practised her magic in years, so I wasn't sure that she would be able to, but I didn't argue.

Two a.m. What would Miss Michaela say if she knew I was up this late?

Cleo and I walked out of Hemlock House as I caught one more glimpse of my family. Mama, who raised me in chocolate brownie recipes and earthly traditions. Grandmama, who raised me in magic and spell books. And Paul, who didn't raise me, but maybe in another life could have. I must tell you, Diary, I wasn't feeling all that positive when we left, and Cleo wasn't, either. The fog forest wasn't too far away from us, only around the corner, really. It was the shortest walk we took all night. The lemontwine tea that we sipped before we continued our journey gave us both an extra spring in our step (it had a special ingredient grandmama wouldn't reveal), but not in our temperament. All we could hear was the *'twit twoo'* of a night owl keeping us company. Step after step, we headed towards the forest. When we reached the point on the map where the entrance was marked (which was in the middle of a dark street that I hadn't recognised), I placed the map on the gravel and stood facing Cleo. We took hold of each other's hands, combining our energies and giving us the strength we needed, to unveil the forest. One of us would not have been strong enough in that moment to do it alone.

Together, we performed the *Paraphysicale* spell, made unique with an insertion of words that also appeared on the back of the map. This was a spell I had never studied, let alone practised. After I set into Dean in the solace of my bedroom some thirty minutes prior, I asked my ancestors for guidance, but I couldn't feel them there; they weren't with me.

Sure, let's keep Lorrie awake nearly every night whispering tales of her prophecy, but then abandon her when she needs us the most! I would be having strong words with them if I made it back.

Cleo and I attempted the spell three times before the forest appeared. Each time, saying the words louder and with more passion, which may have been a disguise for our desperation. But we kept going in an unspoken agreement that we would not give up now; we had come too far and endured too much.

The surroundings of the dark, unrecognisable street faded away and slowly morphed into an expanse of trees. We did it. We were in the fog forest. I appreciated its natural beauty for all of one minute. It felt like autumn there, even though it was summer in the earthly realm. Leaves of yellow and auburn, darkened by the night, glistened as they were kissed with light from the full moon. The tall, overhanging trees struck me as comparable to the ones in the picture of mama and Paul, as he wrapped his arms around her.

"It's beautiful, isn't it."

I didn't realise Cleo had an eye for natural beauty, although its magnificence could not be denied by any unearthly or earthly alike. I just wished we were there under different circumstances. I looked at Cleo, whose face was also reflecting the moonlight. Like me, he was draped in a thick coat that mama demanded we wear. As if getting cold was our biggest concern. He caught my eyes and smiled without baring his teeth, as if he heard my thoughts and agreed that he was also glad he was with me.

"Now where do we go, little witch?"

"Umm I don't know, ahead?"

Chapter 24
Fog Forest

Tuesday 17th September

We walked in a straight line, tunnelled by a stream of trees on either side of us. We were hoping the all-powerful stone I was carrying in my backpack would draw us towards its Keeper, like the pull of a magnetic force. Or at least it would give us a sign. We assumed that if we were travelling in the wrong direction we would be corrected somehow and realigned with the correct path. A little while ago we reached a crossroads. There were three trails branching off ahead of us. One going straight, one slightly right and the other to our left. If there was ever a need for direction, we needed it then. But no, Cleo wanted to go right, I wanted to keep heading straight, so we did the most (or least) logical thing and went left. Our instincts were clearly in contrast with one another, and so we decided they should both be ignored. The leaves were crunching underneath our feet, though it was hard to see them through the thick layer of mist that had formed a blanket over them. We had come too far to go back to the crossroads now. I hadn't timed us, but we must have been going for at least half an hour.

The wind started to pick up and we heard a howl in the distance. Grandmama warned us that there could be any unearthly creatures inside the forest. Some who had entered unwillingly as they stalked an unearthly explorer, and some who evolved from other organisms born in this realm.

"Cleo, this feels like a never-ending path."

My feet were killing me, they had completely lost their lemontwine spring. Cleo's panting and sudden pause corroborated my fatigue.

"Let's have a break, witchy. I need some water."

He untwisted his arms from the loops of his backpack in an awkward motion, as if he had done a heavy workout the day before and his muscles were achy. I had assumed Cleo worked out; his slender upper body was topped with broad shoulders, and his school shirt always sat tightly around his arms, as if the sleeves were about to tear. Maybe he just wore clothes that were too small for him. Anyway, if he wanted a break, I was not going to stop him. He took a gulp of his water as I sat down on a serrated tree stump which was rather uncomfortable.

"Want a sip?"

"Please!"

We rested for only a few minutes and then I stood and brushed the dust off my legs while Cleo remained on the floor, laying in a side position with his elbow propping him up and playing with a twig.

"Come on, little wizard. Let's carry on."

He let out an exaggerated groan and protested.

"Just one more minute!"

"NO! Up or I'll kick you."

"Ergh FINE. Help me up, please?"

I reached out my hand and he nearly yanked my shoulder out of its socket.

"Oof. When you said not to sue you for shoulder pain, I didn't think I would actually *have to*."

"Sorry, Lorrie. Just don't realise my own strength

sometimes," he said with a smirk and I rolled my eyes.

"Pfft, sure."

"Let's carry on shall we, no time to waste!" Cleo slung his backpack around his right shoulder.

"Wait." Just as Cleo took a step forward, I heard a noise.

"What?"

"Shhh!"

"Everything all ri—"

"Quiet!"

We fell silent. At first it sounded like branches rustling in the wind, but then I noticed a rhythm.

"Do you hear that?" I wanted confirmation from Cleo that I wasn't going mad, which at this point was a strong possibility.

"Yeah! What is it?"

"I don't know. An animal?"

"Maybe?" It was getting louder and more pronounced. Footsteps. A few of them. Pounding the unearthly earth. Slow, but determined, like they knew where they were headed — not hesitant, like ours.

I was walking towards the footsteps. Maybe this was the draw I was expecting from the stone, maybe the footsteps belonged to the Keeper.

"Lorrie, get back here!"

Cleo saw it before I did. Two eyes, bright yellow, peeking through the bushes about four metres in front of me, level with my waist.

"Lorrie!" He repeated, but I couldn't move; I was the victim of *Frozay* again. "LORRIE!" Cleo now shouted, snapping me out of it.

I backed away slowly at first, my back to Cleo, but it

followed me out. As it emerged from the leaves, I could see a lean body attached to four muscular legs. A thick mane of dark hair was hanging proudly from its neck, and its sharp teeth were on display as it snarled. It had the basic aesthetics of a panther, or a lion, or maybe something in between. But it also had an unusually long tail which curled in different sized ringlets, a large hump on its back and spiky hair on its head that looked a lot like Stumbles, though a deeper shade of brown. I wasn't sure what it was, if it even had a name, but it terrified the living moonlights out of me.

I continued backing away until I bumped into a tree behind me. The creature was creeping closer and closer towards me, laying out each foot sequentially as if performing a piece in the grand ballet.

"Lorrie, RUN!"

I had the same idea as Cleo and bolted away from the tree, sprinting towards him. We ran back the way we came; Cleo in front of me and the deadly panther lion thing behind.

"Keep going, Lorrie!"

Cleo sensed me slowing down. He turned back to wait for me, and when I reached him, he decisively shoved me through a bush and leapt in after me. Cleo landed just beside me, and I let out a delayed yelp after my leg crashed against a loose branch.

"What are you doing?"

"We'll never outrun that thing, Lorrie. We need to hide!" Cleo scrambled up and helped me to my feet this time, as I whimpered like an injured dog.

"We need trees!" I asserted.

"That thing probably knows this forest inside out, we won't fool it by hiding in any trees! What about the *Vanish*

Aries trick you've been working on?"

"You saw that thing's nose; it'll probably smell us a mile away. And we're far, far less than a mile!" It did have a large nose, I forgot to mention that. "Cleo, it knows the forest the way it is now... so we need to change it!"

"Change it? How?"

"*Rootus Sprowus Treus.*"

Luckily, we were not short of tree roots, the ground was practically dressed in them.

"Hurry then, make some trees!"

"I need a minute."

"Lorrie, you don't *have* a minute, it won't be long till he finds us here!"

I had done the trick in one minute and three seconds, if you'll recall, but Cleo was right; we would be lucky if we had that long.

"Okay, okay. Let me focus."

And somehow, I did. I had managed the trick in thirty-five seconds (Cleo said he roughly counted in his head to calm himself down). I wasn't even sure if any Grade 6 unearthly had ever done that — I think the shortest time on record was forty-eight, and the kid was deemed a prodigy (unless Cleo miscounted, but he would have had to have been massively out, and counting was *not* something I was not something I ever needed to help him with after maths)!

In those thirty-five seconds, not only one, but multiple trees gradually sprouted around us, on every visible root. The already saturated forest grew, and it submerged us. Cleo and I were forced closer to each other as we avoided the wayward branches, until we were practically pinned against each other.

"Shhh." Cleo held his finger to his lips, and we heard the

thud of footsteps again.

After enough time had passed, when we thought it was safe and the creature had given up its hunt, Cleo helped me to weave through the trees until we found a patch of smooth soil. Cleo removed my arm from around his shoulder and lowered me to the ground with my left leg outstretched.

"Let's have a look at you, then."

I rolled up my loose jeans and halfway up my shin was a thick cut about the size of my index finger.

"Ouch, Lorrie. That's a bit more than a scratch!" Cleo pulled out his water bottle and unscrewed the lid. "This is going to hurt a bit."

That was an understatement! I winced from the pain as he poured some water on my leg to clear the dirt from my wound.

"Just a bit?"

"Can you walk on it, Lorrie?"

I moved my leg as a test and let out a gasp.

"Yeah, but I won't make it far."

Cleo sighed.

"I'm sorry, Cleo. Take the stone and go on without me."

"No, I'm not leaving you here."

"You have to, it's a matter of—"

"Life and death? No. You're coming with me."

"Cleo, I can't. When I said I won't make it far I meant I could probably take a step or maybe two. That's it."

I could tell he was thinking of a solution, but I doubted he would find one.

Why do I underestimate my Magus friends? Cleo crouched down beside me and rolled down the hem of my jeans before he placed his hands over where my gash was. He closed his eyes, and I knew he was trying a Grade 7 healing spell. I didn't interrupt him, I remained still. The skin on my leg was getting warmer, until it eventually felt so hot that I mustered every ounce of restraint not to pull it away. We didn't know if it had worked or not.

"Does it feel any better?"

"I'm not sure." I peeled the hem up yet again, and my injury was still there.

"I'm sorry, Lorrie." Cleo dropped his head in shame.

"Wait, Cleo, look!" The cut was shrinking, and the red skin around it was turning back to its normal, pale colour. "It's working, Cleo!"

We were both in awe. I have never seen a healing spell being performed live, only ever on TV.

"How did you do that?"

Cleo explained that his papa taught it to him the first time they went fishing. It was Cleo's first catch, and he didn't expect to feel so distraught after his papa smashed the fish's head on the side of the boat.

"I've killed him Papa, he's dead!" a younger Cleo wailed.

"Don't worry, son. He's fine, look!"

Mr Magus, surprised at his son's distress, clasped the fish in between his hands and performed the same healing spell. In the next moment, the fish flopped out of his hands. Cleo picked it up and put it back into the water.

"And you remembered it, after all this time?"

"Don't tell Papa, but I've practised it a couple times since. When I go into the forest at school, I often come across injured squirrels or birds with broken wings. I've managed to heal them most times, but never tried it on an unearthly!" Cleo was proud of himself, and I was too. I leaned forward and placed my arms around his neck.

"Thanks, Cleo. You're a really good friend."

With that, the giant wave of guilt I was pushing down had overcome me, and I couldn't help but confront the fact that I was not as good a friend, and I wanted to be.

"Cleo..." I moved away from him again. "...I need to tell you something. It's awful, and you'll probably hate me for an unearthly lifetime. It's to do with how we found out about... why we thought..." My eyes were wet as they stared at a blood-soaked leaf on the ground.

"Lorrie, I know."

I looked up at him as he was still crouched in front of me.

"No, Cleo I don't think—"

"You saw me at the fire in the *Fortunaes* trick."

He knew? He *knew* already and he didn't despise me?

"But how—"

"Mel told me, on our way home from Easton's party."

"And — and you're okay with it?"

"Well, I was mad at first, of course. I felt a bit violated. But then I was sort of comforted that you were there with me, in a way. That you felt how I did. Plus, I kind of gave you a reason to be suspicious; I didn't cover my tracks well enough. And just as well, we probably wouldn't have found out about the Keeper, if I had."

I hadn't witnessed that kind of grace in Cleo before. It led me to lose my ability to form words.

"I — I..."

"Don't worry about it, witchy. We have bigger fish to fry, and then heal." With a wink he pushed his hands off his knees and propelled himself up. "You ready to really test that leg of yours out?"

There weren't very many words I knew that could express

how grateful I was to Cleo, for his friendship and his forgiveness, so I chose to say nothing. I cautiously rose to my feet and confirmed that the spell worked; my leg was pain-free.

"Come on then, let's try and avoid running into more scary beasts and find that Keeper!"

We walked out into the path that we had diverted from, and double checked left and right that our predator was no longer lurking about.

"Which way were we going again?"

"I remember that tree over there from before…" I pointed. "Its leaves are a slightly different colour to the rest of them!"

"Umm, whatever you say, witchy." Cleo hadn't paid as *much* attention to the landscape as I had.

Another half an hour or so had passed by, and we hadn't encountered any more surprises, aside from a few harmless little meerkat-looking things. Strange place, this fog forest. We assumed we were headed the right way because the fog was getting thicker, which I thought was a good thing considering the name of the place, and the fog that surrounded Felicity the night she became the Keeper. It was getting harder to navigate, though. We couldn't see our feet so that slowed us down, and there was something playing on my mind, which I couldn't quite put my finger on.

"Ewwww! What on un-EARTH?"

I heard a squelch and was quite pleased that Cleo's boot and lower leg submerged in water before mine did.

"A pond!" I was excited for the change of scenery.

"Yeah, I gathered that!" Cleo stepped out of the water and was shaking his leg like a dog. He removed and emptied his boot as a stream of water gushed out. "Ergh!" Cleo stepped back into his boot and yanked a plastic bag out of his left pocket.

"What's that?" I asked.

"Sandstone flakes!"

"Where did you get those?" I knew the answer.

"Your mama gave them to me! Want some?" He held out the opened bag.

"Never a bad time for sandstone flakes, eh?" I took a handful and shoved them into my mouth.

"Is it me or is this your mama's best batch?"

They were delicious, but then they always are. Our exhaustion, hunger and fear had probably enhanced their taste.

"I've been meaning to ask you a favour…" Cleo began.

"What's that?"

"It's been on my mind, what happened to Mel…"

"And Dean."

"Yeah, and him. Could you… would you set into him again? I just want to know how my sister is doing. It's distracting me is all and I think I could focus more and not step into ponds if I knew…"

I hadn't told him yet about my earlier conversation with Dean.

"Sure." I forced a smile, but I was far from thrilled.

I took a seat and set into Dean. It was becoming easier and easier now that I had connected with him.

"Dean?"

It was quiet at first. Was he sleeping?

"DEAN!"

I imagined being louder, not that he would perceive my increase in volume. His eyelids started to open, and then they fluttered, and then his blinking slowed. He *was* asleep, and when he woke up he was faced with the driver's seat ahead of him.

"Lorrie?"

"Hi. Where are you?"

"I'm not sure, we're driving somewhere."

"Can you see anything? Any landmark out the window?"

"Umm, let me have a look…" He scanned the surroundings outside of the car, but it was still dark and the speed of the vehicle made everything merge into a blur.

"How is she?" I dreaded the answer.

"The same. There's definitely thyme around us, I can smell it."

"And Mr Goddard?"

"He's driving. He's been on his phone the whole night. Probably receiving messages from whatsername. Have you and Cleo figured out that map?"

"Yeah, we're in the forest now. We were chased by something that thought we were a tasty treat, and now we're munching some sandstone flakes!"

"Sandstone flakes? Would I like them?"

"Umm… I'm not too sure you could eat them!"

"Oh."

I could feel Cleo prodding my arm; denying me the same patience I gave him when he healed my leg.

"We need to find the Keeper, Dean. I'll come back. Make sure you look for something you recognise, or something I could use to find you."

"I will. Lorelei, before you go…"

"Yes?"

"Nothing, I just… I'm looking forward to that ballad!"

"Me too."

I hadn't heard (or thought) him saying my full name for a while. I didn't realise that I missed it until then. That I missed *him*. When the spell subsided and I was back in my body in the forest, I slapped Cleo in the arm.

"Ow, what's that for?"

"You keep distracting me! How am I supposed to focus with you poking me like that?"

"Sorry." He looked like a guilty child who was caught stealing sweets from the candy store.

"Is she okay?"

"She's a bit weary, but she *will be* okay."

"Phew, that's a relief."

I hoped it wasn't a lie.

"You okay, Lorrie?"

"Yeah, I just have this feeling…"

"Feeling?"

"This feeling that we're walking into a trap…"

Chapter 25
Good

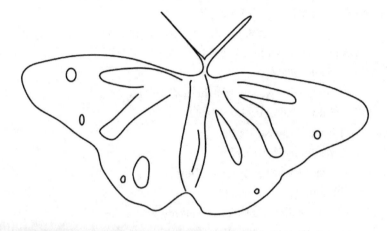

Tuesday 17th September, around 4.00am

"What do you mean, a trap?" Cleo was perplexed by my statement.

"I'm not sure exactly…"

"We've been through a lot, Lorrie, it's not surprising that you're a little… suspicious."

"Yeah, but there's just something fishy — dead fishy — about all this."

"Well, it is all a bit dead fishy. Who'd have thought we'd be doing this right now. I was ready to fail my English test this morning, and now look where I am!"

"Yeah, I *guess.*"

But I couldn't shake it. We took a path to the right of the

pond and carried on, all the while I was contemplating the source of my negative energy. Maybe Cleo was right, I probably *was* just ruminating over all of my recent, foreign emotions. Still, I had those bad butterflies.

The fog was now the only thing in our sight. It surrounded us; swaddled us. We kept walking in the direction which we *thought* was forward, but it was hard to tell.

"We must be getting closer!" Cleo proclaimed.

"I hope so! What was your neighbour like, anyway?" I was curious about the next Keeper.

"Well, she was a little... grumpy, to be honest. Always shouted at papa if he walked on her front lawn, and she seemed like a bit of a scatterbrain."

"How so?"

"Well, once I saw her drop her handbag outside the store your mama works at, and then another time she left her handbrake off in her car and it rolled back into the street."

"Hmm... does she seem protective at least, as the Keeper of the stone?"

"Not particularly... she used to let her Sheebulf off the lead when she took him out for a walk..."

(A Sheebulf is sort of like a bunny rabbit but with short ears and small teeth.)

"...I found it once, in a nearby field, and coaxed it to come to me with some ripped up cardboard that I pretended was a snack. Then I returned it to her, and she didn't seem to care much. I think she had some memory problems, Miss Olave."

She didn't sound like she possessed the qualities of the Keeper, but then what did I know. Before I could properly reason the stone's choice, I detected a figure in the distance. The fog was clearing, and the rough shape became more defined as I squinted my eyes.

"Lorrie, is that…"

The figure started to walk towards us, and with every step it took, a sense of dread consumed my body. My bones felt weak and I was cold, as if it suddenly dropped in temperature. If that was the Keeper, my body was clearly trying to tell me something, I just wasn't sure what it was. I began to have the worst headache, too. The pain was sharp and when Cleo noticed me rapidly placing my hands on either side of my head, he asked me if I was all right.

"I think so, I just have a stabbing pain. It's the strangest thing, came out of nowhere!"

"You're probably tired, Lorrie. You've been through a lot!"

"Does it feel colder to you?"

"Not really, maybe a bit."

The figure kept making its way towards us.

"Should we… go and say hello?" Cleo suggested, not quite knowing how to approach the Keeper of a powerful relic.

He stepped forward and I followed. I could see the detail of her face now as we were only a couple of metres away. It was Cleo's neighbour.

"We did it, Lorrie!" Cleo whispered with delight. "We found her!"

When we were only an arm's length apart from her, we stopped in our tracks.

"Hi, Miss Olave."

Cleo broke the silence to greet his neighbour. I had seen her a few times before taking out her bins when I went to Mel's house, but never had I found myself this close to her. Her back was hunched, and her face looked small in the hood of her cloak. She had lines under her eyes, extending across her cheeks, and her cracking lips were pink with a tinge of light blue. A strand of crisp white hair was placed neatly in front of her right ear, and she stood holding a wooden stick with both hands out in front of her. She looked weary, sure, but not as frail as you would expect for someone who had been lost in a forest for weeks. She must have found a source of food, and a place to rest out of harm's way. She was, after all, able to enter the forest without any map or spell, so maybe it protected her all the more.

"Young ones, you have found me!" Her lips parted as they widened across her face.

"Yes, Miss Olave. We've been on a long journey. It's been quite difficult all things considered, but you're our only hope."

She glided to Cleo and stretched out her hand which she wrapped around his wrist. I felt myself flinch, which she seemed to notice but not acknowledge.

"Dear children, you have done very well. The earth and its inhabitants will be indebted to you forever."

Cleo beamed and stood a bit taller, proud of his achievement. Miss Olave coughed with her handkerchief at the ready, which made Cleo jump.

"Oh, do you need something to drink? We have water, or some food. Lorrie's mama makes these amazing Sandstone flakes, let me get you some…"

"No, don't worry dear, it's just a nasty cold. More importantly, do you have the stone?"

Her appreciative tone transformed into a more serious, formal one. Cleo turned his head to me, prompting me to reply.

"Yes, um, we've kept it safe. I have it in my backpack."

Miss Olave orientated her body towards me and moved

forward. She looked me dead in the eye as she thanked me for protecting it for her. I couldn't transfer my gaze. I was absorbed by her small, dark pupils surrounded by a glassy, grey iris. It was as if she had me in a trance.

"Can I see it, dear?"

I concluded that I was in awe of the new Keeper. I didn't react to her question which, if I'm being honest, I didn't even hear. But I gathered she asked something along those lines as Cleo answered on my behalf:

"The thing is, Miss Olave, we're just a bit worried because, you see, Sereia may be following us and if we take out the stone here, well… I think it's best if we find a safe place which is less exposed, and hand it to you then." Miss Olave tilted her head to the side as she stared at Cleo, with an expressionless face. "Sorry, I know you've waited a while for it, but I think we should be careful…"

"Don't worry, dear." She perked up again. "Where shall we go that's safe? You lead the way and I'll follow."

"I'm not sure. Any ideas, Lorrie?" I couldn't pull my eyes away from her. Cleo cleared his throat as if to prompt me, and when that didn't work, he knocked his shoulder against mine.

"Lorrie, any ideas?" I shook my head.

"Well, not to worry dears, I know a place that should do."

In retrospect, the fact that we blindly followed Miss Olave down an unfamiliar path was a bit naïve, but what were we to do? She was the Keeper after all, hand-picked by the stone itself, and the only one who could stop Sereia.

Miss Olave and Cleo walked beside each other while I lagged behind. Cleo was leaning in towards her as they chatted like old pals in a long-awaited reunion. I hadn't realised they even knew each other that well. Cleo laughed at something she said, and they appeared to be having a wonderful catch up as I caught the odd word here and there.

"Who's that young one? She's pretty."

Cleo looked over his shoulder to me and smiled, as if I wasn't privy to the conversation.

"That's Lorrie, mine and my sister's best friend. She's the main reason we found you."

"Oh?"

"Yeah, it's a long story. But basically, she put everything together and insisted we do something about it."

"Impressive. And you mention your sister, where is she now?"

"We're not too sure. Lorrie set into her boyfriend, Dean, and Mr Goddard — our evil headmaster working for Sereia — was driving them somewhere. In fact, Lorrie, now might be a good time to check in and see if Dean has figured out where they are?"

"Ooh, yes dear, good idea," Miss Olave agreed.

They both looked at me with expectation.

"I'm not sure if now is a good time, isn't it better if we get to the safe place first? I don't want to hold us up."

"Nonsense, dear. We can wait, the earth won't end in the next ten minutes."

Cleo chuckled and I shot him a glare. I didn't feel comfortable with it, and I didn't take much of a liking to being made fun of by an unearthly (Keeper or not) who we had gone through so much trouble to track down, either. Miss Olave must have sensed my unease, as she put on her best reassuring expression and changed her attitude:

"Don't worry, dear. If you'd rather wait, we can do that,

but I can see how distressed your friend is, and I don't blame him. He's only worried for the welfare of his sister."

Manipulation. Miss Olave was good — I did feel guilty after her spiel. Maybe the stone was right to choose her, she was clearly good at persuasion. I sighed and glanced at Cleo whose weary face did not help my predicament.

"Fine, I'll do it."

It was hard to focus with not only Cleo staring at me this time, but also the Keeper. Although I could feel myself becoming stronger, as though I was channelling more energy. Maybe the ancestors had answered my request, after all, and let me borrow some of their powers. I closed my eyes and set into Dean.

"Mr Goddard, please. You need to help her. She's very weak and I'm worried... *please!*"

Oh no, Mel's condition must have worsened. It was strange hearing Mr Goddard speak. It was a voice I recognised in drawn out assemblies and parent evenings, but not in the context of causing harm to my best friends. Did Dean know I was there? He hadn't acknowledged my presence yet.

"She'll be okay, son, but I need to keep her subdued. I'm only following orders."

"Whose orders? Sereia's?"

Mr Goddard was clearly surprised that Dean knew her name.

"Umm, yes." He became skittish as he loosened his stripey blue and white tie.

"Dean?"

He didn't respond, but he looked around the room, possibly trying to show me where he was. The patterned walls around him were painted in a shade of yellowish brown, though there wasn't enough light to see the details. The ceiling was high and large windows let in a hint of orange light from the beginnings of the sunrise. I hadn't checked what time it was, I assumed maybe five-ish. I saw colours of green and purple embedded in the rays, possibly reflecting off something. The stone floor was dusty and cold, and it didn't take long before I heard the echo of Dean's voice.

"Is she coming here?"

Mr Goddard nodded.

"She'll be here soon."

"Good," was Dean's unexpected, unusually brief answer, that had even Mr Goddard intrigued.

"Good?"

"Yeah, I'm glad."

He squinted at Dean and took a while to formulate his response.

"I'm not sure you should be glad, son, you're in a lot of danger. You never should have trusted those unearthlies. I wouldn't have chosen to capture you, I only really needed *her*!" He pointed to someone outside of Dean's field of vision, but I knew he was referring to Mel.

Why did he need an unearthly? What *was* Sereia's plan?

"I *don't* trust them, any of them!"

"What were you doing sneaking around with them, then?"

"Hoping to see you!"

"Me? Why me?"

Mr Goddard and I were both beyond confusion at that point.

"Well, I'm working for her, too!"

My eyes opened before I had a chance to stop them. My body reacted before my mind intervened, and I was back in the fog forest.

"Well, Lorrie… anything?"

I couldn't give an immediate reply. I hadn't a clue what was going on and my mind was doing cartwheels trying to figure it out.

"I'm not done." I snapped.

I closed my eyes once more and was back in Dean's head.

"So, you're saying that you purposefully led them to me, in order for me to capture the witch and deliver her to Sereia?"

I felt Dean's head nod.

"But *why*? I always thought you a liberal boy, hanging around with that unearthly."

"I was drawing her in, getting her to trust me. It was all part of the plan."

"Why did Sereia choose you?"

"Because she knew what happened to my papa."

Mr Goddard frowned, urging Dean to elaborate.

"You see, my papa owns a garage down the road. It used to do really well back in the day; unearthlies even used his services. But he got into a bit of trouble with debt, and when he couldn't pay it back, the unearthly he owed cast a spell on his hands. They were riddled with arthritis in a matter of hours, and he couldn't work his tools any more. It wasn't only his income, it was his passion, too. So, I had to quit music lessons after school and help him out, whenever I could."

"That's awful, son. So, you wanted to get back at them; the unearthlies?"

"Yep, and Sereia promised me we would. She also said she would fix my dad's hands when it was all over."

Mr Goddard pulled up a chair and took a seat, placing one leg on top of the other.

"I have a similar story myself."

"Oh, really?"

"I had a dream, ever since I was a little boy, to build an elite school for earthlies. I was well on my way, too, but then the pact was formed with the council of... what do you call it... and anyway I was given an ultimatum; sacrifice my dream, or my job. So, when a messenger of Sereia's tracked me down and offered me the opportunity to help her wish all unearthly life away in an instant, sparing her life and those of her followers, I couldn't resist. It is time for revenge!"

I couldn't say if I was more shocked at Dean's revelation or Mr Goddard's. Sereia wants to rid the earth of unearthlies? She would be the most powerful being on the earth and there would be *nothing* standing in her way. The earthlies (and her loyal unearthlies who were left) would be her slaves. And Dean... my heart felt like it shattered into a million pieces, but I held onto the tiny hope that he could be bluffing, and it wasn't the terrible betrayal he made it seem.

"Sereia didn't tell me about you?"

"She said it was vital for the plan to work that I didn't expose myself."

"Hmm. Why did you let me tie your hands and blindfold you?" He was testing Dean.

"Well, I thought I should play my part, at least until we reached our destination... which is where, again?

"Vormera Cathedral. Did Sereia not tell you we would be meeting her here?"

"Oh yeah, she did. I remember now."

So that's where they were, and Sereia would be joining them soon. We needed to get there; we were running out of time. I opened my eyes again and leaped to my feet.

"Lorrie, what's wrong?"

"They're at Vormera Cathedral!"

"We must go at once," Miss Olave declared. "We must hurry! Come along, dears."

Chapter 26
Evil

Tuesday 17th September, around 5.30 a.m.

Tuesday 17th September, around 5.30 a.m.

You'll notice I started to put rough timings on my entries again, Diary. It's just to help you keep track. I realise it must be confusing, and it gets even more so!

If Dean was telling the truth, then everything I thought I knew about him, about the earthlies in general, would come crashing down in a dramatic instant. I wasn't sure if I could get over that.

Miss Olave led us back to the area of the forest where we entered using the spell, and it took a LOT quicker to get back than it did to find her. I'm not sure how Cleo and I would have found our way ourselves — we hadn't even thought to leave a trail of stones or something else to guide us back to the entrance. We hadn't really thought of anything other than finding the Keeper, really. Perhaps because we doubted that we would.

The three of us held hands, uttered the words of the spell and found ourselves back in the unidentifiable street. We were greeted by a single *'twit-twoo'* of an owl, perhaps the same one that spoke to us earlier in the night. The sun formed a layer of bright pink on the horizon, and I was relieved to be back in our realm.

"Ooh, where are we, dears?"

I could now make out a street sign, which confirmed that this was a road we had walked many times on our way to the bowling alley we used to go to a lot as kids.

'*Salanzus Rd.*'

There were a few cars on the street now in the unearthly part of town, and a runner in a luminescent jacket dodged us as he panted. How nice it must be not to know of the evil that Sereia had planned for us all. Had we stopped her? I wasn't sure. How were you supposed to know when you had saved the earth? Was there a moment — a definitive outcome — that verified your victory? Maybe when we found Mel and Dean and gave the Keeper her stone, we would find out.

"Lorrie, do you know the way to the cathedral from here?"

"I think so. I think we take the next left and follow the road straight on. It'll take us ten minutes or so."

Miss Olave was leaning on Cleo's arm.

"Can you manage that, Miss Olave? I'll help you out and we can take as many rests as you need!"

"Of course, I'll be okay. Thank you for your concern, you're a good boy." She tapped his cheek with her hand in an overfamiliar grandmama kind of way.

"Do we have a plan for when we get there?" I asked my companions as we began the journey to Vormera Cathedral. Cleo's response was most unhelpful:

"I don't know, witchy. You normally come up with the plans!"

Miss Olave did not offer any suggestions, either.

"I guess we confront Mr Goddard and maybe when he sees that we found the Keeper — you, Miss Olave — he'll surrender?"

"Hopefully, dear." She sounded all too blasé; was she

aware of the gravity of the mission?

"I think you're right, Lorrie. All we can do is turn up and hope for the best. It's worked out okay for us so far." Cleo shrugged.

Still, something felt amiss. I couldn't help but feel a dark energy, and I wondered whether Sereia was getting closer to us. I suspected that she had been watching us from her prison, setting into one of her followers, or receiving regular updates from them as to our progress in stopping her. I was baffled that she hadn't at least attempted to stop us yet. We were so close now. All we needed to do was hand the stone to its Keeper and she wouldn't have a chance at utilising its powers once we rescued Mel and Dean. Or maybe rescued Mel *from* Dean, it wasn't clear.

"So, Miss Olave, how did you survive in the forest for that long?" Cleo was making small talk.

"Well, dear, it's all a bit vague. I can't remember a lot of it..."

"That's okay, the first Keeper couldn't remember much, either. I think she dreamed about it, though, and remembered more over time."

"Oh, maybe it'll come back to me then."

They were walking ahead of me again, side by side.

"I've been meaning to tell you about Mable."

"Mable?"

"Yes, we've been looking after Mable since you... disappeared."

"Oh, yes, thank you ever so much. I was hoping he would be in good hands..."

"He? I always thought Mable was a *she*?"

Miss Olave chuckled.

"Yes, he does appear a bit feminine at times."

"Oh, I could have sworn—"

"Mable is most certainly a *he*, I can assure you."

With that, the discussion around the gender of Miss Olave's Jammer bird concluded. To clarify, a Jammer bird is an unearthly species, resembling a parrot but possessing an incredible ability to repeat thoughts, not only words. I always believed it was incredibly bold to own one; all the opinions you suppressed vocalising would be translated and articulated through a bird.

"Go away, you're a total waste of space", or "I wish I hadn't invited big mouth Claudia to the party."

A Jammer bird would repeat it all, with no mercy.

We approached the trail to the cathedral. It was a narrow, shingle footpath which led to a gothic brass fence. The triangular roof rose up from the ground as we drew near. It sent chills down my spine. How fitting for Sereia to choose such a location for her ultimate curse. Still, there was something that didn't seem... right. Cleo may have been on to something; it may be that I've just been through a lot and nothing about this is meant to feel effortless. But that's just it, it DID feel effortless... *too* effortless! That was it, that was what didn't match up. How could an evil mastermind like Sereria let us get this far into ruining her plan without even an attempt to stop us?

"Miss Olave?"

"Yes, dear?"

"Did you say you wanted to see the stone?"

"Yes, when we find a safe place, dear..."

How did Miss Olave know that she needed to be reunited with the stone? Felicity didn't know she was the Keeper when the stone first found her in the fog forest — it was only later that she found out about her role as its protector.

"Miss Olave, have you ever been to Parisa's caves in the Isle of Dominia?" More Cleo small talk…

"No, dear. I would like to, one day. I've heard that it houses spectacular drawings."

Why Cleo was asking that question right now with everything going on had me stumped, but it tugged at a string which unravelled an entire universe of thoughts in my mind. Cave drawings. Parisa's caves. An astrologist's reading of figures lining up to face a great power. Two figures in cloaks, a mark by their feet, and another drawing to the right. A single figure originally thought to be part of a different marking entirely. A figure smaller than the ones to the left, but in a darker shade of red. With a shadow behind that immersed it. A mean looking shadow, with big teeth and claws for fingers. It looked like pure evil. It was facing the other figures, almost ready to consume them. Two figures in cloaks…

I *knew* the marking perturbed me. Ever since I laid my eyes upon it, it had been playing on my mind like a string quartet. When I slept, I saw the image. And when I thought about the caves, I pictured it. Even when I was thinking about something else *entirely,* my ancestors wouldn't let me forget about the marking.

"The caves," they said. "Look to the caves."

That was it: their power. It wasn't energy or strength that the ancestors had given me, it was *knowledge.* And it hit me like a ton of bricks.

"Cleo," I uttered as I stumbled backwards. He remained with his back to me but answered:

"What's up?" He was distracted by the flower Miss Olave

was showing him, which she picked from a Polyantha rose bush about three quarters of the way into the path.

"Can I talk to you for a minute?"

"Um, can it wait, Lorrie? We're nearly there."

"Not really, it's to do with Dean…"

For some reason I knew that would steal his attention. He spun his head around and walked towards me. Miss Olave began to follow.

"Sorry, Miss Olave, it's quite personal and I'd rather speak to Cleo in private, if that's okay." I didn't quite phrase it as a question. I hoped my fears weren't obvious in my trembling voice.

"What?" Cleo was short with me. Dean was probably the one thing he did not want to talk about right now, but the only thing he would.

"Cleo, listen carefully."

He gestured his arm away from his chest, as if to say: "take it away."

"Haven't you once thought that this was too easy?"

"What do you mean? I thought you wanted to talk about Dean?"

"No, just focus. This entire mission — from finding out about the stone to stealing the map and stumbling upon Miss Olave in the fog forest. It's been a breeze, in the grand scheme of things…"

"Well, I wouldn't say a *breeze*…"

"But aside from the monster thing which nearly had us for dinner, we really haven't encountered too many obstacles!"

"Yeah, I guess it's a bit odd, but we've been lucky!"

"There's no such thing as luck when it comes to good and evil. There's just good, and evil. There's no room for luck. And

276

Sereia's evil would have surely trumped our good."

"What are you saying, witchy?"

"What if this whole time, every step of the way, we were doing exactly what Sereia wanted us to?"

Cleo frowned and shook his head in disbelief, so I continued before he had a chance to label my suspicions as delusions.

"Do you remember the cave drawing, the one I was obsessed over?"

"Yeah, I think you rambled on about it in your sleep!"

"Exactly! Two figures in cloaks, kind of like the ones you and I were wearing, and a blob in front of us, kind of like the stone, and another figure to the right, waiting for us like a huntsman eager to greet its prey. What if Parisa was warning me, warning *us*..."

"Lorrie, you're being—"

"Think about it, Cleo. I know it sounds crazy. But isn't it all too convenient that your papa was accused of dark magic by his neighbour that ended up going missing, and then your mama was recruited with a promise to redeem your papa, and her mission was to steal the stone... and then Mr Goddard showed up after school which he never does, as if he knew what we had planned, but let's us get away while *knowing* that Mel probably wouldn't have gone there without you... and we somehow just stumble upon the stone at *your* house, steal a map from the town hall and find the Keeper in the forest, without even so much as a threat from Sereia herself?"

"Lorrie, you need some rest. It's all been a bit much for you and—"

"No, Cleo, *please* listen..." I was holding his shoulders with both of my hands and shaking him in a desperate plea for validation. It was then that we noticed Miss Olave was gone.

"Where's Miss O?"

"What?" I asked as I looked across to where she had been standing.

"Miss O?" Cleo called out. "Miss Olave, where are you? Look what you've done, you've scared her off with all your conspiracy stuff! She probably thought you were going to accuse her of working for Sereia or something ridiculous!"

"OF COURSE!"

"No, Lorrie, it was a joke."

"No, it's obvious, how did we miss it?"

"Lorrie—"

"She knew about the stone because she ALREADY KNEW ABOUT THE STONE!"

"Huh?"

"Sereia must have found out that Miss Olave was the Keeper, convinced her to make up a foul story about your papa and wander off into the fog forest where we would hand deliver the stone to her. She set all of this in motion, like a puppeteer with strings, and we played right into her hands."

Cleo wasn't disputing me any more. He was considering the possibility that what I was suggesting could be true.

"So, say you're right and this was all just a big ploy that we were unknowingly a part of what happens now? Has Miss O gone to give the stone to Sereia? Is Sereia inside the cathedral?"

We both looked up at the large building towering above us. Only eighteen or so steps to go before we reached the entrance. And although nothing about the cathedral or its grand doors enticed us, we sprinted to it almost as fast as we did when we were chased by the beast in the forest. Cleo shouted

Mel's name as we burst through the doors, which were heavier than we expected and slowed us down as we threw our bodies at them, ignoring the "*shut to public: enter at own risk*" sign. I had never dared to look at pictures of the most haunted construction in Vormera, which had recently been plastered over the newspapers to commemorate the upcoming fortieth anniversary of the teenage wizard's disappearance. It looked similar to how it did when I set into Dean, but far more harrowing now I was there.

"Mel? MEL!" Cleo yelled.

"MEL! DEAN!" I joined in.

The stone columns shouted the names back at us and the stained-glass windows were radiating reds and blues that illuminated sections of the sizable nave (we learnt the technical names of the architecture in P.S., *AKA* Parisa Studies). Not even pews were left over any more; the place was barren. It felt bigger than I anticipated from the outside, and I was half expecting to see a group of lost wizards, in addition to our friends and enemies, but no one was in sight.

"Look, over there!" Cleo pointed at two naked chairs sitting in the far-left corner, with what looked like fragments of rope attached to their legs. "They're gone. We're too late, Lorrie." His eyes were welling up again and I knew mine would follow shortly. Neither of us quite knew what to say and in that moment, swallowed by the enormous, cursed cathedral, we thought we had lost.

And then I remembered that I still had the stone. I yanked my backpack from my shoulders and unzipped it awkwardly in mid-air. I held it with one hand while rummaging through it with another. I frantically threw the contents of the bag on the ground, including my water bottle, torch (which I thought I had lost in the chaos of being chased by the beast), some leftover sandstone flakes and a pair of gloves. They each fell to the floor, one by one, and right at the very bottom of the bag was the stone, covered in a pitiful cloth which was tied around it with some string, as if that would have done anything to protect it. But it was there. I pulled it out and held it up to show Cleo before I untied the string and peeled away the cloth to make sure it was unscathed.

"The stone. We still have the stone…" Cleo was contemplating what this meant, and I had a terrible feeling it wasn't a good thing. If Sereia planned it all out, she must have meant for it to still be in our possession.

As Cleo and I shifted our gaze between each other and the stone, I felt some static in the air and I could see some strands of Cleo's hair coming alive. It was energy, not electrical energy like earthly physics would teach us, but unearthly energy.

"I see you kept the stone safe for me, dears." Miss Olave's voice bounced off the columns and we couldn't trace where it was coming from. "Now, time to hand it over to me."

"Where is she, Cleo?"

"I don't know."

We twisted our heads in all sorts of directions and we desperately tried to place her.

"Come on now, don't be shy."

We backed away together as the voice was growing louder, and I took hold of Cleo's hand.

"Lorrie!" It was Dean's voice. "Get out of here, RUN!"

Just as I turned and bolted for the doors Miss Olave appeared in front of them, like the guards in the Musea.

"Now, now, where are you off to in such a rush, dear?"

I walked backwards and found myself next to Cleo again.

He hadn't moved an inch.

"Look behind you, if you'd like to see your friends."

Cleo turned around but I was stuck in Miss Olave's eyes again, like I was in the forest when we met. But it wasn't awe that held me there, it was fear. I heard the words coming out of my mouth, making no attempt to stop them.

"You're not working for Sereia, you *are* Sereia!"

Chapter 27
Make a wish

Tuesday 17th September, around 6.45 a.m.

"Well, you are a clever little one, aren't you?" Sereia was angry, but she also seemed a little impressed.

"Mel!" Cleo ran towards her. I turned around to warn him, but before I had a chance, Sereia bellowed the words to the attachment spell and next thing I knew his body was flying. He crashed into one of the columns with a great big *'oof'*, where he was suspended at least five metres above ground, kicking his legs out and waving his arms in a hopeless attempt to break free. I saw the small shape of Mel at the other end of the cathedral, before the steps leading to the altar. She was laying on the floor, still weak from the thyme, which I could smell in the air, but hadn't yet suffered the effects of. To her right, Dean was standing beside Mr Goddard, his hands tied together in front of him, and his mouth covered by our headmaster's hand to shut him up.

"Naughty child!" Sereia growled at Cleo after she cast him to the column. "If only you two were less snoopy and did as you were meant to, I might have spared you. But SOOOO many questions and what ifs. It was painful pretending to care for your silly teenage conversations about the Isle of Dominia and Mable, whatever a Mable is."

"I knew Mable was a SHE!" Cleo snarled from above.

"What have you done with my sister?"

"Oh, she'll be okay… I think. Poor thing has just breathed in a bit too much thyme! Don't worry, soon you will have inhaled enough yourselves that you'll miss most of my earth domination."

I observed the grey mist that was slowly filling the cathedral and I followed it up to the high ceiling, where it originated. If I only had a matter of minutes, I wanted some more questions and what ifs answered.

"How long have you set into Mrs Olave for?" I stepped in front of Sereia so I would have her full attention. The fear I previously reeked of had quickly been overtaken by anger. Anger that she hurt my friends, anger that I let her, and anger that she was about to subject the entire earth to the same, dreadful fate.

"Well, in and out for about five weeks. Long enough to report your papa to the unearthly authorities with false claims of dark magic, and then lead her into the fog forest where I visited her body every now and then. I made sure she had enough to eat and didn't get herself killed by any creatures, but it wasn't much fun in there, so I didn't stay for long at any one point in time."

I could feel the fury building inside of me, and surprise. Grandmama never told me that you can take *control* of the being you inhabit when you set in.

"Is she even the Keeper?"

"Oh, so you haven't figured it all out then, Miss detective?"

I'm presuming that meant Miss Olave was not, in fact, the Keeper.

I didn't reply — I was waiting for Sereia to elaborate.

"Well, since yours and your entire family's demise will be on my hands, I suppose I owe you the truth…" She was enjoying the torture, I could tell. It was as though she was pulling a thorn out of my foot, slowly and with no sensitivity whatsoever. "But before I tell you, I just want you to know that although you did not succeed in saving the unearthlies, because of you and your friends and family, the earthlies will have a much brighter future ahead of them under my rule."

"Is that what you told Mr Goddard and all your other minions?" I snapped back.

"Huh, minions, I like that!"

Now Diary, what I'm about to tell you may be one of the more remarkable surprises from that night. It certainly was, for us all.

"Miss Olave could never possess powers worthy of the stone's Keeper; she is far too forgetful and careless with her possessions — I discovered that in the first hour I spent in her body! No, it could never have been her. Rather, a younger sorceress, protective of those she holds dear, with a family and best friend I could manipulate into helping me to take over the earth!"

My hands and my head started visibly shaking.

"Aah, you're getting it, now."

The next word I uttered had me entirely astounded.

"Mel."

"Oh good, I thought I would have to spell it out for you. It's a shame you're on the wrong team, dear, you could have been a great little minion of mine!"

I looked up at Cleo hanging above me, and his face was painted with the same shock. I caught sight of Dean, too, who was staring at Mel's body on the floor. I wonder if he knew if

284

he was part of it all. It certainly didn't seem like it the way Mr Goddard was clutching at his shirt sleeve.

"But... she's just a teenager, how could it be her?"

"I wondered that myself. I was rather underwhelmed when I first saw her walking across the street from Miss Olave's window. A petite, scruffy looking girl — hardly the makings of a powerful protector. The stone has its own reasons for why it chooses who it chooses, foolish as they may be."

I thought about Mel, lying there on the cold, hard floor. Sereia needed two things for her plan to succeed. Mel, the Keeper, and her stone. And we hand delivered them both to her, just without the gift wrapping. Mel was the Keeper. My best friend was the *Keeper*. I was proud of her, and unlike Sereia I recognised the qualities that made her worthy. She was protective, loyal, confident and annoyingly organised. She was also good; downright — to the bone — *good*. And who was I? Someone who let her, and everyone else in the whole earth, down. A tear dropped from my eye, as I realised how much of a disappointment I was to my grandmama, ancestors and the entire Orenda line. Some prophecy of redemption; more like prophecy of shame and humiliation.

"I'd give you another five minutes or so before the thyme does its trick. Did you want to hand over the stone now and save us all some time, or should I just take it from you once you collapse in a heap of self-pity, your choice?"

I wanted the thyme to kick in quickly. I'd rather not bear witness to what I had done, as cowardly as that was.

"Don't do it, Lorrie. It's not too late!"

Sereia roared with false laughter and dropped Cleo from the column. He landed with an even bigger *'oof'* and I swear I could hear his leg breaking.

"Not too late! You do have a sense of humour, dear! I can see you aren't going to hand the stone to me, so I'll wait for you to 'fall asleep', which will be soon." She looked to Mr Goddard for confirmation of this, and he nodded before inspecting his watch.

"Any minute now, your all-mighty evilness."

"That's really what he calls you? How original!" Cleo groaned as he lay face down on the floor.

"What are you going to do with my sister?" He chose *his* final question.

"Well, I'll compel her to wish the stone another Keeper, of course. And you guessed it, that Keeper will be *me*!"

A few minutes had passed, and the cathedral was now saturated in the grey thyme mist. It felt like we were the unwelcome guests at a dinner and the host was just waiting for us to leave, but we were either stubborn or unaware of our intrusion.

"Daniel..." Sereia called Mr Goddard by his first name, how personal. "Why is it not working?"

"I'm not sure, your all-mighty evilness. I know I had the mixture right, I checked it four times before planting the diffusers..."

Diffusers, how clever. No doubt Sereia's idea. She must have been immune to the thyme, somehow. And it turns out so were we. I only later found out that the 'special ingredient' grandmama added to our lemontwine tea was the antidote for thyme, and if it wasn't for her, I would not have been writing any of these entries right now.

"Oh, for goodness' sake I cannot trust an earthly to do ANYTHING!" Sereia stomped over to Mr Goddard, slowed down by the elderly body she had inhabited, and grabbed Dean by the ear.

"Ouch." He winced.

She pulled him towards me in a bid to make a deal.

"Want your boyfriend? Give me the stone and I'll let him go."

I wondered why Sereia hadn't just compelled me to give her the stone or snatched it from me with magic or the swipe of her own hand.

"Well, what's it gonna be?"

"Don't do it, Lorrie…"

Sereia tightened her grip on Dean's ear as a punishment for his discouragement.

"Ow."

I stared into Dean's crystal blue eyes, the same ones that once gazed at me with trust and affection. If I couldn't save my family or Mel and Cleo, could I at least save him? I took a few steps towards him, having made up my mind. But then, out of the corner of my eye, I saw movement on the ground where Mel lay, and indeed her arms were twitching, but it was something else that captured my attention… Stumbles.

Stumbles was on the ground, next to her, licking her face. It was most peculiar, and I rubbed my eyes to make sure that I wasn't just imagining it. Never had I been so excited to see my annoying little pet, and it didn't take long before I realised that he was healing her, somehow. Her legs started moving and her eyelids opened. She even made a sound almost inaudible. It was extraordinary, even if a little nauseating. And then, flooding through the walls and sounding as real and magnificent as Sinthea's ballad, a choir of voices spoke to me.

"Lorelei. You have a purpose and a prophecy, which may be unknown to you, but will one day be known to all…"

"A purpose and a prophecy."

"A *purpose* and a *prophecy*."

"*A purpose and a...*"

For a moment it seemed that even Sereia heard the hymn. At first, I thought they could be the cries of the missing wizards, but my ancestors expressed the same words they had done all along, and it was time I started listening to them. I mean, if Stumbles could heal Mel from thyme poisoning then surely, I could muster the energies to get the stone to her. And I knew that's what I had to do.

I lifted my head, as the powers inside me were awaking with the force of a million butterflies. My arms and legs were tingly, and my closed fists felt like they were burning. I could see everything in high definition. My senses were heightened, and every sound, noise and smell were intensified, but I was totally focused. I had never felt that kind of strength before, and Sereia could feel it, too. She stepped back with an air of apprehension as my arms stretched out from my side and raised up. I couldn't even tell you what spell I channelled or how I harnessed the powers, but in a fell swoop I radiated a force so great that the windows shattered, and the ceiling chandeliers vibrated in a dissonant troupe. Remember how I mentioned about time being a strange thing? Well, it was, and when I asked Grandmama when I would be ready and she told me that "in time" I would find out, she wasn't lying. It *was* in time that I would begin our defeat of Sereia, but in a *different* time.

It's hard to describe Diary, but there in that cathedral where Sereia was about to take over the stone and wish all unearthly beings into non-existence, I somehow entered a different dimension of time. It was an experience I cannot fathom, even on reflection. My body moved at normal speed as I walked towards Mel. But every*thing* and every*one* in my surroundings were moving in ultra-slow motion. Cleo was attempting to raise himself off the floor, Dean was holding his injured ear, Mr Goddard was making a run toward Mel, Stumbles was still slowly plastering her with saliva and Sereia had her arms outstretched with her mouth wide open as if she was attempting to grab me. Glass was falling from above and the doors were closing with the draft. All in about triple the time it was taking me to get to the altar. I couldn't even think of a particular spell that would elicit such a phenomenon, let alone know how to perform it. Maybe I had help from the ancestors, but to this day they will neither confirm nor deny it. I asked them last night, in fact, but they refused to give me an answer.

When I got to Mel I crouched down, afraid to touch her for some reason, so I reached out for Stumbles. He was soft and warm. His tongue was still glued to her face; it made its way slightly into her ear which made me gag a little. As I was about to place the stone in her open hand, which lay out by her face and exhibited a light pink rash, I felt a shift in the energy and the spell was broken. I returned to normal speed, or everything else did, and I swivelled my body towards Sereia who was sailing towards me; her legs barely touching the ground as if she was gliding through the air. Her hand was outstretched in front of her and she was repeating a very unusual, very creepy chant. It didn't sound like Parisa's language though, maybe a variation of.

"Lorrie, watch out!" Cleo shouted, but I had no time or means to react to his warning.

289

Sereia exuded what felt like a tidal wave of energy, and it blasted me through the air, above Mel and beyond the steps of the altar. My body was stopped only by the thick stone wall, otherwise I have no doubt I would have ended up at the other side of the Isle of Vormera. And boy did it hurt! I thought every bone of mine had broken. The collision knocked the wind out of me, and I could barely breathe I was in so much agony. I wondered if my lungs had been punctured by my contorted ribs. I placed my hand on the back of my head and brought it to my eyes to inspect the blood on it. My vision was blurry, and all my other senses were dampened. I could make out Miss Olave's rough shape — a harrowing reminder of our first sighting of her in the forest. Sereia leaned over Mel, their faces almost touching, and compelled her to make a wish.

Chapter 28
Melusine Magus

Tuesday 17th September, around 7.05 a.m.

Nothing happened. I was waiting for the earth to go dark or to witness my friends fade away into nothingness. My ears were still ringing, but I could see things a bit more clearly now. Once I was absolutely certain that Cleo was still there (I saw him hobbling to lean against a column) I stared at my own hands to make sure I wasn't disappearing. Isn't that what Sereia had wished for, after all; the instant evaporation of all unearthlies? I looked at her curiously, and she looked at the stone the same way.

"Try again, Keeper!" Under complete mental control of Sereia due to her weakened state, Mel mumbled the very same words she must have done the first time:

"I hereby appoint Sereia Vanderguard as the new Keeper and wish for the total demise of all other unearthly beings." Sereia hadn't even thought to spare her lover's life. Ruthless.

"WHY IS IT NOT WORKING?" Sereia became enraged and flew one of the abandoned chairs across the room by merely looking at it. "Come on witch, SAY IT AGAIN!"

No matter how many times Mel uttered the words, the stone did not seem to grant her wish.

I thought about whether Sereia could have got it wrong, and Mel wasn't the Keeper. Or that maybe because it wasn't

Mel's *true* wish, it would not be granted. Different possibilities swarmed my sore head, and the same ones were no doubt taunting Sereia's. In the next instant, I saw movement in the far corner of the cathedral. Dean ripped the ropes from his raw wrists, and it wasn't until the other day he told me how. There were sharp fragments of glass lying at his feet from when I confidently exuded a mass of energies and crossed through a time dimension (as well as some cuts on his face which I am still constantly apologising for). While Sereia was unsuccessfully compelling Mel to wish unearthlies away, Dean knelt, picked up the sharpest fragment and manoeuvred it between his hands, angling it to chafe the rope. It frayed first and then the glass cut straight through. When his hands were freed, he raced towards Sereia with not an ounce of reluctance, striking her as she stood peering down at Mel, facing towards me, with her back to Dean.

I caught a glimpse of Miss Olave's startled facial expression as she face-planted the floor, with Dean lying on top of her. I felt for Miss Olave — she would have a ton of unexplained bruises and deeply disturbing memories if Sereia ever released her body back to her. She was in there, still, just lying dormant, in a sense. The stone rolled from her palm as Dean tried his best to tie her hands together with the same, recycled piece of rope that once restricted him. I had nothing but admiration for him. And you may think he was naïve to expect fragile, concurrent pieces of string to hold one of the most powerful of sorceresses, but he kept her distracted for a moment, and a moment was all we needed.

Just. One. Moment.

While Sereia was preoccupied with swatting *her* fly, I forced myself to rise to my feet with the ambition of rescuing the stone from its prolonged, circular roll. I had gotten up a bit too quickly and staggered from left to right before finding my balance, but I leaped down the stairs, missing one or two, fell to my knees half deliberately and clasped my hands over the stone. Mr Goddard was now making his way towards me, but Cleo had him sorted in a matter of seconds with a simple discarding spell which hauled him across the floor and right out the door.

"Just getting rid of the garbage, Mr G." Cleo proudly recalled saying to him, after it was all over. Irony, at its finest.

Once I felt the stone firmly beneath my palms, I picked it up and took it straight to Mel. At that point, Sereia had recovered from the surprise of what had happened to her and propelled Dean away from her, like she did with me, but a fair bit more gently so as not to waste any energies.

I dropped to the ground in front of Mel, placed the stone in her hand and asked her to make another wish. I couldn't find the words, but I had a feeling Mel knew what to do. I trusted the stone, I trusted my ancestors, I trusted myself and I trusted my best friend. Mel made not a single sound, but just as Sereia was uttering the words to her next, devious spell, Miss Olave's body tensed up as though she had received a shock and fell to the floor in her heap of self-pity. Mel lay there, still, for another few minutes. Dean pushed himself from the ground and walked over to give Cleo a hand as he stumbled down the nave, pausing to catch his breath and struggling through the pain of his gory, crooked leg. Cleo sat down next to his sister, shaking her shoulders and crying.

Mel's eyes were closed, and she hadn't moved since Stumbles licked her face. Speaking of Stumbles, he had hidden behind one of the columns in the chaos of bodies flying everywhere, but he came out and perched himself next to me while I sat next to my friends, and I was comforted by his presence.

"The healing spell, Cleo. Teach me the words and we'll do it together."

He wiped his tears and shuffled closer to me as Dean, who was in the middle of us, moved away and knelt behind us. We held hands, spoke the words, and harnessed all of our energies to save our friend. But it wasn't working…

"Come on, Mel." Dean whispered under his breath.

She gave us no sign that she was still with us. Tears were streaming down my face as Cleo ripped his hands from mine.

"It isn't working, Lorrie." He looked at me with desperation. "Please, PLEASE Parisa if you can hear us, help my sister! We did everything we could, *please!*"

Dean crawled behind me and placed his arm on my shoulder as I took hold of Cleo's hand and placed my other on Mel's head.

We were all connected, and the bond we now share will never be broken because of that. What we went through that night… over the course of that week… can never be explained to anyone who did not witness it. When we thought we had lost Mel, I only had one thought in my mind, and I asked the boys what they were thinking in that moment, too. What would my life look like without Mel in it?

I pictured myself, sitting at my desk while Mel's name was called by mistake, until the teachers got used to her not being around any more, or before the excuse of Mel visiting her cousins was realised as a more permanent arrangement.

Melusine Magus.

I would wince every time I heard it. At lunchtimes, Cleo

probably wouldn't sit with me any more as memories of the past would torment him. He would probably spend all his time in the forest, or he would drop out of school after he abandoned his intentions to attend more lessons and try harder with his work. I worried he would end up doing unearthly community service one day, cleaning out Bob and his families' enclosure. Dean probably wouldn't want to speak to me ever again, for getting him into this mess. And if what he said about his papa's curse being true (which I later found out, it was), then he certainly would want nothing to do with me. I was puzzled that he even did, in the first place.

I may go to the forest occasionally to check on Cleo, and spy on Morton raking the leaves on a continuous loop, with or without Ozzy by his side. I would so miss casting harmless spells on him with Mel, although my time spent with Dean taught me that I should think twice before tricking an earthly and focus on spending more time bridging the divide between kinds, somehow also resuming my role within the EPS. Without Mel, I wondered whether I would ever laugh at a funny film or talk about crushes on boys or figure out what to say to Jessica next time she makes fun of my ears. Without Mel, I would be destined to more insults, more boys pushing me off swings (obviously I mean that figuratively; I've outgrown the park, of course). I would live a long, unearthly life of misery, without magic or mischief. It would be worse than if Mel never forgave me for the spell on Cleo. At least then I would hear her voice in the halls or see her name written on the notice board when she signed up for the next school play, which she always did. I couldn't bear to think of what it would be like without her, but I punished myself in doing so.

Cleo said that, when he was shaking her and pleading with

her to wake up, he thought about what he would regret. He would regret fighting with her over stupid things like what to watch on TV or about how she took the last jelly biscuit without asking. He would regret not being there for her when she needed him the most, how he hid with me in Mr Goddard's office that night instead of running after her and condemning himself to the same fate. Mostly, he would regret not making her prouder. Not being the brother she deserved, and the son his parents deserved. With Mel gone, he would be the only one to carry the family name, and he would forever bring shame to it. "Mel is the best part of our family, she's the light. Without her, it's dark. And I couldn't ever make it any lighter." He was hard on himself, that was one thing I discovered about Cleo, amongst others. *Far* too hard on himself.

And then there was Dean. He said he wasn't thinking about what life with be like without Mel; he didn't really know her, and he hardly interacted with her before. He wouldn't have regretted not helping her more, not trying harder to prevent her from this fate, because he knew from the start that he wouldn't have been able to. The one thing Dean thought about when we didn't know if Mel would come back to us, was a memory. It was the first day of school for us unearthlies, three years ago. Dean was sitting at his desk when Mel and I, along with a few other unearthly students assigned to that class, walked in. "Here's some new classmates of yours. You'll notice they are wearing different coloured collars to yours, which means they are unearthlies. Please make them feel welcome." The hypocrisy of pointing out our differences and then asking our classmates to make us feel welcome escaped me at the time.

Mel sat down in front of Dean, and he couldn't remember

which desk I was allocated to, but I reminded him it was at the back. When another unearthly student held their hand up to answer a question, which they did with great success, an earthly student named Jessica laughed at him. When prompted by the teacher to share with the class what she found so funny, she simply shook her head and said:

"Nothing, miss, just another unearthly pretending they know more than us."

The boy's face went red as the rest of the earthlies in the class laughed hysterically, but in a way that obviously showed that they were pretending. Dean said he felt guilty for pretending, too, while he noticed that Mel had been muttering a few words almost silently. Next thing he knew, the chalk sitting on the shelf attached to the bottom of the chalkboard began to float, mid-air, and drew the letters:

"We don't need to pretend."

To this day, he hasn't told another soul that he knew it was Mel who did it; he respected her for it. He said he enjoyed the silence that fell upon the room before the kids that were laughing at the unearthly boy started gasping with amazement instead. He knew, from that day, that Mel was a good unearthly and as much as he was taught to hate her kind for what they did to his father, he decided he didn't hate this one. She stood up for her friends, which was more he could say about Jessica. One day I would ask Dean about Jessica, and whether he reciprocated any of the feelings she had towards him. But that is so far from being relevant, so I'll continue with what happened after we all sat together with Mel, waiting for her to wake up and not knowing what we would do if she didn't.

Cleo asked Dean to help him up so that he could retrieve his backpack and call his mama and papa (somehow his phone still had some battery life left). He wanted help but more than that, he wanted his parents to be with him. Dean tapped him on the shoulder and said:

"Sit tight, I'll get it for ya!"

In moments of darkness, kindness is the greatest gift.

I leaned in and gave Cleo the third — or maybe fourth — hug of the evening. I wanted him to know that I would always be there for him. I could never compare to his sister, but I would *be there*, right beside him, and I would have his back. I would try my very best to dissuade him from bailing on his lessons and cover for him when he did. That's what Mel does, so I would do it too. I would do everything I thought she would have done. I would try to be brave and stand up for other people, and I would try to have more fun and come out of my shell every once in a while. She always told me I should.

"Lorrie, is your head all right?" Cleo noticed a spot of blood on his shoulder when I retreated from his embrace.

"Yeah, just a bit sore."

Dean jogged back with Cleo's backpack and laid it by his side.

"There you go, buddy!"

"Thanks, Dean." Cleo glanced at him and nodded his head.

"Lorrie, your head is *bleeding*!" Dean dropped down and crouched behind me, separating my hair as I flinched.

"It's okay, really." I pulled away, not wanting to be made a fuss of in that particular moment of time.

"No, it's not. Let me look!"

Cleo dialled his mama's number and placed his phone to his ear while Dean took off his blue hoodie and used a sleeve to pat the back of my head.

"Hold this there, it'll stop the bleeding!"

"Thanks."

"You really need to watch where you're being thrown into, Lorrie. Would hate for you to lose your head over all this."

While I shouldn't have appreciated his humour considering the state of Mel and everything we had been through, I found it comforting. It reminded me of the days before, when I would have laughed without a care in the world at a joke told by Dean.

"Dean..." I didn't make any attempt at repositioning myself to face him. "When I was in your head, earlier on, you said to..."

"Mr Goddard!"

"Yeah, you told Mr Goddard that—"

"No, I mean he's over there!"

Mr Goddard wobbled through the doors using his hands to steady himself. He probably expected to find a very different outcome — one where his 'almighty evilness' was alive, instead of us (it turns out Sereia *is* still alive, but I'll come to that later). Cleo hung up the phone after it went straight to voicemail and turned to face Mr Goddard. I really wasn't sure what he would do, so I pre-empted the situation and tried to stop him from doing something really silly.

"Cleo, I want him to pay as much as you do, and he will. But your family needs you... *I* need you... and you'll do us no good if you're sitting in an unearthly prison somewhere."

Cleo snarled like a wolf had set into him, and his eyes went black. So, before he could make any move, I thought of the first spell that came into my mind and turned Mr Goddard into — you guessed it — a frog. I told you I could do it, Diary, if I wanted! Mr Goddard was now all but a dirty green toad, and he was trapped as the doors shut behind him again. Cleo initially looked at me with rage, but then Dean let out a laugh, and Cleo looked at *him* with rage instead.

"I'm sorry, I don't mean to be—"

Cleo looked ready to attack someone, but then Mr Goddard the frog let out a *'rubbit'* which multiplied into fifteen *rubbit's* as it bounced off the walls, and even Cleo couldn't help but smile.

"It's probably for the best — what I would have done to him would have been far less amusing."

Mel must have found it funny, too, cause she let out a groan and then her eyelids fluttered.

Chapter 29
Chrysalis

"Mel?" I yelled a bit louder than necessary.

"Mel! Mel, are you okay?" Cleo shuffled closer to her and placed his hand on her shoulder.

"Umm... I think so, what happened?"

"You... it doesn't matter. You're okay and that's all that matters!"

Mel stared at her brother as she tried to sit up. I swooped in beside her to support her back. She scanned her surroundings first, and then focused in on each one of us.

"Well, you all look rough!"

We all let out a chuckle, mostly one of incredible relief.

"You don't look so good yourself, Mel!" I teased her, like the good old pre-saving the earth days.

Cleo gave her a sip of his water and we sat there in silence together. For a haunted cathedral, it felt pretty peaceful. If I visited the grounds on any other occasion, I most likely wouldn't have made it through the doors, afraid of coming to the same fate as the wizards. But that Tuesday morning, the evil in the earthly realm was greater than any others. And we defeated it.

"Isn't this place meant to be very haunted?" The innocence of an earthly.

"Yup, but don't worry, we'll protect you." Cleo was actually being genuinely nice to Dean, and I thought maybe one day they could be friends. Ambitious?

"Lorrie…" Mel did her unsubtle whispering trick as she stared at Dean, prompting me to lean in. "Is he following me…"

I laughed so hard I couldn't even form a reply. It was an inside joke, but one I had only with myself, and there was something special and even more hilarious about that.

"Also, is there something in my hand?"

The stone. We all forgot about it, despite it saving our unearthly lives.

"Mel, there is a WHOLE lot you need to know…" Cleo began, but just as he paused to take a breath, the stone rattled in Mel's hand.

She dropped it as if she was holding a hot potato. It rolled forward a bit towards Dean and I, and we jumped back, wary of its unknown potential. It stopped in the centre of the four of us as we peered over it.

"What's it doing?" Cleo asked.

"I don't know?" I replied. We turned to Mel; she was the most likely one to have the answer.

"Don't look at me, I don't know!"

"Maybe it just had additional energies left over from granting Mel's wish?" Dean was catching on to this magic lingo.

"I made a wish?"

"Well, not consciously…" I didn't know how we would begin explaining this all to Mel.

"Look, it's moving!" Cleo shrieked as he pointed at it and shifted further away.

It wasn't so much moving as it was *morphing*. Its shape was changing, and its colours became more vibrant. It was also more transparent than before. I tried to think back to its appearance when I removed it from its cloth after we entered the cathedral. It did look *different* than before, but I couldn't quite explain how.

"Is something... is something coming out of it?" Dean had a look of horror and fascination on his face, which was shared by us all.

"Is it... *hatching?*"

I wasn't sure what I was expecting to come out of the stone — or what we later realised had been a chrysalis all along — but it became clear when four wings emerged.

A butterfly. A beautiful, radiant creature which showed off delicate but proud wings, with exquisite shades of sapphire blue and emerald, green enhanced by the unfiltered light from the broken windows as they spread. We sat and watched it in awe. The butterfly was small and took about ten minutes to fully appear from its cosy abode (although that is a VERY rough estimate because I was totally *not* paying attention to the time). It was spectacular. And confusing.

"Um..." Cleo broke the silence. "Did anyone else know that the stone had a butterfly inside of it?"

"It's not a stone, it's a chrysalis, which you would know if you paid attention in biology!"

"Well, *excuse me* for having better things to do than watch a pointless video about an earthly insect that only lives for a week!"

"Earthly butterflies can actually live for up to a month. Now shh, you might scare it!"

I never thought I would say this, but it was nice to hear

303

Mel and Cleo argue again — it felt like the balance of the universe had been restored. They were both wrong, though. This was no earthly butterfly. It had survived decades, dormant in its hard exterior, and it was the source of the extraordinary wish-granting power. You see, it was Mel who started to slowly piece together the unearthly life cycle of the butterfly through her dreams, like the Keeper before her, and before her, too. It was knowledge that only *she* could acquire, and not something Grandmama and Paul discovered in their conversations with Felicity's daughter. She shared them with Cleo and I, and with Dean, and swore us to secrecy. If anyone ever found out that the stone was a chrysalis, and that every time a new Sorceress is appointed as its Keeper it releases a magnificent butterfly as a symbol of birth and then rebirth, the consequences could be far greater than they were when we all thought it was just a mystical stone.

Try to keep up with me, Dairy. I'll slow down if I don't feel that I'm explaining myself well. Sereia tried to wish for the extinction of unearthlies and possession of a power *greater* than the earth has ever known (greater than Parisa's), but it simply could not grant that desire for two reasons. Firstly, and very simply, Mel had not wanted it to happen. She uttered the words, but it was not her true desire, like I suspected. Secondly, and more confusingly, the chrysalis can only wish for the *enhancement* of a feature or property, which must already *be there*, such as when its inhabitant (the butterfly) reaches its full potential, and the process of metamorphosis is complete. So, in the earthly care home where Felicity spent her later years, the lady who was losing her memory was granted its restoration. The man who lost his voice had it returned to him. And the small child with the terrifying illness was healthy again. Not only that, but all of the wishes that the Keeper shared did not merely return one to their original state, but it awarded them an enrichment beyond what was there before. The lady's memories were sharper, the man's voice was utterly mesmerising, and the child's other co-occurring health conditions were also cured. And Sereia... well... Sereia's powers were never *great*. They were always very, very rotten.

While the chrysalis transforms the wishes of those who have sought approval by its protector, what remains unchanged are the powers of the Keeper herself, which may sound strange. But as the butterfly retains its promise even after it leaves its chrysalis, so too does its Keeper. The butterfly chose Mel because she is reliable, caring, protective and pure, and always was. The butterfly chose her because she didn't *need* to be transformed. It wasn't her powers that awarded her the role, it was her character. It was *her*. So, when the chrysalis was united with its new Keeper, the butterfly that lay inside it was born, to signal the end of the cycle, and the beginning of the new one. Mel only told me last night (as we stuffed our faces with popcorn and drooled over the lead actor in the romcom we were watching) that she realised, in a recent dream, a new butterfly was growing.

In the cathedral when the butterfly emerged, we stayed seated on the hard stones, appreciating the very miracle of it. Once it paraded on the spot, showing off its splendour and perhaps finding its feet, it flapped its wings slowly at first, but then it gained momentum and raised from the ground. We watched it as it sailed higher and higher towards the ceiling of the cathedral, before it found a breach in the glass of one of the squares forming a once large, multicoloured window, and flew out. I stared at that same gap long after the butterfly departed through it. Only when I heard a quiet rattle did my focus shift. The remains of the chrysalis, now a clear, soft entity of broken skin, began to reform. The process defied everything I had learned about butterflies, but then this *was* an unearthly one, and I hadn't studied those — they didn't exist, according to extensive research and common knowledge (which needless to say was wrong).

It's hard to describe, but the vague shape of a caterpillar formed as the skin of the chrysalis wrapped around it, and it transfigured until an identical chrysalis was formed. All in a matter of minutes. I wished I had a microscope to observe the unnatural and yet entirely natural event, but my wish was not granted. We've talked about it a lot, amongst ourselves, and we're eagerly awaiting new epiphanies to visit Mel's dreams. We have so many questions:

How long does the butterfly remain in its chrysalis? Until the new Keeper is assigned? When will that *be*? *Who* will that be? Did the last Keeper know about Mel? And the butterfly who flew away, what happens to it now? Did it lose its powers? Did they transfer to the one who took its place? None of these have answers yet, but I'm hoping they will, one day.

After Mel wrapped the old but new chrysalis in a piece of cloth I handed to her, she placed it in her pocket and Dean and I helped her to her feet. She was dizzy at first, but she recovered her strength fairly quickly. It turns out that Grandmama had given Stumbles a *massive* bowl of left-over honey roast chicken infused with the thyme antidote. He must have thought he had struck gold! Grandmama then performed a tracking spell and compelled Stumbles to embark on his mission to join us at the cathedral. In slobbering all over Mel, her body absorbed just enough of the antidote to make her conscious. Then, when she wished on the chrysalis and officially became its Keeper, its energies bound to her energies in a reciprocal process that revived her and triggered the release of the butterfly.

Once Mel stood up, Dean hauled Cleo from the floor. The four of us, arm in arm, stumbled through the big grey doors of the cathedral. We sort of forgot about Mr Goddard the frog momentarily, until Dean saw him hopping along the path at an impressive pace.

"Oh well, let's hope he gets eaten by a bird!" Cleo muttered with scorn, which we all found amusing.

As we started to make our way down the path, Mr Magus was running toward us, followed by two strangers. He paused when he saw us, presumably taking a long-awaited sigh of relief before approaching Mel and Dean and flinging his arms around them. I could hear Cleo wincing in pain as his body was squeezed like the last bit of toothpaste in the tube, but he didn't ask his papa to stop. I could tell he needed the embrace just as much, if not more. Once Mr Magus was convinced that his children were all right (after looking them up and down and pulling at their cheeks fervently) he came over to me and offered a hug by extending his arms. I accepted — I also needed one. It was Dean's turn, and although he was a total stranger to Mr Magus, he knew of the boy who was with his daughter when she was captured. So, he declared:

"Come on, you too, kid!" He grinned as Dean fell into him, awkwardly.

Mr Magus explained that grandmama told him where we were after the tracking spell.

"Is my family okay, Mr Magus?"

"Yes, Lorrie. Your mama, papa and grandmama are just fine! They stayed at the house in case Sereia came after them as a diversion to keep her away from you!"

"And Mama?" Mel clung to her papa's side.

"Yes, darling. She's all right, too."

After everyone felt reassured enough, the two strangers walked up and stood next to Mr Magus, prompting an introduction.

"Oh yes, these are agents from the Council of the Mother of the Wand. I told them I'd take them to you after they discovered Sereia's plot... What happened, is she here yet?"

You would think by looking at the state of us he would assume that she *had* been here.

"Yes, Papa, but not any more..." Mel began. "Papa, I think I..."

Cleo interrupted her.

"I think I killed her papa. I didn't mean to, but she was about to hurt Mel and all of us and take over the earth. I'm sorry." Cleo taking the blame was one of the many, unexpected things he did over the course of the two days.

"Did you?"

The female agent spoke while her male counterpart was wiping his shoe on the grass, smelling rather dubious. I hid Stumbles behind my leg at that moment.

"Umm... yes, yes I did!" he said, confidently.

"Well, we received word from the *Soulas Lossesta* penitentiary that Sereia's lover, Draven, was ready to testify against her for her recent... escapades. Then, just a few moments ago, I had a call from a guard who was terrified when Sereia returned to her body — having undergone a lengthy channelling spell — with a horrifying scream, before proceeding to destroy the limited number of possessions in her cell, including a picture of that actor from the romcom everyone's talking about, bizarrely! He is rather handsome..."

"She's... she's alive?" Cleo needed to hear it again.

"She is, so I'm not sure how you think you might have killed her, son?" The smelly-footed guard jumped in.

We explained everything to them as they furiously scribbled some notes on a tiny notebook, leaving out the part about Mel being the Keeper, of course, although I had a feeling Mr Magus sensed we were hiding something, as he kept prying on the way home.

"What happened to the stone? Where is it?"

"Oh, we lost it Papa. Lorrie and I..."

"We lost it in the forest, Mr Magus, when we were looking for Miss Olave."

If you're wondering what happened to their neighbour, of course we called the unearthly paramedics who cautiously entered the cathedral (so as not to disturb the evil souls that reside within) to find a rather spritely but very puzzled Miss Olave. Sereia *must* have looked after her, in a totally egotistic 'I need you fit and strong to help me take over the earth' sort of way.

We went to visit her in the unearthly hospital a few days later, and of course she had no recollection of the bizarre events, aside from feeling very cold in some strange forest somewhere and worrying that she was going to lose a toe or ten. She was rather enjoying the attention I suspect, and she said the food was half decent. More than that, I think she enjoyed the company. She even found herself a boyfriend after being flirted with by the unearthly man in the bed next to hers.

It was quite romantic, really. I received an invitation to their wedding in the post this morning. I will most definitely be going, and I may even take Dean too, seeing as he didn't get an invite. It took him a while to come around to everything that had happened, and the entire unearthly earth that had been opened to him, so he didn't spend much time with us over the next few days. We're okay now, though, and he joins us for lunch sometimes if Mareck is at football practice. Cleo pretends he isn't *too* fond of Dean, but I caught them laughing at the same joke the other day, when they thought I wasn't listening.

Oh, and we had a meeting (just a video call) with the actual Mother of the Wand, who thanked us for our services and made us sign some papers to say we wouldn't tell a soul about the events of, well, the past two weeks. And when I got home after our adventure, the first thing I did was drift away into a ten-hour sleep. Mama let me off school the next day, feeling quite sorry for me, and Mel said they got to stay home, too. I hadn't heard much from Dean, as I mentioned, but I think his papa was so glad that he came home. Mr O'Malley feared that his son had run away because of the pressure he had been under, taking on extra shifts at the car shop. Oh, and Dean lied about all that stuff with him secretly working for Sereia, obviously, but he wasn't lying about his papa's hands. Luckily, the Mother of the Wand was so grateful to us that she promised she would reverse the curse and restore the functioning of his hands and start a man hunt for the unearthly who did that to him, in the first place. I started to warm towards her, though I'll never forget what she condemned my family to.

And my papa, well, he stayed with us for a couple weeks after it all went down. He said he would stay to help Mama look after Grandmama, who was becoming more poorly, without any explanation as to her condition. Then, he started renting a small room nearby, and he visits us frequently. I suppose he is trying to get to know me a bit better and make up for lost time. I'm enjoying it, though. I like Paul; I even slipped up last week and called him 'papa' by mistake. He was beyond chuffed. He also made some brownies with mama and I and showed me some of the music he likes to listen to, which is not all that different from mine.

"Oh no, not you too, Paul!" Mama teased. "I already listen to enough of that stuff!"

I promised him I'd show him a trick that my friend quite likes when he got back from closing his carpentry business wherever he lived — he wanted to make the move down here more permanent. I introduced him to Dean the other day; they got on well.

So, Diary, that just about covers it. What a whirlwind the start of the new school term had been. There's a little more that I thought I would share with you before I say goodbye (I need to put my head down and study for my Grade 6 test in January). If you'll accept just one more entry, then I'll see you tomorrow. I'm watching a new play at the theatre with the Magus family tonight. Oh, and Mama and Paul said they would come too, while Stumbles keeps Grandmama company.

Chapter 30
Metamorphosis

Tuesday 15th October, 1.15 p.m.

I can't say it was the best production I'd ever seen, but the theatre was certainly an experience and it was nice to spend time with the Magus family. Papa took Mama and I out for dinner afterwards at our favourite pizza restaurant. I saw them holding hands when I came back from the public toilet. Mama had moved to the chair next to him and placed her hand on top of his. I purposefully coughed to warn them of my presence, giving Mama the chance to fly back to her chair across the table, like a naughty child who got caught stealing from the cookie jar. We took a few slices of grandmama's favourite pizza home (beetroot and pickle) and I even let Stumbles have a nibble of my margherita. Although it is still uncertain whether Stumbles has any powers or not, he did us a great service that day, and I'll never forget it. Still, I will never stop reprimanding him for being a pest.

I have a few more things planned for this half-term. I challenged Dean to a rematch of Skittles, though I said he could come to Hemlock House as his papa is still a little bit suspicious of unearthlies. He said that if I won again, his forfeit would be organising a picnic for us at the beach. I told him I would win, and he may as well start packing for it now. Then, I promised Mel we would go shopping for some new boots (not for her, for *me*). She's been on at me for ages to upgrade my old scruffy ones, and I think I'm still so overjoyed that she's alive that I've agreed to practically *everything* since that day. I *even* let her do my makeup once, which Cleo graciously said made me look "like an earthly clown who had her makeup done by an eight-year-old". It was then that Mel threw a makeup brush towards him and slammed her bedroom door in his face.

We'll probably have a sleepover too; Mr and Mrs Magus are going away for a few days to spend some time reconnecting. They realised, after they independently plotted to steal the same relic from the same museum, that they should probably start communicating a bit more with each other. It's the first time they've let Mel and Cleo stay home by themselves without asking their eccentric aunty to babysit them. Since we were able to save the earth from a crazy, evil sorceress, our parents are a little more trusting of us, though maybe they shouldn't be. We did, very nearly, set the garden alight the other day by attempting a Grade 8 spell of igniting a fire. Mama came running from the house shrieking at us while she carried a hose pipe. Speaking of mama, she has been revisiting some of her spells. I spied on her as she tried to remember a simple floating spell with some dried-up leaves. It took her a few tries, but she managed it in the end.

I also promised I would make more time for *my* spells, although Grandmama is spending most of her time in bed these days. I've been spending lots of time with her; I visit her bedroom everyday where I resume my position in her cosy armchair in the corner by her window, reading my new book aloud; *'The trials and tribulations of Earthly people: How to bridge the divide with the mortal kind.'* Mel asked Easton if I could borrow it from his papa, but then had to bluff her way through explaining how she even knew he had a copy. I'm already on Chapter 11: 'How to have an open and honest conversation with an earthly', and I am really getting into it. I think Grandmama is, too, though she falls asleep every so often.

After I read the concluding paragraph of the chapter this morning, Grandmama asked me to retell her about our experience in the cathedral. She's curious as to whether we witnessed any paranormal experiences with the lost wizards, and I like to think she's a little proud of me, too.

"No, Grandmama, no spooky teenage wizard encounters I'm afraid!"

"Oh, that's disappointing. And how was the big bad wolf? As scary as they say?"

"Sereia? Well, probably not as scary as she would be if she wasn't in Miss Olave's body... but, still scary."

I'm not sure I told you, Diary, but I heard from Mr Magus, who heard from the Council, that after the chrysalis sent Sereia back into her body, it locked her in there. So, no more channelling spells for her. It also revealed a massive flaw in the 'Soulas Lossesta' prison; while the inmates were confined by the tall buildings and an assortment of anti-magic shielding spells, who knows how many found ways to break free and channel other earthlies and unearthlies to wreak havoc (although not many in there are powerful enough to do so. Call it: *connection* issues). After what happened with Sereia, a group of Grade 12 and 13 witches and wizards from the Council visited the prison and made sure the safety measures were robust and up to date with modern magic. Hopefully, nothing like that ever happens again.

Oh, and then there's my powers. So, I told Grandmama about the way I altered time in the cathedral — about how strong the energies inside me felt — and I expected her not to believe me. But, like my ancestors, she grinned with a kind of wise, 'I know more than you do' smile, and it made me think that she probably wasn't surprised that I could have done it. I wondered what else she supposed I could do... I spoke to the ancestors last night, thanking them for trying to warn me and apologising to them that I didn't listen.

"I'm sorry I let you down, ancestors of the Orenda line. I'm sorry I wasn't clever enough, or strong enough. I'm sorry it was Mel instead of me that was worthy of being the Keeper. I'm just sorry for being such an overwhelming let down to my prophecy."

I was enjoying a pity party for one, as I was hit by a wave of guilt and shame that left me panting for air. They ignored me as I fell asleep, but when I woke up at five a.m. with a numb arm that I had been sleeping on, they answered with an all-too-familiar reply:

"You have a purpose and a prophecy, which may be unknown to you, but will one day be known to all."

I'm still figuring out what it means.

I think we're just about there, unless I'm leaving anything out... Oh, yes, how could I forget! The stone — I mean the chrysalis. It remains in Mel's possession. We felt a little bad about it, but after telling everyone that Cleo and I dropped it somewhere in the fog forest, swarms of scientists, explorers, officials and members of the unearthly community fled to the forest to try and find it. They somehow got a hold of copies of the map, which some unearthly kid, who once was expelled from school for setting into an unearthly and stealing her answers during an exam, had found crumpled on the ground outside his house on Salanzus Road. Oops. He was caught by the unearthly authorities, but not before he made hundreds of photocopies and sold them for a high price to anyone willing to pay. What did he spend it on, you may ask? Copious amounts of birch sap pancakes from the breakfast café at the top of the street. I heard that's where they arrested him: sitting at a table stuffing his face with the very last forkful and dripping the sap EVERYWHERE.

I shouldn't really tell you where the chrysalis is kept, Diary, in case someone else takes a peek in you. But I can assure you it is safe, and we were only tempted *once* to use it on Morton. We didn't, though; we still have a *little* bit of fun with him, coming up to candy cane season, but never using the chrysalis. Only the four of us know about it, and Cleo didn't once suggest that I attempt to wipe Dean's memories, who he still refers to as my "boyfriend".

"Cleo, he isn't my boyfriend, you know!" I said to him last weekend when I was helping him with his maths (which he is getting quite a bit better with).

"Oh, really?" He seemed a little relieved, though it was hard to tell with Cleo. "Cool. Also, I have something for you to say thanks."

"Thanks?"

"Thanks for not suing me for your shoulder injury!" He winked as he removed a small box from his pocket.

My shoulder did kind of hurt for a few days after everything that happened in the cathedral, but I couldn't tell if that's because my body was launched at the stone wall or because of Cleo.

"What is it?" I stared at the box that Cleo handed to me,

shaking it a little near my ear to try and guess, but I never would have been able to. It was a magnet of the cave marking that I had seen in the souvenir shop.

"I saw you looking at it and, although I didn't realise at the time it was basically a warning to us, you seemed to like it. So, when you left the shop, I got it for you."

Mel walked into the kitchen at the time and uncomfortably poured herself a glass of water from the tap before walking out. She is still determined that Dean has a crush on her. He asked me the other day (after she told him frankly that she likes him a lot but isn't interested in being his girlfriend) whether I had ever said anything to her to make her think that.

"Nope." I was obviously holding in a roar of laughter.

"Lorrie?" He sighed and shook his head before laughing with me.

I gave him his tuba, eventually. He liked it a lot.

One more thing you might enjoy. We went on another school trip to the Zoo last week and I saw Bob. I would recognize his furry, brown polka dot tail anywhere. I don't think he remembered me though; when I walked to the fenced section of the enclosure that he was sunbathing next to, he didn't even glance in my direction. The closer I got, the less I remembered him too. But I thought I owed it to him to tell him that we defeated Sereia, and that he helped us. Wow, even thinking back on it all now, what a crazy adventure that was. And we lived to tell the tail; the furry, brown polka dot tail.

As I said, Diary, I need some time out to focus on my Grade 6 test. It's less than three months away and as much as I've enjoyed your company over the past couple of months, I do find you slightly… distracting. I kept my promise, though,

I even made it *more* than a month! I really have enjoyed our time together, and I am glad mama gave you to me, not that I will admit it to her. Thanks for letting me word vomit all over you, and sorry again about the grammatical errors, I really will try to improve! I will miss you, Diary, and I hope you will, me. You still have tons of pages left — you're a thick chunk of tree, and I mean that in the nicest way. So, you will see me again. I'll be back before you know it, right after I (hopefully) smash that test! You'll never guess the latest trick I'm working on actually... It's called *"Metamorfous"*, meaning: Metamorphosis.

Chapter 31
The Note on the Wall

Friday 27th January 2021, 8.20 p.m.

Friday 27th January 2021, 8.20 p.m.

I was sitting on my bed, flipping through the certificates in my 'Spell Grade Certificates folder', each sitting in an individual plastic sleeve, protecting them from lemontwine tea spillages and brownie crumbs. The folder, a shiny golden colour to reflect the pride of its contents, was slim, but getting heavier now. I flicked to the last certificate, which represented my proudest and most recent achievement. It read:

'Certificate of achievement: This is to certify that Miss Lorelei Orenda participated in the January 2021 official Grade 6 test of sorcery and unearthly Law and can hereby practice as a Grade 6 sorceress. Your hard work, dedication and commitment to your craft is admired and cherished.'

Signed, Mother of the Council of the Wand and the Chair of the Official Society for Education and Training in Sorcery.

The creaks in the wood still whisper to me, and this old oak house has witnessed many more secrets. Over the last three months, it has observed countless spells, creations of potions, recitations of the Laws of Sorcery and conversations — many conversations — between its occupiers and their guests. I threw everything I had into the Grade 6 test yesterday, and despite the obstacle of Grandmama's poor health, I passed it with flying colours. The only thing I stumbled on was the

Oath I made to our Lore, promising my ongoing commitment and protection of our values and responsibilities. It is spoken after every test, but it's easy to slip up because it's long and has so many big words! Con-se-crate. I pronounced it as "concentrate" by mistake. What does that even mean, consecrate?

I was exhausted after the test. It was a four-hour affair in total, and although Papa promised he would treat us all to a takeaway in celebration, I practically passed out on my bed as soon as we got in (not before saying goodnight to Dean, though, we've got into a bit of a habit of that). Instead, I woke up to a full breakfast spread, and had company, too. Mel tucked in straight away to the pastries, and Cleo guzzled some muesli topped with a scoop of yoghurt, a drizzle of honey and a few handfuls of sandstone flakes. I had a sprinkle of Mama's fresh batch of flakes too, but on top of pancakes with birch sap syrup.

"Want any pancakes with that syrup, witchy?"

"HA, HA. Says you with enough sandstone flakes to fill a bath-tub!"

Mama and Papa ate with us too, but the table still felt empty without Grandmama. Stumbles was trying to launch onto her chair and failing miserably, so I picked him up and sat him there. He tried to lick my pancakes, prompting me to regret my decision instantly.

"How's the new headmistress, kids?" Mama asked as she reached across the table for a croissant.

"Yeah, she's all right, Mrs O. Just a little… uptight."

"She's the first unearthly one the school has had, right kids?" Papa added.

"Sure is, Mr…"

320

"Call me Mr P." He winked in a sort of 'trying too hard to be a cool papa' type of way.

"Um… okay, Mr P."

Mel smiled as everyone sensed the discomfort.

"Hopefully, she doesn't go all evil on us!" Cleo joked.

"Yep, wouldn't want to have to turn her into a frog, too!" When I said that it prompted fits of giggles, aside from Mama and Papa who are still none-the-wiser as to what we did to Mr Goddard.

"What ever happened to the old one of yours?" Papa asked.

"Who knows, he's probably floating on a lily pad somewhere trying to bring himself to feed on flies!" Cleo was practically crying with laughter.

"You kids make no sense!" Mama was confused, but also joined in with a small chuckle, having been infected by ours.

After breakfast, Mel, Cleo and I went for a walk in the local woodland area. Then, I spent the rest of the day finishing off the book that Easton's papa leant me. Mel was desperate for me to "hurry up and read it already" so she had an excuse to stop by Easton's house and return it. The book taught me a lot of lessons, which perhaps I will share with you one day. In fact, I'll tell you one now, call it a sneak preview. There's only one way for the kinds to truly get along: show each other our earth or, rather, our *versions* of the earth. That's what did it for Dean and I, after all, and I've shown him Sinthea's ballad at least fifty more times since.

I think Papa's coming around to unearthly magic, despite all it did to him and his family. In fact, the most bizarre thing happened the other day. I saw Papa outside with floating leaves, too, although I couldn't spot Mama anywhere. I meant to ask him about that but then the day flew away like our little butterfly friend out the cathedral window.

We watched a TV programme a couple hours ago, one about hidden earthly realms, and I remembered that I wanted to visit one someday.

"I think it could be fun, Mama, if we all take a trip to a mystical realm!"

"We don't have a map for any, Lorrie."

"Nope, but I know someone who does…"

Cleo *might* have slipped a map for a hidden beach in his pocket before we left the archives, but I don't feel too bad about it… For everything we went through that night, we deserved a little reward, I reckon.

"First, go pop your certificate in with the others, then we can talk about unearthly trips!"

"Sure!" I beamed as I raced upstairs, feeling excited about the year ahead.

I hadn't made any resolutions, though. Maybe to be nicer to Stumbles, but that was about it. Our most recent Parismas was different than usual. It had its ups and downs, but it was wonderful overall. It *definitely* is my favourite holiday.

I was out of breath (although you'll be proud, I started running the other day, for ten or so minutes before collapsing on the grass). I crashed onto my bed where my folder awaited me. Just as I finished inspecting my recent addition and basking in my success, I noticed some movement in front of me. I redirected my gaze and almost couldn't believe what I was seeing. The cream wall which stood opposite me, on the far side of my bedroom, was vandalised with the formation of dark lines. It looked like someone had taken a black marker pen and scribbled carelessly all over it. The lines seemed

random at first, but then I saw it, and it's like I was subjected to the *Frozay* spell again. Bad butterflies were hysterical in my stomach, and I felt the way I did when I met Miss Olave in the fog forest. A devastating sense of doom. It read:

"*Lorelei, I need your help.*"